You can feel the compassion and love for the Lord in Harold's writings and his characters.

—Lindale Ranches-Linda Jensen

THE WAY
BACK HOME

THE WAY BACK HOME

Harold Southwick

Tate Publishing & *Enterprises*

Published by Tate Publishing & Enterprises, LLC
127 E. Trade Center Terrace | Mustang, Oklahoma 73064 USA
1.888.361.9473 | www.tatepublishing.com

Tate Publishing is committed to excellence in the publishing industry. The company reflects the philosophy established by the founders, based on Psalm 68:11,
"The Lord gave the word and great was the company of those who published it."

Book design copyright © 2009 by Tate Publishing, LLC. All rights reserved.
Cover design by Cole Roberts
Interior design by Joey Garrett
Edited by Christopher Sommer

Published in the United States of America

ISBN: 978-1-60799-751-1
1. Fiction / Christian / General
2. Fiction / War & Military
09.07.14

ACKNOWLEDGEMENTS

To the entire group at Tate Publishing who have been so helpful in my first attempt at writing a book and getting it published. Thanks Trinity Tate, for your initial interest in the manuscript and subsequent contact. Next, thanks to the entire production team, in particular Rachael Sweeden for her cheerful and ever-helpful correspondences and to Dave Dolphin, Curtis Winkle and Kylie Lyons for their contributions. I especially want to thank Christopher Sommer, my Conceptual Editor, for his guidance and instructions for improving the overall content. His expertise and guidance were greatly appreciated, as were his encouraging comments. Next, thanks to Cole Roberts for the work he did in creating the front cover design. My wife and I enjoyed that endeavor a lot and learned a great deal. Last but not least, my appreciations goes to Melanie Hughes and whoever else will be involved in the layout, printing, and marketing phases. If I have missed anyone, it was not intentional. It is great to be a part of the Tate Publishing family.

To Emily Albright and Linda Jensen (two very dear friends) for the time they took from their busy schedules to read the manuscript and to submit an endorsement for the finished product.

Last but not least, to … my dear wife, Sue, for proof-reading, for giving insight and the on-going encouragement to see it through from beginning to end! Also, to my daughters for their help in understanding how to use this computer more effectively.

Over and above all those previously mentioned … to The Lord for his inspiration to even attempt this endeavor!

FOREWORD

When I was eight, I asked my mom if I could marry my dad. My mom said he was taken, but she promised to tell me how to find a man even better for me than my dad. Her plan was Jesus. Following church, she shared with me that I had a Savior who would never leave me or forsake me. And she promised that if I delighted myself in him, he would give me the desires of my heart. (Psalms 37:4). God's plan worked. I gave my life to Jesus that day, and I started praying—and not just for the man of my dreams.

As an eight-year-old girl, I never imagined Christ would use me to lead my children to him. What a difference prayer makes. Through seeking his kingdom and all these things in my trials, my losses, and even my joys it made life more precious knowing I have a Savior who intercedes on my behalf.

Through this book you will see the power of prayer first hand. You'll learn that being a Christ follower isn't something that's just for Sunday mornings or good times. These characters face tough choices and trying circumstances. Southwick tells us a story of a young man's amazing journey through life. As Eddie grows and experiences many avenues, the Lord's hand guides him through the trials of loving, loosing, and finding love. However, none of that was too much for God. He is able to sustain us and ultimately make us more than conquerors in all situations. (Romans 8:37)

It is my prayer that you will be strengthened and encouraged through Southwick's story. Just like Eddie, the Lord will use your life circumstances to guide, love, and use you. The Lord wants to give you the desires of your heart.

—Emily Albright
Home school mom of three

Why are thou cast down, oh my soul ...
Hope thou in God.

Psalm 42:5(KJV)

To Sue, who has stuck with me through thick and thin,
And to Michelle, Lisa, and Amy

PROLOGUE

The Greyhound bus came to a stop on the edge of the highway opposite the lane leading down to the ranch house nestled among the old cottonwood trees. At first glance one would have thought the man who stepped off the bus and waited as the bus pulled away was in his late thirties. His face was drawn, and he walked with a visible limp. He carried his battered duffle bag in his right hand and held his left arm close to his side. Each step he took was an effort that brought pain to his eyes and caused him to grimace. When he reached the midpoint down to the house, he stopped and put his bag down. Reaching into his back pocket with his right hand, he brought forth a large blue handkerchief and mopped his face and neck. He was determined to make this last leg of his journey home on his own, using his battered body to return to what he had been running from or fearing for the last three years.

As he stood staring at the house situated in front of the out-buildings and corrals, memories flooded his mind, and a lump lodged in his throat. His gaze stopped on the suspended swing on that front porch where he and his family had spent so much time together when he and his siblings were growing up. A vivid memory of the first time he had sat in the swing with the most beautiful girl he ever knew overwhelmed him. He hung his head and prayed that God, who he had blamed for so many things and who still kept pursuing him, would give him the courage to finish this long journey back home.

He picked up the duffle bag and continued slowly toward the house, hoping as he went that his family would welcome him back in spite of his past actions and attitudes. There was someone in that house he had to become responsible for, and he hoped God would give him grace and wisdom to do that the way it should be done. As he reached the front gate, he noticed the fence could use some new paint. The thought idly ran through his mind, *Dad must be slowing down.* The squeaking gate brought someone to the front door. He saw the curtain part and his mom look out to see who was there.

PART ONE
THE EARLY YEARS

CHAPTER 1

The little boy looked out the window, let out a yell of glee, and bounded out the screen door and down the steps of the front porch. He raced as fast as his little legs could carry him and jumped up into the arms of the man he loved more than life itself. Daddy was home! Hal grimaced as he picked his little guy up, the residue of those old wounds. Sue came to the door to see what had caused all the excitement. Hal had told her on the phone early yesterday morning he wouldn't be home from Billings until Monday. The rodeo ended on Saturday night, and he was going to sleep and then drive home on Sunday. She ran out the door as fast as little Eddie and joined them in the yard. She clutched Hal to her with great joy and tears of relief that he was going to be here for the church picnic tomorrow afternoon. She had an announcement to make.

"Oh, Hal, I'm so glad you're home," Sue said as she released him and looked at his tired face.

Little Eddie clung to his daddy and just smiled. As Sue looked at the two of them, she couldn't help but see how much they looked alike, and her heart filled with pride and joy. She had some more great news to share with him, and she hoped he would be as happy as she felt about it. Hal was eyeing her with a curious look.

"Let me come in and clean up, and then you can share it with me, babe!"

"How do you know I have something to share with you?" she asked.

"Because I know you," he smiled.

Later, after he had showered and eaten his favorite meal, he said, "Okay, now I think I'm ready for what's put that gleam in those big, baby blues of yours."

She picked little Eddie up off his chair, came over, and snuggled up to him on the couch and said, "I am so proud of the daddy you are to this little guy! He looks just like you, except for his hair of course, and he loves you with all his heart. I just hope this one I'm now carrying is that little blond-haired girl we both want so much! I just hope you will love her as much as you love both of us."

A look of surprise and wonder came over his face, and then a big smile spread across his features. In that instant, she noticed again how the cleft in his chin seemed to deepen when he experienced strong emotion.

He gathered them both in his arms and exclaimed, "Ah babe, you know how to touch a man's heart. I love you so much! You're such a wonder with this little guy, and I can't wait to watch you with a baby girl that looks just like you."

Later that night he lay in bed beside Sue and listened to her soft, contented breathing following their lovemaking. He thought again how blessed he was and how his responsibilities were calling to him. He also thought again about another calling that had been made on his life, and as usual, he felt he was inadequate and unprepared for that calling.

HAROLD SOUTHWICK

CHAPTER 2

Hal still did some calf roping and team roping around the country and made some pretty good money at it, but it became harder each time he had to leave home to head for another city. His younger brother Stu and he had been "rodeoing" since they had gotten out of school and on their own. In fact, that was how and where he had met Sue. She was a little blond-headed beauty with big blue eyes sitting on the front row in the grandstands, if you could call them grandstands. They were just rows of two-by-twelve plank bleachers located behind the fence that surrounded the arena in this little southern Idaho town. He first noticed her as he picked himself up off the ground where he had landed after having been thrown sky high from that horse called Old Red that he just "had to ride." As he dusted himself off, he heard this sweet voice mockingly say, "Nice ride, cowboy!"

Fighting the urge to respond with a comment of his own, he looked deep into her eyes and felt as though he was suddenly swimming in a sea of baby blue. Confused by this sudden and unexpected emotion, he gave her a wink and strutted back toward the chutes, glancing once over his shoulder to see if she was still watching him. She was, with a shy half smile. In that instant he knew he had to get to know this girl!

That was the beginning of a whirlwind relationship that would encompass the rest of that summer, a growing awareness of just how much he loved Sue and just how much he needed her approval of him and who he was, or at least of who he was trying to be. He wasn't always sure just who that person was, but he felt she could help him find that identity and become that person. That quest ran into a roadblock, however; her mother insisted on her finishing her schooling and going on to bible school before she got serious about anyone, especially some young cowboy.

Because of that, Hal served a hitch in the US Army in Germany and had returned home to be put on standby recall for the Berlin Wall Crisis. He and Stu who had also just returned from a hitch in the army, decided they wanted to hit the rodeo circuit one more time before they settled down to whatever life had for them. Stu was two years younger than Hal and they had been close growing up. Even though they had fought a lot as brothers, they always looked out for each other. The chores they were required to do when they were small were usually shared. Because of that, whatever Hal did, Stu usually tried to do as well. They became interested in rodeo as a result of being tied on to the back of some young calves by their older brothers, A.J. and D.D. They had no choice but to hang on and learn to ride. Life was good, and he was enjoying it, but he still had this longing in his heart for that pretty little blond-headed girl with the big blue eyes. He got to see her sometimes that summer, and they were making some tentative plans for the future; but there was a hang-up that entered the picture since he had been overseas. She had become a "born-again" believer in Jesus Christ as her Lord and Savior, and she said she couldn't marry him unless he "gave his heart to Christ." She and her mom attended a little Baptist church in Glenn's Cove, and her mother taught a Sunday school class of little kids. Hal decided that if he wanted to see much of Sue Hightower, he was going to have to go to church with her at times just to pacify her and Momma!

Little did Hal Edwards know what lay in store for him on more than just one front. He could tell the first time he attended church with Sue that she was well thought of and that these people seemed to be real friendly. That surprised him. He had always thought "church people" were stuffed shirts who never had any fun and thought they were better than other people. He found that he kind of enjoyed visiting with most of them and that they were actually interested in him and what he was doing. The preacher was a little guy with a big nose and liked to laugh a lot. He could also get wound up when he was preaching a message. Sometimes it seemed that he was talking just to Hal, and that bothered him more than he wanted to admit to Sue.

CHAPTER 3

Hal had grown up in a family of six: four boys and two girls. His dad and mom had always taught all of them to look out for each other and to especially show their mother respect. If someone treated the girls in a way the boys didn't think was appropriate, they didn't hesitate to confront them. This didn't always sit well with the girls; sometimes they enjoyed the attention they were receiving. Down in Southwest Idaho where he had gone to school, people knew that if you got into a fight with one of the Edwards boys, "you was in a fight with all of 'em." He had learned early on in his life to be self-sufficient. Therefore, it was a real struggle for him to admit to himself that he might need something or someone outside of himself to make it through life. He felt that there must be a god. He wasn't sure if there was a heaven or not. That was a curiosity for him, but he had never spent much time thinking about it. His whole family had always loved the outdoors, so he knew someone must have made all the beautiful places they had seen and enjoyed together. All that "baloney" he had heard others sometimes argue about that man had evolved from a bug, or whatever it had been, was just that, "baloney." He had to admit, though, there were some people who acted like their ancestors were of a different species and that they hadn't been an improvement on the line. He had always just felt a man had to make allowances for those kind, but sometimes that was pretty hard to do.

HAROLD SOUTHWICK

It was in that setting that he and Sue struggled in their relationship. The preacher preached that God had a son. He said that this son was a "begotten son." Hal wondered what that really meant and also what that had to do with God. The fact that this "begotten son" had come to earth and died on a cross for mankind so that people could have the opportunity to go to heaven didn't sit well with Hal; he felt that a man was responsible for himself and his own.

He asked Sue one night as they sat in his truck down by the river where they liked to park, "What's so wrong with the way I am? I try to do the right things most of the time. Mom does her church thing and since D.D. got killed she has Dad going with her. I guess if they need that, it's okay. It's just not for me." He knew that all the people in the church were praying for him every day, and that kind of made him nervous. He didn't understand why that was, but he knew that it was a fact! His going off to rodeos on weekends sometimes helped him get away from the people and from Sue's quiet pressure, but it didn't seem to help him get away from the unease that was invading him down inside. What was happening to him? Where was his self-assurance going?

There was one thing he knew for sure, though, and that was he did not want to live his life without this beautiful little gal. So, in order to solve the roadblock, he "went forward" one night at a Sunday night service and went through the motions of accepting Christ as his Savior. The joy that everyone showed took him completely by surprise, and he felt confused and guilty of his ruse.

Later, on the way back to Sue's house, she said, "Pull down here by the river where we like to watch the moon and dream. I have something to tell you!"

He parked his truck under the old cottonwood tree along the Snake River and turned to her, "Well?" He was apprehensive, to say the least.

"Yes!"

"Yes, what?" he gulped.

"Yes, I will marry you!" she cried and threw herself in his arms. "I have waited for this day since you first winked at me that day at the rodeo!"

"When?" he asked.

"When, what?" she exclaimed.

"When can we get married?" he asked, his eyes filled with wonder.

"Take me home so I can tell Mom. She'll want to help me plan all of this. She's going to be as excited as I am. Oh, sweetheart, I love you so much! Thank you, God, for answering my prayers." Sue was in tears, and Hal was torn because of his joy and his confused sense of guilt.

The next week was one of high activity at the Hightower house as Sue and her mom and younger sister made plans for the upcoming event. Sue and Hal wanted to get married in just three months, but both moms thought that it should be at least a six-month engagement for appearance sake. Sue and Hal wondered why since they didn't have to get married. Besides, they were both adults and were anxious to begin their life together and to be able to enjoy all that being married would enable them to share. They had been very careful to not engage in any activity that would dishonor their relationship and their families, as well as God. But, needless to say, it had not been easy, especially for Hal. Sue was a very attractive little gal, and he was a red-blooded American boy.

CHAPTER 4

All of those plans were about to undergo drastic changes. The Berlin Wall Crisis had pretty well worked itself out of the emergency stage in the past year, but the French Foreign Legion wanted to get out of Southeast Asia, and they wanted the good-old USA to bail them out. So, American military advisors were being sent to Vietnam to assist the French in their fight with the Viet Cong and the North Vietnamese. Hal had been becoming more and more concerned about this because he knew that his military occupational standard qualified him to be recalled to go to assist these military advisors. As he was coming in from the field with his dad and brother for lunch, just a week after Sue had set a date for their marriage, his mom handed him a registered letter from the Department of Defense. Hal didn't have to open it to know what it contained. He felt sick to his stomach. He tore open the envelope and read that he had thirty days to wind up his civilian affairs and to report to Ft. Lewis, Washington, for preparatory training and for shipment to Vietnam.

How was this going to affect his and Sue's plans? Why did this have to happen now? Then another thought jolted him. *Is this happening because of my not-quite-honest decision to accept Christ? What should I do? Should I tell Sue about my lack of honesty?*

He finally went to his room and for the first time really tried to pray. He had heard the pastor say in a sermon that sometimes good could come from unfortunate events in people's lives. *Could any good come from this?* He needed to talk to Sue and let her help him with all of this. *Would she want to wait for him? Did he even have the right to ask her to?* And then, somewhat unexpectedly, the thought entered his mind: *What would God have me do?* Finally, after much agonizing, he bowed his head and prayed, "God, if you are who they've been telling me you are, please prove it to me. I don't know the first thing about you or what you want from me; but I love Sue, and I want to be her husband. Because of that, I want to belong to you also. This is about all I know to do right now. In Christ's name. Amen."

With much concern about what was ahead for him, he finally decided he better call Sue and ask to talk to her and her folks. He had shared the letter with his mom and dad, and they both thought that was the next thing he had to take care of. They promised their prayers. Stu, being the ornery younger brother he was, told him he would gladly step in and be Sue's "guy" while he was gone. That thought didn't cheer him much, but it brought a bit of a smile to his face.

"Why would she want to spend time with you when she'll have her memories of me?" Hal asked. Because of the example their folks had been to them, they had always been able to joke and jab at each other and to share each other's concerns. Now it helped him to start gaining some perspective on all of this.

CHAPTER 5

Sue was devastated when Hal told her of his recall. "What are we going to do now? Can't you get out of this? You've already served your time; it's someone else's time now!"

He slowly replied, "You know how I feel about that, Sue. If my country needs me, then you know I feel I have to go. But I want for us to go ahead and get married, and I hope you want that, too. But only God knows what will happen over there, so I don't know if it would be fair to you to do that since we don't know if I will come home."

"Sweetheart, that doesn't deserve an answer. Yes, I want to get married before you go! We'll have our wedding next Saturday afternoon, even if we don't have time for invitations and all the other stuff. Then we'll have a week of honeymoon wherever you want to go. Let's go tell Mom."

———————————

The next week was a nightmare and a time of great anticipation for both of them. Their families went into a frenzy of activity, and with the help of the church people, the wedding came off without a hitch. There was much grumbling about our country going to Vietnam, and people thought it was unfair that their kids had to go fight someone else's wars. Hal and Sue's thoughts were focused on the week they had to spend together as husband and wife now. They agreed to not let the uncertain future intrude upon this time of intimate sharing they had faithfully waited and longed for. This was now their time together, and nothing, war or anything else, was going to take away from this special time together. Hal's family owned a nice little cabin up on Trinity Lake in the Sawtooth Mountains, and they loved the lake and beauty and solitude of the place. That was where they decided to spend their honeymoon. Those six days spent together sharing all that was now theirs to share would become the sustaining anchor that would carry them over the long and uncertain months ahead.

Sometimes, though, it seemed that it wasn't enough. That was when they both began to find that there was another source of strength for them that they hadn't counted on. For Sue, it was during the long hours of darkness as she lay longing to hold Hal in her arms that she found that Christ would comfort her with his presence! For Hal it would be that, but more than that, it would take on a whole new meaning he had no idea about at that time.

CHAPTER 6

As Hal lay there in bed beside Sue, he thought again of those lonely days at Ft. Lewis and how glad he had been for the rush to get him and six other men trained for their new life in the "jungle." It kept him from having too much time to think. The month he had been going through jungle warfare indoctrination training, Hal had been sustained by his frequent phone calls with Sue. Then, Hal was taken to McCord Air Base and put on military air transport and flown directly to Saigon, South Vietnam.

His first sight from the air revealed a sprawl much bigger than he had thought it would be. There was everything from some more modern building in the downtown district to tin and clapboard shanties, filthy mud holes, and every other condition that people back home had no idea about. The thought went through his mind uninvited: *What are we fighting over a place like this for?*

After they had landed, they were met on the tarmac by a big, burly sergeant in army jungle fatigues who had them grab their gear, load into the back of an army four-by-four, and told to hang on; they were going for the "ride of their lives." He wasn't lying. Before they got to the compound in the northern part of the city, they had been down crowded streets filled with pedestrians, people on bicycles, slender men pulling shays by a long pole on each side, and an occasional vehicle that looked as though it had seen better days. They had been yelled at by people who had to scramble out of their way. They had observed many little street-side businesses interspersed with night-life establishments and houses of ill repute. There were even some people who yelled what they learned later was a welcome to them!

At the compound, they were told to put their gear in a billet-like building and then come to the assembly area, which they did. Waiting for them had been a US Army major dressed in jungle fatigues and wearing a beret. He had a red throat bandana around his neck. Hal knew from his earlier experiences that it represented a specific military unit with specific capabilities. The major introduced himself as David Self, and said he was the information spokesman for the Southeast Asian US Military Combat Advisory Detachment. His job was to brief them on what the full range of their duties would be. He also informed them that they no longer were being attached to the French Foreign Legion but that instead they would be assigned to US military officers attached to the South Vietnamese Army as advisors. They could be used in any way that the SVA and their officers agreed would benefit the war effort. Their job would be to see to personal needs of their particular officer, to keep records of the efforts engaged in, to dispatch information to superiors on the ongoing war efforts, and to also be available to engage in combat efforts if their individual attachment officer deemed it necessary.

When there was a break in the briefing, Hal turned to the soldier next to him, "They don't want much from us, do they? I reckon we can handle it though, that's why they sent us."

"It's going to be a learning experience, no doubt," Jake Miller said.

"It already is for me. Germany sure didn't look like this place. I guess we're here now so we'll just have to make the best of it." Hal murmured as the briefing sergeant called for their attention. Hal thought, *Let's get it going so I can get done and go home.*

They were introduced to the officers they would be assigned to next. Hal's man was a fourteen-year career captain from western Wyoming. He stood about six feet tall, about an inch taller than Hal, and had an air of quiet competence about him. Hal liked his direct look and firm handshake, and he felt that here was a man he could trust. They both were to learn that being from the same general part of the country and lifestyle was going to be a plus for their relationship. Coming events would soon prove how very important that fact was and how the friendship that just seemed to naturally grow would help them to fulfill their responsibilities.

Hal saluted and said, "Sir, I look forward to serving with and helping you do your job in any way I can. This is new and different from my last assignment, so I'm sure I'll need a lot of advice from you."

Captain Green's eyes showed amusement as he replied, "It's not like any of my past assignments either, so I guess we'll have to learn together, soldier." His return salute was as crisp and precise as the rest of his manner.

Hal thought, *I can learn a lot from this man.*

CHAPTER 7

The first couple of weeks were spent in getting oriented to the routines, learning the drill of how they were to relate to the South Vietnamese Army teams, and establishing a working relationship with their individual officers and how to interact with each of the other six advisory teams. This was especially important for when they entered into actual combat conditions. This was getting down to the critical aspect of their mission here in this strange land, and it was about to become a reality.

Actual combat conditions hadn't reached Saigon but were becoming heavily involved in outlying areas. On the streets of Saigon, they were told that you couldn't tell, especially at night, who were "friendlies" or who were undercover Viet Cong. The best advice was to not trust any of them and to watch each other's back. A lot of the South Vietnamese people had relatives in the north and really did not know where their loyalties should be given. So, to say the least, Hal and his buddies knew they were in one heck of a dangerous situation. Because of that, they became a very close-knit group and knew they had no choice but to depend on each other with their very lives.

That became especially true between Hal and Bob, his advisor officer. A lot of the distance that the army encouraged (actually demanded) between officers and enlisted men didn't exist to a large extent here because of the very nature and execution of their mission. Each of these men, both officers and their assis-

HAROLD SOUTHWICK

tants, had been chosen for this job because of their personal as well as their military qualifications.

The officers were well versed in military tactics, logistics, and combat maneuvers and had proven their courage in extremely stressful situations. All had been battle tested in one way or another. As for the enlisted men, all of them, including Hal, had extensive administrative military experience, military maneuvers training, were well versed in weapons care and usage, and had proven themselves capable in stressful situations. Hal had worked for the top operations officer at V Corps Headquarters in Frankfurt, Germany, and had firsthand experience in what went into war operations planning. They all knew that they were in a whole new ball game here in the jungle and in the execution of this kind of warfare. But that was also part of the attraction that motivated them in what they were being called to do here, and it gave their mission meaning. They had also been trained in how to administer basic emergency medical assistance. This was going to become a very important aspect of their support for each other since there was no large-scale medical attachment from the US military yet in place in Vietnam.

There was something else Hal was becoming convinced of, though. They were going to need more than just their own experience and cunning to survive this period in their lives. It was a gut feeling, and it was causing him to reevaluate his commitment to Christ and to begin praying for a deeper understanding of just what all that required of him and what all it involved. He was beginning to see that he needed to learn how to really pray and to do more of it. That was really brought home to him the first time he was asked if he wanted to go out with Bob and the SVA unit to assess the size of the Viet Cong guerrilla unit they had gotten reports of moving into the province just up the Ho Chi Min Trail from Saigon.

After Captain Green returned to their compound from his briefing, he asked Hal, "Do you want to go out on this patrol and get a taste of what this jungle fighting is like? We're going on a recon patrol. What they want us to do is find out how many guerrillas are in that Viet Cong unit up the trail."

"Yes sir, I do want to go," Hal answered without hesitation.

Of course he wanted to go. He wanted to see for his own satisfaction if he was the man he felt he was and that he could do the job! His older brother had been a marine in Korea and had experienced the battle of the Chosen Reservoir and much that followed before being sent to Japan to recover from his wounds and frozen hands and feet. Hal had always admired him and had always wanted to prove to A. J. that he could do it too. That might sound stupid to Sue back home, but it was just something he had to find out. But he also felt a tight feeling in his gut and a strange sense of what he thought must be fear. He wasn't alone in that feeling though, for Bob came to him before they broke camp and asked him if he believed in prayer.

"More so all the time," he replied. "Why do you ask, sir?"

"I just felt there was something about you that was a little bit different from the other guys, and I've seen you reading your little New Testament Bible a couple of times. I … uh … well, I just feel that we could use a little help from on high, or … um … something," he confessed.

"My pastor back home told me that it was no sign of weakness to ask God for help in times like this or any other time, for that matter. He says it shows that we don't know all that is in front of us but we can know the one who does and that he will help us. So yes, sir, I will try to pray. I'm not very good at it yet because I'm still pretty new at this lifestyle. But here goes, so everyone bare and bow your heads, please!" He bowed his head and prayed, "Lord, I don't know the right way do this is, so I'll just ask if you will please protect us as we go try to fulfill this mission. We're all a little scared and we need your strength, so if you would do that for us we would sure be thankful. In Christ's name, Amen."

Bob slapped him on the back, thanked him, and said, "Let's go get this done."

CHAPTER 8

That first time out was an experience. Although they didn't come under direct enemy fire to begin with, they were able to get close enough to enemy action to see from a hillside that these Cong guys knew what they were doing and that they meant business. They had a small squad of the SVA pinned down in a small depression around what looked like a mud hole. Hal realized later that it was an old abandoned rice paddy that could no longer be worked because of the war. They had been dropped in behind a hill some distance to the south by South Vietnamese Army helicopters and had been led through dense brush and stunted trees toward the sound of the small arms fire. Hal's pulse had been gaining momentum as they had gotten closer. He made dang sure he did everything he saw the rest of them doing to not be seen. The little SVA lieutenant slipped back to where Bob and Hal were and motioned them all back. After conferring he said, "Let's slip around the far side of the hill and come up that draw over there to lay down support fire for those pinned down around the water hole."

As they were approaching close enough to engage the VC, they spread out in the dense foliage and brush. When they were all in position, the signal was given, and they began a heavy barrage of small arms fire. Hal saw one of the Cong slip off to the left and disappear. Several of his buddies were down, and Hal thought he was getting out of there. As they started to advance forward, they started coming under gunfire, and Hal realized the guy he had seen disappearing had snuck around and was opening up on them. Suddenly, one of the SVA near him screamed and went down. Bob slipped up beside Hal and motioned for him to follow. They slipped back through the brush and circled around behind where the rifle fire was coming from.

Up ahead, Hal could see flashes of rifle fire through the grass and brush. Bob motioned him to the left behind a small tree. When he was in position, they both rose up and opened fire. Hal wasn't sure who hit him or if they both did, but he felt bile rise in his throat as he watched the soldier fall and twitch and become still. His knees turned to jelly and he dropped behind the tree as the contents of his stomach spewed out his mouth, filling his nose and causing him to cough. Captain Green came to his side and asked, "Are you okay?

When Hal could answer, he said, "Yes sir. I didn't think killing someone would affect me this way."

"Be glad it wasn't you, Hal. You need to toughen up." Bob grinned at him.

"Yes sir," Hal answered, thinking to himself, *I am glad it wasn't me, but this is still a hell of a way to settle disputes. That's the first one, though, and now I know I can do this.*

Bullets continued to fill the hot steaming jungle air and Hal was soon fully engaged in the battle. During a lull in the firing, Captain Green peered through the brush to where Hal lay. Seeing that Hal was over his revulsion and into the engagement, he gave him a thumbs-up.

"I think they've had enough. Let's back out of here," he said with satisfaction.

The Cong pulled a quick retreat, and those who had been pinned down were able to make contact with their unit and disappeared into the jungle. Bob and Siah, the SVA lieutenant, conferred and decided they had accomplished what they came for. They made a quick exit of the area and returned to the drop-off point and radioed for the choppers to pick them up.

After they had returned to the compound and were debriefed, Hal and Bob completed the report of the action required of them, and Hal dispatched it through channels back to their control officers in Hawaii.

Thus began an oft-repeated routine of taking care of various duties required of him. Sometimes he went on patrols with Bob and the unit, and at other times he was left behind to take care of the personal needs as well as the administrative part of the mission. The other six teams had similar experiences, and there was much talk about all of that when they had off times to relax. They all came to agree that this was like no other combat action that they had studied about or had heard stories about.

The action was starting to get more intense, and more fighting was moving closer to Saigon. As 1963 moved into the fall season, it looked more and more like US military involvement on a larger scale was going to become a reality. The information concerning enemy numbers, actions, and capabilities that the advisors were sending back to the military strategists in the States had a lot to do with this. These were uncertain times not only in Vietnam but also at home.

CHAPTER 9

Hal had letters from Sue and from his mom on a pretty regular basis and they always helped to ease his loneliness, but they left him feeling that he was missing out on a lot at home. The other guys expressed similar feelings, so Hal knew he wasn't the only one. In the fourth month of his recall, he received a letter from Sue that he somehow knew contained some special information for him, along with her expressions of missing him and longing for the comfort of his arms. On opening it, he read news that filled his heart with a sense of wonder as well as joy and a feeling of sadness that he wasn't home to share in this time with his wife. Sue wrote,

> "Hi sweetheart, I miss you so much. I wish I could tell you this with you here by me. I went to the doctor today and he confirmed what I was sure was true. You're going to be a daddy, and I'm going to be a mommy. No more dolls for me. We'll have the real thing in several months. I'm so excited. I hate it that you're missing out on this time in our family life. When are they going to let you come home? Mom is happy for me. She say's this will give me something to focus on while you're gone. Your folks are ecstatic; they're going to be grandparents. Come home soon, my love. I need you."

This news brought a new awareness to Hal's thinking. He had observed all the seemingly homeless children that roamed the streets looking for shelter and something to eat, and it had left

sadness in him. He and his buddies gave C rations to them sometimes and tried to make friends with them. Many of them acted
as if this was the first time anyone had shown them any concern.
The news that he was going to be a father made him wonder
where their parents were and why they weren't being helped in
any way. He was left with a feeling of anger that he couldn't quite
define. He knew that if the fighting reached the streets of Saigon
these kids were going to be the ones who suffered the most. They
had no one to give them care and protection. He found himself
asking God where the fairness was in that. God seemed to be
silent.

He also wondered for the first time if he would make it back
home to be a responsible daddy to this little one Sue was carrying. He prayed that God would please let that happen. His next
thought was, *Will it be the little boy they had talked about wanting
first.* Only time would tell. As he pondered where his life was
heading , he became aware of how it seemed to go much deeper
than just being a daddy. In his mind's eye, he kept seeing what
looked like a hand pointing toward home!

In his next letter to Sue he wrote,

"Hi, Babe. I just read your letter telling me we're going to be
having a baby. I sure wish I could be home with you. This
place is a hell hole. It's hard to grasp what you must be feeling now, but I couldn't be more excited. We're going to have
a baby of our own! You don't know yet whether it's a boy or
girl, do you? To answer your question of when I'll be home, I
don't know. Things are getting more hostile all the time. We
aren't allowed to write home about all we're going through,
but it's not good. Please pray for us. I was just thinking about
us having a baby. I see so many little kids on the streets here
in Saigon with no homes to go to. They are ragged and don't
know where their next meal is coming from or if there'll even
be one. It makes me angry; where are the ones who brought
them into this world? Some of my buddies and I give them
C-rations to eat, and try to help them, but it's never enough.
The war is going to be here on the streets of Saigon before

very long and these kids are going to be the ones who suffer the most. There must be some way to help kids who are left on their own, whether they are here or somewhere else. You and the church family know a lot more than I do about what can be done. So, would you have them pray with you about it? I've asked God where the fairness is in them being left alone like they are but I've never got an obvious answer. God seems to be silent. I guess I've got a lot to learn about God answering prayer.

Give everyone my love and tell my family I want them to help you any way they can, since I'm not there. I love you and miss you more than I can tell you. Your Hubby."

HAROLD SOUTHWICK

CHAPTER 10

The next months brought heavy fighting up toward Da Nang. His buddy Jake's unit came under heavy fire near there, and his advisor officer was killed. Jake was wounded and had to be evacuated to a field hospital located at the compound where they were billeted. Hal was able to go see him, and they both agreed that there was no more excitement to this situation and that there sure didn't seem to be any "glory" to fighting a war.

His unit had been enjoying some rest and relaxation time away from the stress of combat for a few days and was now being sent up to relieve the unit Jake's team had been attached to. They were chopper lifted to a staging area just south of Da Nang, where they unloaded, formed up, and set off up a trail that led into the dense foliage that surrounded the rice paddies along the coastal highway. They began to encounter sporadic rifle fire, and several of the SVA were being hit. They still hadn't spotted any of the Cong, but Hal had a sense that they were about to be hit with a lot more than anything they had experienced before. A foreboding seemed to settle on him. He tried to fight it off but soon realized that prayer was the only thing that was going to help him. He said a quick prayer in his mind and then realized that Bob was next to him.

Bob said, "Say one for me too!"

Hal thought, *Somehow God wants to use me to speak to Bob's heart.* This was a new insight for him, and it scared him for a moment; but it just as quickly gave him a new sense of a larger mission in this encounter. He thought, *Lord, am I up to all of this that I'm finding myself faced with?* Then he remembered parts of a scripture he had heard the pastor say one day in church. He said that a person could do everything that God asked them to do by the strength that God himself would give them. Hal knew that he sure was going to need a lot more than his own strength for what he felt was ahead of them. Suddenly, all hell broke loose. They were down on their bellies crawling through tall grass, brush, and some small trees, in mud that clung to everything. Hal was trying to keep his rifle up out of the mud and still stay down so as not to draw fire when small arms fire erupted out of the tree line to their left. Fear gripped his gut. He didn't want to die here in this Godforsaken place. He was going to be a daddy and his wife needed him. He tried to see Captain Green's face but he was too far in front of him. A shudder went through him and he felt all alone. Scenes of family times flashed rapidly through his mind. These were followed by scenes of the few brief times spent with God's people in church. He remembered their promises of prayer. *Oh God, I need those prayers now.* A fervent urge to pray took hold of him and he cried out in his soul, *Lord, please help me.* In spite of the din of the battle raging around him as he lay there praying to God, an unexplained calm slowly eased his fears. He sucked in a deep breath and moved forward. Bob whispered to him that they were in trouble and for him to stay back behind him. Bullets were sending up geysers of mud in front of him, and he felt a graze on his left shoulder. In the same instant, he saw Bob flinch and heard him groan. Captain Green grabbed his side and stopped moving. Hal knew that Bob was hard hit, but he didn't know how many times. Keeping as low as he could, he crawled up beside him and looked at him through the grass and mud. He could tell that Bob was in bad shape, but that he was still conscious. Hal tried to look around to see if he could locate a medic, but the enemy fire was still too intense and, to make matters worse, rocket propelled grenades were now being directed onto their position. The explosions were deafening, and Hal felt fear grip him again. The SVA were trying to put up a return fire,

HAROLD SOUTHWICK

and some were doing a good job and they didn't seem to panic. It went through Hal's mind that these guys were good fighters. But he also knew they were in big trouble and that he had to get Bob out of there and into the trees behind them so he could stop the blood flow.

He asked, "Bob, can you move at all? I'm going to try and get you back into the trees behind us and see what all is wrong with you. If you can, try to turn around. I'm going to try and pull you back."

Bob tried to twist his body around, but Hal could see that the pain was almost more than he could take. He was a true soldier, however, and he wasn't going to give up without giving it his "all."

Suddenly, a grenade exploded to their right, and Hal felt a ripping pain shoot through the back of his right thigh. *Oh God, now I'm hit*, he thought!

"Hal, get the heck out of here. Don't … worry about … me. Take care of yourself," he groaned.

"I'm okay, just nicked, I think. Just get turned around, and I'll get us out of here. Come on, sir! With God's help, we can do this!" Hal replied, trying to ignore his own wound.

The shelling was increasing, and the situation was going down-hill fast. Hal fought back his own pain and started pulling Bob backwards through the mud and grass. His own pain was causing him to cramp up in his leg, and he had to stop. Another spray of bullets started dancing toward them; one of them slammed into Bob's lower body, causing him to groan again. He looked at Hal and said weakly through his pain, "Hal, you've served me as well as anyone ever has … but … there's one more … thing you need … to do … for me!"

"What's that, sir?"

Gathering himself, he exclaimed, "You need to tell me how … to find this Jesus … I know you have in … your heart! I … don't think I'm going … to make it … and I don't want to end up … in … hell!"

Motivated by something beyond himself, Hal quickly said,

"Okay, sir, here goes. I guess the way I under stand it is that all we have to do is admit to God we're sinners. They told me at church that I needed to do that and I needed to believe Christ died for us; that his blood paid the price for our sins. After that they had me pray and ask him to be my Savior. The way I understand it that's all you have to do."

Hal saw Bob's lips moving and heard him ask for God's forgiveness and for God's help in getting out of this mess. A look of peace came over his face, and Hal knew that God had answered again. Unbidden again, he sensed a hand pointing toward home and a beckoning in his soul. Feelings of awe come over him then, and he knew that in spite of the mud, the blood, and the pain he was going to be okay. He was acutely aware that Bob's wounds were critical and that he had to get him some help. Inspired by what had just taken place, he renewed his efforts to get them both back in the trees. He was sure that Bob's soul was okay now, but his body sure wasn't. Bob needed more help than he could give him, and he needed that help quickly. Hal knew that it was up to him, that this was also part of his mission in this seemingly God-forsaken place, to help Bob in his most urgent and immediate need. His own wound was secondary as far as he was concerned and was not a factor in his efforts to help his new brother.

He somehow got Bob pulled back far enough to where he could start caring for his wounds. He had to lay his rifle down and felt naked without it in his hands. Bob had lost consciousness by now and Hal did the best he could with what he had. An SVA medic was working his way back to them, and Hal turned Bob over to him. As he was crawling back down in the grass to get his rifle, he saw movement to his front. Just as he grabbed his weapon, a young guerrilla jumped up and opened fire on him. He felt a bullet tear into his left shoulder as he returned fire. Another bullet broke his left arm, and he fell back, expecting more bullets to riddle his body. His whole left side seemed lifeless and numb. The pain in his right thigh was now forgotten in the aftermath of these new atrocities. He squinted through tear-filled eyes to see

HAROLD SOUTHWICK

the Viet Cong soldier lying in the grass and mud not twenty feet from him. His enemy was now gasping for breath, and blood was running down from an open wound in his scull into his eyes. As Hal watched, horror stricken, he could see the fear and anguish in those eyes that were a reflection of his own feelings. That look sent shock waves through him. As Hal struggled with his own emotions and pain, he suddenly sensed that this enemy soldier was trying to reach across the gulf of their differences and connect with him in their pain and suffering, their aloneness together in this tragic setting. In a flash of intuition, Hal suddenly realized that this soldier did not want to die all alone. His wants weren't that far from what Hal's own wants and needs were. The last thing that Hal was conscious of was the shuddering gulp for air as the young man's eyes rolled back into his head as he died.

CHAPTER 11

Hal regained consciousness briefly after receiving treatment for the flesh wound in his right thigh, a bullet hole in his upper left shoulder, another one that had broken a rib and punctured his left lung, and the one that had broken his left arm just below the elbow. The pain from the one in his shoulder had made him unaware of the broken rib and punctured lung. He wouldn't know the extent of his injuries until he woke up in the US Army hospital that had just been set up in the outskirts of Bangkok, Thailand. Both he and Bob had been transported there after preliminary surgery at the Saigon compound hospital to stabilize them. They both underwent extensive surgery in the Bangkok hospital to get them on the road to recovery. If and when their conditions improved, they would be evaluated and most likely flown either to Hawaii or a West Coast military hospital for further surgery and rehab.

Hal's condition seemed to improve well over the next week, but Bob had lost so much blood and had suffered extensive damage to internal organs that he was slower to improve. In fact, he wasn't responding well to his treatment. Doctors were reluctant to let Hal know about Bob's condition until he was more stable himself, but because they came to understand Hal's sense of responsibility for Bob, they finally told him things didn't look good. They wondered why Hal cared so much.

HAROLD SOUTHWICK

There was a lady from Texas who had come to Thailand to teach in a Christian school there who felt led to visit soldiers in the hospital. One day as she checked in at the hospital front desk, she was made aware of this young soldier from Idaho. She was asked if she could maybe pray with Hal and talk to him about Bob. As she entered the room and looked at the young man lying there in the bed with all his bandages, the oxygen line, IV drips, and all the other gadgets hooked up to him, with his eyes closed, she felt an overwhelming connection to him that she didn't understand. She thought, *God has something special in store for this young man.*

She sat down by the bed and prayed, "Dear Lord, please help me to minister to this fallen soldier the way you want me to. You have put a path before me. Please help me to follow it and to give this young man a sense of what you have for him. May this help him to recover and to become what you want him to become. In Christ's name. Amen."

When she looked up, she saw Hal looking at her with a tired, questioning look.

"Hello, Soldier. My name is Leslie Davis, and I'm here to visit with you, pray for you, help you correspond with your family back home, and anything else you need. I'm a teacher in a Christian school here in Bangkok, and I also have a ministry with homeless kids on the streets. How are you doing?" Leslie smiled warmly at him.

"Well, right now I'm not sure how I'm doing, ma'am. But hopefully I'll get better," Hal replied. "How did you know of me being here?"

"I have come to the hospital three times a week since it opened here to visit with soldiers from back in the States. It gives me a sense of connection with back home that I need. I love serving God over here, but I get very lonesome at times. This helps to relieve that. When I came in this morning, they told me about you and also about your friend Bob. They indicated that you are a Christian. Is that right?"

"Yes, I am, thanks to my wife back home," Hal replied.

"Do you know if your wife has been notified of your injuries, Hal?" Leslie asked.

"I don't know for sure. Could you find that out for me? I think the Advisory Detachment in Saigon is supposed to notify the Department of Defense, and they notify people at home when something like this happens. I don't know how long that takes, though," Hal said wearily.

He gave her his home phone number when she asked for it. He was impressed that she would call home for him from clear over here.

She then asked, "Hal, I have been asked to talk to you about your relationship with Bob, your advisor officer. He is in the intensive care section and is in grave condition. You keep talking about him in your sleep. What's that all about, or can you tell me?"

"Ma'am, we've become pretty close working together like we have. He saw me reading my little bible a few times when we were in our quarters at the compound. I guess he started wondering what it was about me that seemed different. I told him that I had become a Christian before I came over here and was trying to learn how to live it. It wasn't easy to do being away from home and church, but I was trying. He asked me to pray with him and the men a couple of times before we went out on patrol. When we were in the middle of this last battle and I was scared to death, he saw me praying and asked me to pray for him too. I did that and we moved on," Hal said.

"Were you under fire then?" Leslie wanted to know. As Hal answered, his memories of the event were evident to Leslie, "Yes, it seemed like hell had opened up and was about to swallow us. Later, after he had been wounded and didn't think he would get out of the mess alive, he asked me to tell him how to become a Christian. I had never done anything like that before, but I just told him to do what the people at home had told me to do. He did that and we both felt a lot better about things. I feel like he's my brother now. That's probably why I talked in my sleep."

As Hal shared about leading Bob to Christ during the battle they were wounded in, Leslie began to see that this young man had what God looks for in those he wants to use in his work. This encouraged her to share the truth about Bob's condition. She knew that Hal would want to know this so that he could pray specifically for him.

"Do the doctors think he is going to make it?" Hal asked.

"It's touch and go right now. So why don't we pray for him now?"

"Go ahead, ma'am, you pray."

Leslie prayed a short but beautiful prayer, and Hal felt a lifting of his spirit. He asked her if she would try to see Bob and say "hi" and to "hang in there," for him. Leslie could see that he needed rest, so she patted his arm and left him. She met a WAC nurse in the hallway and asked her to show her to Bob's room. When she entered the room, she saw that he was awake but in a great deal of pain. He watched her as she came up to his bedside and laid her hand on his arm.

"Hello, Bob. I'm Leslie Davis, and I've just come from Hal's bedside. He wanted me to come and pray for you. Would you like that?" she asked.

He nodded weakly and closed his eyes. As she prayed, Leslie could sense a warmth pass between her hand and Bob's arm. When she had finished and looked at him, his eyes were filled with tears. He tried to talk around the tubes in his nose and the oxygen mask on his face. She leaned down and made out that he was thanking her and that he wanted her to thank Hal for saving his life. He gave her a feeble thumbs-up and closed his eyes. As Leslie left the room, she prayed to God that many more would not have to end up in the same shape these two young men were in. However, before many more weeks had passed, she would be making many more such visits to this hospital. The war in Vietnam was about to begin in earnest.

Just days later word came to Bangkok that President Kennedy had been shot to death in Dallas, Texas. *Dear God, what is this world coming to*, she thought.

HAROLD SOUTHWICK

CHAPTER 12

In the days following, Leslie made many such visits to see Hal and Bob. Their conditions were improving slowly, but Hal developed an infection in his lung and was going to have to be kept there longer than they first thought. Leslie had called their army unit in Saigon and found out that Hal's wife and family had indeed been notified that he had been wounded in action. She just felt she should call Sue and tell her that she was visiting with Hal and that he was going to recover but that he needed a lot of prayer. This was a first for her, and she was nervous about making the call. But then she thought, *this is God's work, and I can do it.* As she waited for connections to be made on the overseas call, she remembered once again the call she had received about her own husband's death in Korea. The memory was still as painful now as it had been back then.

"Hello," a soft voice answered from far away.

Leslie could hear the concern in the voice. She knew that Sue had been made aware this was an overseas call.

"Sue?"

"Yes!"

"Sue, my name is Leslie Davis, and I'm calling from Bangkok, Thailand, on behalf of your husband, Hal."

"Is he okay? How do you know him? Can I talk with him?" the anxious voice asked. "Is he in Thailand? We weren't sure where he was sent from Saigon. I'm just going crazy with worry! Our baby is due in just a few days, and I need him here so bad! Will he be able to come home soon?"

"Sue, I don't know what the army had told you, but your husband has four serious wounds. He has a shrapnel wound in his right thigh, a bullet wound in his upper left shoulder, a broken left rib, and as a result, a wound in the left lung, as well as a broken left arm from another bullet. In spite of all that, he is doing quite well. He does have some infection in his left lung, but he's responding to treatment for that. The doctors say his chances for full recovery are good but that it will take time.Sue's soft, worried voice interrupted her, "You say your name is Leslie Davis. Are you married to someone over there? How did you meet Hal?"

"I'm a Christian teacher at a school here in Bangkok, and I visit the wounded here at the hospital, so that is how I have met your husband. I pray daily for him and with him and his friend Bob. Bob says if it wasn't for Hal he wouldn't be alive. He also told me that Hal led him to Christ in the heat of battle after he had received his first wound. Sue, your husband is quite a young man, and you can be proud of him!" She could hear the soft crying on the other end of the line. "Sue, I know how difficult a time like this is. I received a call like this during the Korean War telling me that my husband had been killed in action, and it devastated me. You have my prayers. I can assure you that Hal loves you and he can't wait to get home. That will happen in due time. Stay close to God and let him strengthen you. He will, you know. He did it for me, and that's why I serve him. Hal sends his love and says he will call as soon as these "yahoos," as he calls them, let him."

"Thank you so much for being there for me, ma'am! God is still looking after him, and I'm so thankful. I'm sorry about your loss, Leslie. Someday I hope I can thank you in person for what you're doing for those men. Please give Hal my love. Tell him everyone here is praying for him. His dad is going to be so proud of him, as we all are," Sue replied with strong emotion in her voice.

"I'll call again in a few days and let you know how he is doing. Please just stay close to God and keep everyone there in prayer for these two fine young men. God will send him home to you. May your baby be a wonderful homecoming present for Hal! Take care and God bless." With that, she broke the connection.

HAROLD SOUTHWICK

CHAPTER 13

In the weeks that followed, Hal gained strength and an interest in what Leslie was doing with the young street children in the slums of Bangkok. He told her about the little kids on the streets of Saigon. They spent much time in prayer for this need, and Hal was beginning to feel a need to get involved some way in this ministry that Leslie was doing. He also learned that Leslie had a daughter back home in Texas who was attending college.

He had talked to Sue several times on the phone by now and was eagerly waiting for the call to let him know he was a daddy. It seemed to him that she was overdue.

Bob's condition had improved greatly since Leslie had prayed for him that first day. He was wheeled into Hal's room one morning while Hal was sitting at the window looking out and longing to go home.

"Hey, partner, why the long face?" Bob asked.

"Oh, hi, sir. I was just sitting here wondering when I was going to hear that I'm a daddy," he replied. "You remember when your first one was born, don't you?"

"I sure do! I was stationed in Germany at the time, and Bet was at home in Jackson Hole. It was a difficult time for both of us. I love my career in the army, but it's a hard life on the family at times. I just came in to tell you that I'm being flown back to the States tomorrow for further rehab. I'll be going to Ft. Ord, California. They don't know if I'll be able to return to active duty or not. Right now, I'm just ready to go spend some time at home with my family and to do some fishing and ride some horses. How about you?"

"I'm with you. I want to get out of here and get home. I guess I'm being sent to Madigan Army Hospital at Ft. Lewis, Washington. They tell me my lung is about well enough that I can take the trip home. My arm and rib still hurt; and my shoulder is sore and stiff, but they're getting better. My leg will always be stiff, the doctor says. Let's get together and do some fishing and riding when things get settled down and we're able to do those things again. I'm hoping my tour of duty is going to be over when I get all of this rehab taken care of," Hal answered.

"Hal, I just want you to know again how much I appreciate your being there for me and for leading me into this relationship with God and Christ that I have now. I can't wait to get home and share this with my wife and kids! They're going to be there in California when I get there. Hal, you've been a good soldier. I just hope the people back home appreciate what guys like us are doing to help secure their lifestyle. From the sound of things, though, I doubt it. Take care, and I'll see you back in "God's" country." Then, with a handshake and a wave, he was gone.

Hal sat there in deep thought. He remembered his selfish motive in asking God to be his Savior and then having the audacity to ask him to prove who he really was to Hal. He thought about all the people that he had come into contact with since that time and about all the events he had been involved in up to this moment in his life. Getting to share Christ with Bob Green and a few others had given him much satisfaction. God had brought this precious lady, Leslie, into his life to encourage him and help conquer his loneliness while he was so far from home. She had taught him much as they studied God's word together. He had listened to her pray and learned from that. He was sure he would never have met her and become aware of her commitment to Christ if it had not been for the things that had happened to him since he first selfishly accepted Christ! *God really does have a plan for our lives*, he marveled. He would always treasure the joy he had experienced upon getting to lead Bob to Christ in spite of those terrible circumstances and the sense of peace that had filled him then. He realized in those quiet moments of reflection that God had more for him than just a life with his precious wife that he had asked for. God had something else for him to do. Again he sensed that "heavenly hand," as Leslie had named it, pointing him homeward.

Later that same day Hal's doctor came to him and said they had made arrangements for him to be loaded on a plane the next morning. He would be taken by air force medical transport to McCord Air Force Base, Tacoma, Washington. From there, he would be taken to Madigan Army Hospital to finish his rehab. Hal was more than ready to go. When Leslie came later that afternoon, he told her of his transfer. She was happy for him but also saddened. They had become very close. Hal told her he felt as though she was his big sister even though she wasn't very big! She had been a big influence in his spiritual growth and was a great help in his recovery so far. She had helped him to see how his attitude about his circumstances could affect everything else in his life. God was in the details of life here on earth. He promised to stay in touch with her and to make future contact concerning becoming involved in her ministry with the slum kids. Their good-byes were painful for both. Hal's going was leaving an empty place in Leslie's heart. She was soon to find that there was going to be many more wounded soldiers to give solace to and that would help her with her loss. None of those encounters, however, would prove to be as special as this one she had shared with Hal. She just prayed that some day in the future she would get to see him again in better circumstances and also get to meet his wife.

CHAPTER 14

Sue hadn't been made aware that Hal's transfer to Madigan Hospital would take place so soon. She knew that her time was very near when she started having cramps during the night a day after their last phone call. She woke her mom around five a.m. and told her what was going on. That was the call to action for the family. Everyone had been anxiously awaiting the arrival of this first grandchild. Because of that, everyone had insisted on being on hand for the baby's arrival, especially since Hal couldn't be there for the big event. Sue called her doctor in Mt. Home and was told to get to the hospital as soon as the pains started coming about four minutes apart. She then called Mom Edwards and asked them to call Hal in Bangkok to let him know what was going on. She had been staying with her mom, who was a widow, since Hal had gone back into the army. This was a blessing because this was a big, scary event for her and Hal wasn't here to help her through it. She hardly ever swore, but she thought, *damn the army*. Her next thought was to ask God to forgive her. Hal was paying a price for her protection, and she should be willing to sacrifice some too. But that still didn't make this easier. She didn't want her husband to miss out on this special moment in their family's life. If she could have only seen at that moment her husband's physical condition, it would have eased her mind concerning her own burden to bear.

Those nine months since Hal had been gone had been hard to take. To have experienced those first two weeks of their marriage

HAROLD SOUTHWICK

and the wonder of their togetherness had been a taste of heaven. To have their closeness come to such an abrupt end had been a shock to her. Her relationship with the Lord and with her family had helped her bridge the gap, but her family couldn't replace what she had shared with Hal in those few short days. She knew God didn't intend for them to, so she had learned to depend on him more and more. She had stayed busy with her work at the post office and at church, and that had all helped. She had also been collecting items to set up housekeeping if or when Hal got home and they could move on to that. The uncertainty of his situation had been a heavy burden. When she had gotten word of Hal's being wounded, she feared she would lose the baby. Much prayer by her, her family, and the church family had helped her survive that. When she had gotten the call from Leslie Davis, she somehow knew that God had heard her prayers and that Hal was going to be cared for. She longed to meet her personally. Leslie's care for Hal had been God's way of transferring her longing to care for him in his wounded condition, but now she needed him to hold her hand and reassure her. Her heart wanted him here, but her mind knew that wasn't possible.

She muttered, "Please hurry and get well and come home to us. We both need you so much!"

Hal's mom had finally been able to reach the hospital in Bangkok by phone only to be told that Hal was no longer there. They told her Hal was being shipped to Ft. Lewis, Washington for further rehabilitation. His arrival time was not known since the plane he was on carried other wounded men. They were going to land in Hawaii so the wounded on board could be monitored. If any needed treatment before continuing on, that would delay the trip on to Ft. Lewis.

Sue and her mom had already left for the hospital in Mt. Home so she was unaware of these developments. Both moms had been through this experience several times and knew Sue didn't need this added stress now. When Mom Edwards got to the hospital, they decided Sue could be told later that Hal was on his way to Ft. Lewis. Sue's contractions were coming about every two minutes now, and she knew it wouldn't be long. She sensed God's presence, but she sure wished Hal was here to hold her hand. She was anxious about this unknown experience and just needed him with her. Her mom understood this; she too had been there. Because of that, she knew that God's strength was sufficient, and she told Sue so. They prayed, and then she went to get an attendant to bring a wheel chair for her. The doctor was waiting in the delivery room and did a quick exam. It wouldn't be long now. Sue's mom waited with her in the room just off the delivery room. She shared her own experience of when she delivered Sue those twenty-one years before. Medical practices had come a long way since then, she said, so everything was going to be okay. Nurses came to monitor Sue every so often and prepare her mentally. The next hour seemed to take forever, and the pains were becoming stronger and closer together. *Wow, this is going to be more difficult than I imagined,* she thought. *I think I understand what some of the pain Hal has been going through must have been like now. Dear God, please let him be okay.*

Another hour passed, and she suddenly said, "Mom, it's time! Tell them to get me in there and get this over with."

There was a flurry of activity. Everyone knew what to do, and soon she was positioned on the delivery table. The doctors and nurses were in place, and she was being encouraged to bear down. She had been asked if she wanted a shot to lessen the pain but had declined because she didn't want anything to hinder the whole experience. Searing pain shot through her and she could hardly hear the encouragement she was getting.

"Here comes the head," the doctor said matter-of-factly. "Everyone, be in place. Sue, give another big push; we're about there!"

Summoning strength she knew was not her own, Sue gave a big effort and suddenly felt the baby come forth. She felt as though she would pass out; but she didn't want to miss any of this, so she hung on.

Suddenly she heard the doctor exclaim, "It's a boy! Good job, Sue! Here, ladies. Let's get him all wrapped up."

The next several minutes were a blur for Sue as the rest of the process was taken care of. Finally, the head nurse came and laid a beautiful little boy all wrapped in a little blue blanket in her arms! This new momma took one look at the baby boy; in that moment, her heart was forever captured by the wonder of this God-given gift! Somehow, she knew he was special.

"How much does he weigh?"

"Eight pounds, four ounces," the nurse replied.

"How long is he?"

"Twenty-one inches," was the reply.

"I did it, Hal, I did it! He's here! Oh babe, where are you? Please come home!"

Pride for this new addition to their family filled her heart, and she wanted to share it with her dear husband.

"Has Hal been told yet?" she asked.

The nurse went to the door and motioned for the moms to come in. Mom Edwards said that the hospital in Bangkok told her that Hal was being transferred at that very time to Ft. Lewis. She said that they would be stopping in Hawaii and perhaps she could contact him on the ground there. Hawaiian time was about four or five hours ahead of Idaho time, so he should be getting in there soon. They decided to call the Army Information Office at Ft. Lewis to see if they could get a phone number at the hospital on Oahu or have Hal call them at the number at the hospital in Mt. Home. Prayers were offered that this would happen.

Later, after Sue had received all the attention a new mother requires after giving birth, she was wheeled to a room, and "little Eddie" was brought in. The rest of the family was allowed in to meet the new member of the family. Everyone agreed he was just about "the cat's meow"! While he was being passed around for everyone to hold for a minute, the phone in the room rang. Sue's heart was in her mouth! Stu answered it while everyone quieted and listened. The hospital switchboard asked for him to hold for an overseas call. Stu quickly passed the phone to Sue and told her it was coming from overseas.

"Hello," a questioning voice said. "Who am I talking to?"

"Hi, Daddy, this is the momma of your precious new baby boy!" Sue cried.

"He's here already? Oh babe, I'm sorry. I wanted to be there," Hal said in a tired voice.

"Where are you now? Are you doing okay, babe? We were told when your mom called the hospital in Bangkok that you were being flown to Ft. Lewis. You're not there yet, are you?"

"We're on the ground at an Army medical center here on Oahu, Hawaii. They're making sure we're all doing okay. We should be into Ft. Lewis sometime tomorrow morning. I wanted to get there and see if they would let me come on home, but it's too late for that now. I don't think they would've allowed it anyway. I'm still pretty weak and have a lot of healing to do. I'm not sure when I'll be able to get home, Babe. I miss you all so much, and I'm just sorry that I'm missing all of this," Hal sighed. "I can't wait to see all of you and to hold our little guy! Are you doing okay, love? I'm proud of you!"

"Now that I've talked to you and shared our news, I'm fine. He's special, Hal! You'll see when you get here. Well, they all say to tell you they love you and can't wait to see you. We're all very proud of you, sweetheart! I miss you so much. I'm being told I have to hang up now. Call me when you get to Ft. Lewis and can do so. Bye-bye and we love you," she said as she hung up.

"Mom, somehow we've got to go to Ft. Lewis to see Hal. He's hurting, and he needs us there to help him get healed up. It's more than just his physical wounds; he's wounded in spirit too. I just know it. He needs to see his little boy! That will help do the trick. Besides, I need to see him so bad too. Can you help me make this happen?" Sue was crying as she finished her plea.

Hal's dad, C. D. was a, tall, raw-boned man. He was always pretty quiet, but he just had a way of getting things done. He loved his family and would do anything for them. He knew what Sue was saying about Hal's need, and he decided that he would

HAROLD SOUTHWICK

make this happen for her and the baby. Besides, he and his wife both needed to see him as well.

He stepped out of the room with Dot, his wife, and said, "Let's see if Stu will take care of things at the ranch for us for a week."

"What are you up to now, Dad?" Dot asked.

"Sue needs to go up there to see Hal. And Hal needs to see his baby boy! We can make it happen. So let's do it, okay? Besides that, we both need to see him too. God has let him get back here from all that mess he's gone through, and we need to show him we care. Those guys have been over there for all of us, and most people don't give a hang about that! As soon as the baby can go, we'll load Sue and him and her mom up in the van, and we'll all head up there. It'll be just what we all need. These last nine months have been hard on all of us.

"Well, C.D., let's do it then," she said."Good, that's settled." C. D. said with resolve.

His wife just smiled and nodded her agreement. They went back into the room, and Sue looked at them expectantly. She loved Hal's family and was thankful for all the help they had been for her and her mom.

"Well, young lady, I think we can get that done for you. Let's find out how soon this little guy can travel!" C. D. drawled in his slow, deep voice. He had a big twinkle in his brown eyes. Sue was reminded again how his eyes and Hal's eyes were so alike. *No wonder Hal's the kind of man he is,* she thought.

CHAPTER 15

As Sue lay there in bed beside Hal, she knew that he was thinking about all that had gone on in their lives since that day they first saw each other at that rodeo. She also knew, instinctively, that Hal had something else that was tugging at his heart. *He'll share it with me when he has it nailed down in his heart,* she thought.

As she lay there, memories of that trip to Ft. Lewis came back to her. The doctor had told them that if everything went well they could take little Eddie up there in a couple of weeks. She had recovered quickly and was out of the hospital in two days. They were able to bring Eddie home on the same day to a big welcome from church family and friends. The following days were filled with learning how to care for this new member of the family. She had a lot of help with that chore from both grandmas. Plans were being made for the trip, and it was a time of great anticipation. She couldn't wait! She remembered the call from Hal when he had gotten into Ft. Lewis and had been placed in the hospital there. He sounded tired and down in spirit but tried not to let it show. She wanted to tell him they would see him in a few days, but C. D. wanted to surprise him, so she prayed with him instead.

The trip to Ft. Lewis had been an interesting one. None of them had ever been to the Seattle, Tacoma area, so they were seeing how pretty the rest of the Northwest was. All the traffic and activity, as well as the size of the place, made them a little nervous. Glenn's Cove wasn't even a drop in the bucket com-

HAROLD SOUTHWICK

pared to this place. They all agreed, however, that that was why they liked home so much. It was late at night when they got to the motel Gramps had reserved, and they were exhausted by the time they got checked in and unloaded. Everyone was surprised that the baby had been such a little trooper during the long ride. They had made several stops so he could be tended to and fed; he had done very little fussing, and, of course, everyone was proud of that.

Sue was up early the next morning feeding Eddie and getting him ready. She wanted to get to the hospital! Her mom said that they better call ahead to see when they could get in to see Hal. She finally found a phone number for Madigan Hospital and dialed the front desk. She was told that Hal would be in therapy from seven thirty to eight thirty and would be returned to his room by nine a.m. She told them that they wanted to surprise him with being there so please not to tell him. They agreed and said they would have everything set up for them when they got there. They were to be there at nine thirty. His doctor would meet them at the front desk and escort them to Hal's room. After getting directions how to get to the base and then to the hospital, they decided to go to Denny's across the street from their motel and eat some breakfast. Sue was so uptight that she had trouble eating. Her mom said she had to keep herself nourished so that the baby would receive the nourishment he needed. Sue thought, *Oh boy, Eddie, nothing is going to be left to chance where you're concerned, little guy.*

Grandpa Edwards proudly showed his grandson off and told the waitresses that he was going to see his daddy, home from the war and in the hospital! That brought a lot of well wishes. Finally, it was time to go see Daddy! Suddenly, Sue was nervous. She could not have told anyone why, but she just hoped Hal still loved her like before and that he was going to be proud of her and this baby she had bore for him!

She hugged everyone and said, "Hurry, let's go see him. He'll be better in no time. Please be with him, dear Lord!"

"I sure hope he doesn't pass out from surprise!" Dot suddenly exclaimed.

"Aw heck, Mom, he's a man!" his dad returned. "Come on. Let's go make his day!"

Hal was back in bed in his room, being hooked up to the pain-medication IV drip when his doctor came through the door.

"Hal, someone is here to see you. Are you up for visitors?"

"Well … yes. Who is it?" he asked.

"Let me go bring them in from the waiting room."

Hal wasn't aware that anyone was supposed to come see him. Maybe it was someone from the advisory group wanting to check up on him. He was hoping that Sue would call sometime this morning and let him know how she and Eddie were doing.

The door opened, and the nurse held it for someone to follow. The nurse stepped aside and watched his reaction, ready to respond if need be. His expression went from curiosity to wonder, to complete surprise as he watched Sue step through the door with a little blue bundle held tightly in her arms! He tried to catch his breath, and tears filled his eyes. He was speechless! His eyes searched her face, and he reached for her with arms that had craved to hold her for so long. He was vaguely aware that others were crowding into the room. Everyone was watching him with smiles and tears as he clutched Sue to him and then reached to see this precious new gift from God. Sue leaned down and opened the little blanket and proudly extended her arms filled with this little guy they had brought into the world to Hal. She waited expectantly for his reaction. His face registered wonder, joy, and then pride as he looked at the baby. Then he leaned down and tenderly kissed Eddie on the forehead. As he looked up to Sue, he was struggling to maintain his composure. Finally, he just let go and wept tears of joy! He was back where he belonged, with his family. Suddenly, in the midst of all these emotions, he sensed in his mind the presence of that "hand" again. This time it seemed to be caressing his back. When he could find his voice, he

HAROLD SOUTHWICK

spoke with such feeling that all hearing him saw how powerful this moment was for him. In that moment, Sue and C. D. knew they had given him the best coming-home present he could have received.

"Oh, my gosh, babe! I love you! He's great. What a gift and what a surprise you've brought me. I can't believe you're here! You are just beautiful! You look great!"

Finally, he noticed everyone else crowding around the bed. His mom leaned down and kissed and hugged him to her and just sobbed. Then his dad was clutching his hand and beaming at him. Last, but not least, Sue's mom was hugging him. Hal's cup was full.

The nurse checked his vitals again and observed his level of engagement with his family. Sue took note of her efficiency and was impressed. After asking Hal if he was doing okay, she said to page her if he needed anything and left. The rest of the morning was filled with catching up, talking about the baby being born, Hal's time in the hospital in Bangkok, and his getting to know Leslie Davis. When his dad began to ask questions about his combat time and the battle in which Hal was wounded, he was reluctant to talk much about it. His mom noticed this and laid her hand on his dad's arm to quietly interrupt these questions. They all noticed that he seemed relieved to not have to try talking about it right then. They could all recognize a difference in his demeanor from what they remembered about him. He seemed more reserved, and, at the same time, they sensed a resolve and a depth of something they couldn't put a name to just yet. This young man of theirs had come home changed in ways they had yet to come to know and understand. He had been aged by more than just the months that had passed since they had last seen him. They saw sadness in him and wanted to know more about that. Dot knew her son well and knew that encompassed more than just his combat time and his injuries. Sue seemed to sense this as well. Later, when they had left the room to get some lunch, they talked about those feelings and agreed there was a lot more to learn about the changes in Hal and what had brought them about. His obvious love and pride for his little son was heartwarming. Sue ached for the day when he would be released from the hospital and was able to come home. She needed her husband in so many ways. She knew that she could help him heal quicker and better than this hospital could. By the end of their five days there, when they had to leave and go back home, Dot could tell that Hal was on the mend. She knew that was so in both mind and body. God was good.

HAROLD SOUTHWICK

CHAPTER 16

The trip back to Idaho was uneventful, though somewhat wistful. The good-byes had been difficult, especially when Hal had kissed Sue and then held Eddie for the last time before they left. He had hid his face in the little guy's neck and whispered in his ear how much Daddy loved him and his mommy. Everyone else had left the room by then to give the three of them this time alone. Sue had watched that moment between father and son and understood that she was watching the beginning of a very special relationship. She found herself hoping then that her relationship with each of them individually, as well as together, would not be diminished somehow. She vowed then to do all she could to enhance the relationship for all of them. She knew that would always be accomplished by prayer. God was both the author and finisher of all of this.

When they arrived back home, they set about getting ready for when Hal would be released and come home. They had decided that Sue and Hal should set up housekeeping in the little two-bedroom second house on the ranch. That would make it possible for Dot to help Sue with the baby if she needed it and also with Hal if that might be unexpectedly needed. Sue's mom was only a couple of miles away and could check in when she was off work at the post office. C. D. thought these plans were just right. Stu had taken a job working for a big fertilizer conglomerate over in the Magic Valley. Because of that, C. D. was hoping that when Hal got back on his feet he would want to become a full time partner in the ranch operations. He knew all of that still hinged on whether Hal was released from active duty when he was released from the hospital and completed his home rehab time. It was getting along in February; he would have to start planning the coming year's work and what help he was going to need.

Sue wanted to do some repainting and put up new curtains and do some other things that women just seemed to always want to do to a place before they moved in. So, the women all got together and decided to make it a project for the ladies group at church. Sue hoped Hal would be able to come home in about three weeks, so they got right on the project. It was a fun time, and much prayer went into the preparation of this new first home for these two young people and their new baby. The second bedroom was turned into a nursery for Eddie with all the things that went with that. Sue made sure that Hal's rodeo trophies, ropes, etc. were displayed for his viewing pleasure. Last, but not least, she added her own special touch to the main bedroom; this would be their own special hideaway. Soon all was ready and waiting for Hal's return. A special welcome home was being planned at the church.

CHAPTER 17

Hal was being kept aware of all the goings-on at home and was looking forward to getting out of the hospital. His rehab had been going very well and his doctor had him scheduled for release the first of March. He would have to go through a debriefing time for his service in Viet Nam due to the nature of their mission with the SVA. Then he would have to process out of active duty. The army had informed him that he had served his country well and he would be released from active duty. He would be eligible for disability compensation and continuing military medical care. This made him a happy man. He wanted to get on with this new chapter in his life. He was to be awarded a Purple Heart, a Meritorious Service ribbon, and a South Vietnamese campaign ribbon by the post commander on the day of his discharge. Hal was sorry that none of his family would be there for that; but it would be videotaped, so they could see the ceremony that way. He was all right with that. He wanted to go home. The "hand" was urging him that way.

The last few days of February were cold and wet in western Washington, but to Hal they were beautiful. He was given a last physical and therapy session on the twenty-sixth, then driven around the base courtesy of the motor pool and cleared those stations he needed to clear for release from active duty. The following day he was able to get a pass and go up to Whidbey Island to see A. J., his older brother, for a few hours. He returned to base and spent that night in temporary duty billeting. Those were sleeping quarters where those who were only going to be staying for one night or a very short time slept. Early the next morning, he called Sue and told her he would be leaving for his awards ceremony and given his discharge papers at nine a.m. After that was over, he would be transported by motor pool vehicle to Sea-Tac airport and would be on the eleven thirty Northwest flight to Boise. He had already told her all of this before, but he just wanted her to be sure to be at the airport with "bells on"! At last this time in his life was over, and he was going to be free to move on to whatever it was that God wanted him to do next. He knew it began with becoming the husband and father he had watched his dad be. Beyond that, he knew God had something specific for him to do. He had a lot to learn yet, and he looked forward to the journey. He remembered asking God to prove to him that he was who the church family had told about. Wow! Had God ever been doing that in the last year! He felt humbled and in awe that God wanted to use him. He was just a country boy from Idaho. All he had to offer God was himself, and he was about to find out that was exactly what God wanted.

His awards were pinned on his uniform by the base commander, and he was thanked for his service to his country. This left him feeling humbled and yet proud that he had done "his duty." When he was handed his discharge papers, the thought ran through his mind, *This is what I've been looking for.* An hour later he was at the Seattle-Tacoma airport, waiting to board the plane. The flight home was a time of quiet anticipation and reflection for him. He just thanked God for keeping him safe and helping him to be able to be with his family again. He wondered how Bob was doing and if he would ever see him again. He thought of Leslie Davis and what she had come to mean to him. He would call her the first chance he got at home. Somehow, he knew he would see her again.

The sight of Sue holding Eddie and pointing down the ramp to him, saying, "There comes your daddy" filled him with great joy! Their embrace and kisses completed the journey; he was back. In a few more miles he would be home.

HAROLD SOUTHWICK

As they walked down to the baggage claim area, Hal was carrying Eddie and trying not to show that his left shoulder and arm were not as strong as he thought. Sue noticed his discomfort and said, "Let me take him, babe. You'll have lots of time to carry him when you get your strength back. By the way, I brought your truck up to get you. I knew you would be anxious to drive it again. I think you love that thing more than you love me sometimes!"

"Not hardly, pretty girl, but thanks. I haven't driven much since being called up, and I've missed my truck. I'm surprised Stu hasn't worn it out by now."

"Stu has his own new truck now. He makes good money at his new job."

"Maybe I'll borrow some and buy me a new one."

"I doubt that. You love this truck too much to trade it off!"

"You're probably right, love. Let's go home!"

They retrieved his baggage and left the airport. Hal felt great behind the wheel again, and to have his beautiful wife and his son there beside him made him aware of how precious life was now. The ride home to Glenn's Cove was filled with catching up on news and family things and with laughter like the old days when they were dating. Soon, they were home, and as Hal drove down the trail from the highway to the house, he saw his mom and dad sitting on the front porch waiting for them. He stopped the truck, and then, before getting out, he hung his head and silently thanked God for this scene before him. He had wondered several times while in Vietnam if he would ever see his folks sitting there on that porch again. The weather was still cool but not bad for early March, and his dad had his arm around his mom. Sue and Hal looked at each other and smiled.

She said, "There is us in forty years!"

"Yup, that's special."

They got out of the truck as his folks got up and came down the steps to greet them. His mom gave him a hug and cried on his shoulder.

"I feared I would never be able to hug you here on this porch again. I'm so glad you're back!"

Hal embraced her with tears of his own, "Me too, Mom."

His dad took his hand and pulled Hal to him. He said with a catch in his voice, "Now you're truly back home, Son! We've prayed for you every day since you left, and now we have much to catch up on. Let's get you unloaded and spend the afternoon just being family."

The afternoon was spent in eating, talking, playing with little Eddie and phone calls. People from the church welcomed him home; the pastor and his wife wanted them all to come for a meal as soon as they got settled in. He called his older sister, Peg, in Montana, and his younger sister, Leah, in eastern Idaho. Those were emotional calls and left him wishing they were here. He and Leah had been especially close as kids and had shared in each other's adventures and everything else. They had grown even closer after their brother D. D. had been killed in a hunting accident when Hal was fifteen. His mom and dad had suffered so much from that, and it had motivated them to keep the family closer together since. That had been the push that had finally caused his dad to start going to church with his mom. He had never tried to push the kids into going, but Hal could tell that the tragedy had caused him to start looking beyond himself for some solace. At the time, Hal had felt no need for that, but looking back now after what he had seen and experienced in Vietnam, he had a deep appreciation for how God could calm and mend a hurting soul.

CHAPTER 18

The weeks that followed his return home were filled with getting settled into their little home and learning how to be a daddy to his son. That first night of his return, having Sue finally in his arms again had been more than he had hoped for. Their passion and fulfillment finally quieted the longings they had endured those long, lonely months of separation. It sealed the bond between them and cemented forever in Hal's mind his commitment to provide for his God-given family. He began a routine of reading the Bible every morning before working out to help restore his strength and the use of his shoulder and arm. Sue was quick to see his need to understand God's Word better, so she bought him his own special study Bible. She longed for the day when he would feel free to share with her what all he had experienced that day when he was wounded in combat. She resolved to pray for him every day to be healed of the pain of those memories. She thanked God for the newness of their precious baby to help in that process. She thought, *God's timing and his provision are miraculous. He knows what he is doing. I just wish I knew more about what he is doing. I don't think Hal even knows for sure; but he is searching and he wants to be ready for what it brings.*

Hal was slowly working his way back into the ranch routine. He had always enjoyed working with the cattle and was glad when he could get back on his horse and help with the cutting and branding. He was also glad to get back on a tractor and do some field work. He remembered his dad taking him on the old tractor and combine when he was a little boy and showing him how to operate them. He had been as proud as a peacock. Now he looked forward to the day when he could do the same with his son. Some people thought that this kind of work was too hard and dirty, but Hal found great satisfaction and a sense of providing a need in this work. Besides, it now gave him solitude where he could think about the things of God. It had a spiritually maturing effect on him. He was impatient to get back to his old physical condition so that he could do his full share of the work. And also he wanted to do a few more rodeos! He hadn't told Sue about this yet, but he hoped she wouldn't give him too much resistance. He knew he wouldn't be able to ride broncos anymore, but he could still do some roping.

CHAPTER 19

Hal called Leslie Davis in Bangkok shortly after he returned home and talked to her a few more times as spring moved into summer. She had been pleased with his recovery. She shared with him that she had been visiting several other soldiers who had been wounded in Vietnam at the hospital where he had been. She admitted though that she missed him and their conversations. She promised to keep him informed of the work and to continue to pray that God would show him what it was he was supposed to do in answer to the beckoning he sensed. Sue and Hal took little Eddie up to the cabin at Trinity Lake and spent a week in early August. The fishing was good, and the time they spent hiking and playing with Eddie was great therapy for Hal, not only mentally, but physically as well. They reminisced about their honeymoon there fourteen months before. It was a very special place for them. That was where Eddie had been conceived and their life together had begun. By the end of the week, Hal felt he was finally getting back to normal, both mentally and physically. He knew it was time to take the load of the ranch off his dad's hands and let his folks slow down a little if that was what they wanted to do. He also knew now was the right time to talk to Sue about wanting to do some roping at a few rodeos as well. While out hiking the last morning along the lake, he brought it up.

"Suzy girl, how would you feel about me doing a little week-end roping at a few rodeos? I feel that I'm about ready to get back to doing some of the things I loved doing, and that's where I want to start."

"I figured you were about ready to test yourself out pretty soon and that was where you would want to start," she said with a grin. "I know how much you loved the sport, so I say go for it!"

"You really mean it? Thanks, babe. I want to try a couple of rodeos this fall and then maybe do several next year. I promise to not get too involved, and I'd love to have you and Eddie go with me when you feel like you can. Also, I know that Dad and Mom want to slow down and get away from the ranch more, so I'm going to make Dad a proposal. If he agrees, I will take over management responsibilities during the week if he will look after things one or two weekends a month. That way I could try my luck at roping again. I won't start doing that until next rodeo season though. I want Dad to break me in on managing things the rest of this year. What do you think?" Hal was a study of earnestness.

"That sounds good to me. There's one thing that we should think about, though. We're going to need more living space if we have another baby," she replied.

His answer surprised her, "I've been thinking about that too. Mom and Dad don't need all that room in the big house any more, and it's more work than Mom needs to keep up with. How about if we pray that God would help them to see our future needs and theirs too? I love that house and especially that front porch. We've spent many wonderful times out there."

"Where would they live then?" she asked.

"We could fix up our house the way they might want it, and they could live there. It would be plenty big enough for the two of them," Hal replied.

As the summer moved into fall, Hal began to realize just how much was involved in the long-range planning to make the ranch a viable business, as well as the day-to-day operations. His proposal to his dad had been met with cautious agreement. His mom thought the idea was a good one. She looked forward to being able to do some short-term missionary trips, and she wanted C. D. to go with her. She and Sue's mom had been talking about doing something like that for a good while. C. D. told Hal he already knew enough to take on the majority of the day-to-day work. For the most part, their two hired hands knew what was required of them each day and were very good at doing it. His job would be to see that they had what they needed to get the job done and to organize the timing of the work, etc. Hal had watched his dad do all that stuff for years and pretty well knew what to do. What surprised him the most was the weight of the responsibility for the decisions that had to be made. His dad had never talked about that very much, and it had seemed a natural thing for him to do. Hal knew that with experience he would feel comfortable with the responsibility. In fact, he felt excited about the job. As for doing some more roping in rodeos on a few weekends, his dad thought that was okay. It still let him have a hand in the ranch operation. He still needed that.

CHAPTER 20

As Hal lay in bed beside Sue, he thought about how much he had really enjoyed his time on the ranch and the time he had been able to spend roping in rodeos over the last two and half years. He had really come to appreciate his dad more and more for the patience and enthusiasm he had shown in helping Hal learn the ropes of managing the ranch work and for letting him have those weekends off to enjoy his favorite sport again for a while. He also really appreciated Sue for bearing with him. She had taken Eddie to a few of the closer rodeos, and they had shared some of the old romance of those first days when they had met and he was rodeo riding. But now as he thought about it all, he knew that it was time he moved on and finally answered the call on his heart. He was now pretty sure what it was that God was asking him to become involved in. He had been growing in his understanding of God and what he wanted from those who called him Lord; and he loved the Sunday school class he attended, but he knew now that it was time to get involved in his own ministry. As he had watched Eddie grow and change, he became more aware that he needed to be home so he could be involved in Eddie's spiritual development. A plan had been coming to mind that intrigued him. He had gotten involved at church with the junior boys group a little bit, and he had this idea about bringing young boys, and girls too if they wanted, out to the ranch and teaching them about horses and other ranch animals. They were part of God's creation, and Hal thought it would be good to teach the

HAROLD SOUTHWICK

kids how to care for the animals as well as the different uses God had created them for. Some of the boys had some experience with animals, but they could still learn a lot more about them. He decided to talk to his dad and mom, as well as Sue in the morning. As he prayed before he went to sleep, he knew it was time to give up his rodeo participation and go ahead with this. With that decision made, peace settled on him, and he fell into a deep, contented sleep. His earlier feelings of inadequacy were suddenly gone, and a sense of direction had taken away his fear of not being prepared. God was calling him to use the very things he knew best to begin his journey of service!

The next morning at the breakfast table, he told Sue about the decision. She gave him a big smile.

"As I was laying there beside you praying last night, I knew God was bringing you to an important decision! What all are you talking about?" she asked, happy that he would be home most of the time now.

"Well, I feel that God would like for us to start a ministry to the young kids in the church using the horses and other animals out here as the teaching focus. I want Mom and Dad to be involved in it as well. Why don't we have them over for supper tonight and talk about it. I'll tell you what I'm thinking about then. Is that okay with you? I'm still trying to piece it together myself," he grinned.

"I think that is a great idea, love! What ages do you plan on working with?" Her mind was already kicking in to gear.

Hal hadn't really thought about that aspect yet but realized it was something to consider. "Good question. What do you think?" He was already seeing how others could fit into the whole project. "Think about it today, and then we'll both lay it out to Dad and Mom tonight."

That night at supper, his parents were taken with the idea right away. It all kind of amazed Hal; he guessed that when God was ready for some ministry to get under way he quickly prepared the hearts of those he wanted involved.

Sue was quietly thrilled that Hal was moving into the potential she had always known he possessed. By their response to the idea, she could tell his folks felt the same way. C. D. suggested that they ought to talk to Pastor Don about it and encourage his involvement as well. He had three young kids that might like something of that nature. Sue said she would be the coordinator with the families and would try to recruit some of them to help out at times. If some kids needed transportation, she could take care of that. Mom said she could be in charge of refreshments and tending to scrapes and bruises. There was sure to be some of those to deal with. That brought up the need of insurance coverage on the ranch for the project. Dad volunteered to take care of that. He also said he would take care of which animals to have involved each day. They all decided that one afternoon each week would probably be best.

Pastor Don liked the idea and approached the church about it. For the most part, they seemed in favor. Some moms were a little reluctant because they saw a potential for injury to their kids, but others said that was a part of life and that kids could be injured doing about anything. As the church people watched the plans take shape, they began to see that this ministry could be a good way to keep their kids off the streets and become involved in something that might help them later in life. Hal began to feel a deep sense of gratitude to God about this whole thing. Deep emotion welled up in him as he watched the Lord work through the Holy Spirit to bring people together in making the endeavor happen. He also began to see that this ministry could expand into a far wider effort than just the ranch and animals! He was going to have to pray about all of these ideas that were coming to him. He suddenly knew that he would have to run all of this by his dear friend and spiritual mentor in Bangkok. She would have some insight for him.

HAROLD SOUTHWICK

Thus began what became a great outreach tool for the church and a source of great satisfaction for Hal. Sue and his folks were also learning how rewarding it was to see these young kids go from anxious curiosity to fascination and into deep enjoyment of what they were doing. They soon grew to love the animals, especially the horses, and their whole demeanor evolved into a sense of being a part of something that was worthwhile and just plain fun. Hal and Sue watched them change and knew that they were being changed along with the kids. They came to realize together that this was God's ministry for them and that was its own reward.

Those first few years were especially rewarding for them as they watched Eddie grow from a little boy and come to love the ranch and the animals along with the other kids that became a part of the program. Added to that was the beautiful little dark-haired baby girl born into the family eight months into the outreach program.

Sue's pregnancy had gone well, and the baby was born in early February. They named her Audra Sue. She had her daddy's darker hair whereas Eddie had blond hair like his momma's, but her features were a carbon copy of her mommy. She soon became the apple of her daddy's eye, and Eddie took to her like flies to honey. She took time from Sue's involvement in the "Ranchin' Kids Outreach" as it became known; but soon everyone in the program adopted her, and she became a part of the whole deal.

Eddie became close friends with a young boy who had been one of the first kids to join the "RKO." His mom and dad had started coming to church shortly after Hal had come home from Vietnam, and they had become good friends with Hal and Sue. Their names were Bob and Joan Johnston, and the boy's name was Jimmy. Bob was from Minnesota and had been in the air force, stationed at Mt. Home Air Force Base when they first came to Idaho. He had been released from active duty but was still in air force reserve. He was pretty sure he would be called back to active duty as the war in Vietnam escalated. They had moved to Glenn's Cove because they liked the rural setting and the outdoor recreation opportunities. Joan worked at the school as a teacher's aide, and Bob had a civilian job at the air base. He commuted with several others in town who worked at the base. They had come to love the ranch outreach activities and had become two of the most dedicated helpers along with others from the church. This whole endeavor had led to a great fellowship and many camping trips and other field trips had been enjoyed by everyone.

CHAPTER 21

Hal had always loved being out on the Snake River in a boat. So, when he was able, he had bought a seventeen-foot outboard boat, which soon became another feature of the ministry. At the time, no one knew that it would also become the one part of the ministry that would lead to heartache and tragedy. When God is at work in people's lives and much is being accomplished for his glory, Satan hates it and will do anything he can to hinder the work. Hal had heard the pastor make the statement several times, but he had not yet experienced direct personal implications of that fact. He knew that the ministry was a very effective effort and that sooner or later they would come up against Satan's efforts to kill it. Because those involved in it knew this, they had formed a prayer team that spent some time each day praying for everyone and everything connected to "RKO." They all knew that the reason everything had flourished the way it had was directly related to God's answer to those prayers.

The long front porch of the ranch house had become the most favorite place for the group to meet and pray together if the weather permitted. It gave everyone a view of the corrals and the activity going on there and was a place where God just seemed to come and visit with them. The kids also just loved spending time there as well. Many memories of time spent there would become a beacon to a certain young man experiencing troubled times in the distant future.

Bob had grown up around all those lakes in Minnesota, and his family had always had a boat. So it was only common sense for him to head up the boat part of the outreach program. The kids were taught how to swim, use of life jackets, water ski when they were old enough, safe use of a boat, and also the dangers that were a part of boating. In a few short months, the boating had become almost as popular a part of the ministry as the horses.

It was with great disappointment that Bob came to Hal one morning and said, "Hal, I finally got that same nasty little invitation like you received one time before! Uncle Sam wants my help in the mess in Viet Nam."

"Oh, no! When do you have to report?" Hal asked.

"I've got thirty days to get everything in order and report to Mt. Home Air Base for reassignment. I don't know where I'll go from there."

"I can picture Joan's reaction to that," Hal said, remembering Sue's response when he had told her about his own recall. Thinking back, he could hardly believe that it had been six years since that time. Eddie was already five years old, and Audi Sue was moving along toward two.

"Well, I reckon we better call everyone to come to the porch and cover you and your family in prayer." Hal drawled. "That sure was a comfort for Sue and me back then."

Hal's folks and he had traded houses to live in shortly after Audra Sue had been born. Dot had seen the need for the kids to have more room with the new baby and had discussed it with C. D., who had readily agreed. In fact, the double move had been accomplished with the help of all those on the "RKO" team. That turned out to be a fun time as well as a big help. It had been C. D.'s suggestion that they make the front porch the prayer altar.

The response to the call to prayer for Bob and Joan was what the whole group had come to be known for. It never failed to amaze Hal how those who loved the Lord and were committed to serving him rallied around each other when a need like this came upon one of their own. The thought went through his mind again that those who didn't want anything to do with God were their own worst enemy. If they could just get a glimpse of what God had for each of them if they would only trust him. Hal was overwhelmed anew that God had not been put off by his own less-than-honest acceptance of Christ those several years ago. Hal remembered asking God to prove himself to him. He had certainly done that through the events in Vietnam and everything leading up to and through this children's ministry.

With those thoughts and memories in mind, Hal led the group in prayer for their friends and coworkers that evening on the porch. They had all shared in a pot-faith supper and had then got down to the greatest ministry they had the privilege being a part of: *prayer*. By the time they had all prayed, tears were freely flowing, and a sense of calm confidence had come over all of them; that was evident more so in Bob and Joan. Joan would be staying in Glenn's Cove, and Bob knew she would be well looked after by the church family. He knew his friends and trusted Hal and Sue to lead in that effort. He also trusted the Hal and Eddie would be a big help where Jimmy was concerned. His son loved being around the two of them and the horses, so this continued relationship and the RKO activities would help keep him occupied while his daddy was away. God was at work. Bob and Hal could already see that the Lord was answering their prayers as the group rallied around the Johnston family. That support would come to be a great comfort in the trials that would soon be coming upon many in the group. It would also be sorely tested to persevere.

CHAPTER 22

Bob having to leave the ministry placed an added load on Hal. The need to keep the boating as a part of the program going was essential because the kids loved it. Every effort was made to figure out who would take Bob's place. Hal really didn't have the time to do it because of all the time the ministry with the horses and other animals required. In addition to that, running the ranch required a great deal of his time, and he was committed to doing that correctly because he felt he owed it to his dad and the family to provide for all of them. While they tried to get someone who was qualified to lead that part of the ministry, C. D. decided he would fill in as best he could. Hal had some reservations about that because of his dad's age; but he didn't want to hurt his feelings, and the need had to be met. For several weeks all went along pretty well, and everyone started to relax a little bit. His dad seemed to have a knack with the kids, and he had learned a lot about boating from watching Bob. Still, Hal worried about his ability to keep up with the kids. His eyesight and hearing weren't what they had once been either.

One afternoon several weeks after Bob had been recalled, Sue came running down to the corrals, where Hal and several boys and girls were practicing currying the three horses that were used for that purpose because of their disposition.

HAROLD SOUTHWICK

"Hal, come quickly!" she screamed. "I just got a call from Bets. Something has happened out on the river in the boat!"

C. D. had taken Eddie, Jimmy, and two other kids out in the boat to do some skills training. Betty Bourne was along as his helper. The training included getting to sit in the co-driver's seat and steer the boat with C. D. in the driver's seat, teaching and encouraging. Betty was an experienced swimmer and was always in the boat when these sessions were in progress. The boat was equipped with a mobile radio so they could communicate with Sue at the ranch house if the need arose.

With a sinking feeling in his gut, Hal quickly turned his tasks over to Pete Woodson, his pastor's dad and his assistant with this part of the ministry. He left on the run with Sue.

"Did Bets give any indication what was going on?"

"Just that something was wrong with your dad!" Sue sobbed.

"Let's go, babe. Come with me in case I need your help. Do you have the mobile radio?"

Hal was thinking as they jumped into the pickup and took off for the boat dock on the river about a mile away at the south end of the ranch.

"We better call for the ambulance to meet us there."

"I already have. You know we have our action plan in case of emergencies, and I've followed it," she exclaimed. "I've called the prayer chain as well!"

Hal slid into the parking area at the boat dock, and they jumped out of the truck as several others started to arrive. They had been trying to raise Bets on the mobile as they came down to the dock, but there had been no response. Hal tried to reassure Sue that Bets may have been too busy to answer the radio. As they were getting the small back-up boat into the water, Eddie's young voice came over the mobile radio on Sue's belt.

"Mommy, can you hear me? Grandpa's hurt!"

"Where are you, sweetheart? Daddy and I and others are at the boat dock getting ready to come help you. What's wrong with Grandpa? Is Aunt Bets okay?" Sue tried keeping her voice calm.

"We're down river toward town, around the bend from the dock, Mommy. Aunt Betty is working on Grandpa," came back the terrified young voice. "Tell Daddy to hurry!"

"Are you in the boat, or where are you?" She was trying to get as much information as she could so she could let the ambulance crew know what their response effort would include.

As Hal and Sue were loading the little boat, he asked their neighbor Jake Dean, who had just arrived with his boat, to wait for the ambulance and bring them to the scene. Jake also had a radio in his boat so they could keep in contact. With that done, Hal gunned the outboard motor, and they took off down river. They were both fearful of what they would find. The information from their frightened seven-year-old was very sketchy, to say the least. The training they had given the kids on how to use a radio along with the other emergency training had paid off so far. They were sure that Betty needed all the help she could get and in a hurry. As they came around the bend in the river and could get a sight on down-stream, Sue focused the field glasses on the river ahead. The boat came into view, and it appeared to be sitting at an angle with the front end up out of the water. They were about twenty or thirty feet from a little island that sat out in the river some forty feet from the south shore. As Hal and Sue drew nearer, they could see some of the kids leaning over the side of the boat looking toward the shore of the island. What was going on there was still hidden from Hal's view. As they approached, one of the kids heard them and turned and started waving frantically. As Hal brought the little boat up closer, he could tell the larger boat had hit a gravel bar that ran at an angle out into the river from the island and had lurched over to one side. He pulled in below the larger boat, taking care to stay away from the hidden bar in the water. They could see Betty as she bent over his dad. He lay partially out of the water on the edge of the island.

"Jimmy was thrown out of the boat, and Grandpa jumped out to help him!" Eddie was yelling and pointing. Sue could see Jimmy on the shore. He seemed to be holding his left arm. Sue quickly jumped into the water and went to the larger boat to calm

HAROLD SOUTHWICK

the kids while Hal rowed over to Betty and his dad. Her radio came to life, and the ambulance crew asked for an update. They were loading gear into Jake's boat and wanted to know what was most needed. Hal took one look at his dad and knew he was having a heart attack. Betty explained she had pulled him out of the water as far as she could and had been trying to clear water out of his lungs, but he was a large man and had been a heavy load for her. As Hal took over for her, she ran to Jimmy and started checking him out. He had been crying and holding his left arm. Upon examination, she could see that he had a nasty bruise on the elbow and was bleeding from a gash on the forearm.

"Tell the EMTs Dad is having a heart attack!" Hal yelled to Sue. "Betty, what do you have over there?"

"Jimmy's left elbow and forearm are injured. I can't tell if it's broken or not!" she hollered back.

Sue heard the exchange and relayed the information to Jake's boat. They radioed back that they were on their way. She warned them about the gravel bar and where to approach the island from. Hal could hear her and was proud of how she was responding under all this stress. Once again, the emergency training for their ministry efforts was paying off. C. D. was starting to regain consciousness; but his lips were blue, and Hal knew he needed oxygen badly. He gave his dad a couple of breaths mouth to mouth, and that started C. D. to coughing. More water spewed out of his mouth, and he began to thrash about so Hall dragged him farther up on the bank. He quickly checked for broken bones and then rolled him onto his side so that his mouth could drain. He put his hat under his dad's head and took off his shirt to cover him as much as possible. Hal knew that loss of body heat was a big factor in bringing on shock, and his dad had been in the cold water a long time. He silently thanked God for Betty and her presence with his dad in the boat.

"Hal, your dad saved Jimmy's life! He landed face down in the water and was not moving when he was thrown out. C. D. killed the motor and jumped out and got his face out of the water. I could see something was happening to him, because he started coughing and gasping by the time he got Jimmy close to shore. I got the kids calmed down some and jumped out to help him, but the water is swift below that gravel bar. We're about frozen!" Betty was shivering as she explained.

Hal could tell that she was in need of some attention herself. They could hear Jake's boat approaching and soon Jake had the EMTs on shore. They quickly started doing what they did so well. One immediately put a nasal cannula on C. D. and started oxygen while another went to tend to Jimmy. Hal grabbed blankets that Jake tossed to him and covered his dad and then went to wrap Jimmy in one. He started to put one around Betty's shoulder, but she began to protest.

"Bets, you're blue from cold, and you need to warm up some!" Hal exclaimed as he draped the blanket around her.

She stood there trembling, and tears fell from her eyes. Hal gave her a hug and thanked her for being there. She gave a nod and bent to help with Jimmy. Hal helped get his dad on a backboard and loaded in Jake's boat as Betty and Sue got Jimmy loaded on as well. Time was very critical, and they hurried to get headed back to the ambulance at the boat dock. Hal's dad needed intensive care immediately. Jimmy needed further checking, and they all needed to be warmed up. The questions could all be asked and answered later. Hal desperately wanted to go with his dad, but he knew his first responsibility was to get the kids and the boat, along with Sue and Betty, off the gravel bar and back to the boat dock.

He decided the first thing to try was to take the tow rope in the big boat and see if he could pull it off the bar with the smaller boat. They decided to put Eddie and the other two kids on the island with Betty while they tried this maneuver. Hal was just glad they had all had their life jackets on when the accident happened. Jimmy probably would have drowned before his dad could get him out of the water if not for that. Hal still didn't quite understand what all had gone on. Betty would have to answer all those questions when they had time to get to that. The sheriff's department would want to be involved in that also. Hal was sure they would be here soon, if they weren't already at the boat dock, waiting for the ambulance.

The thought suddenly crossed his mind, *Where was Dad's life jacket?* He had seen Jimmy still in his. Hal anchored the tow rope to the back of his little boat and then maneuvered it behind the big boat as Sue waited in the back of the larger boat. When he was able to back it up far enough, he threw the rope to Sue. After two tries, she was able to get it tied to the rope bracket on the back of the boat. The propeller was partially out of the water, so they couldn't start her motor to assist in the retrieval. Hal knew he would just have to quickly accelerate forward and see if he could move the boat back a little at a time. He knew the fast current where he was would help that some. It would be tricky, but if they could get the back of the big boat in the water enough for the propeller to be covered, she could start the motor and put it into reverse and help with the process. She would have to be quick in shifting to forward when the boat came off the bar to avoid colliding with Hal's boat. That way she could accelerate enough to keep the current from carrying her back into Hal's craft hopefully. The leaning of the big boat worried Hal especially since Sue was in it and he didn't know if there was damage to the underside where it rested on the bar.

After prayers, Sue said, "Let's hurry up and get this done. We need to get these kids back to shore and go see how Dad is doing!"

Hal accelerated about half throttle, and the boat hit the end of the rope with a pretty good tug. They could tell that it moved Sue's boat a couple of inches, so he backed up and gave it more throttle for the next try. This time it moved a little more. In the back of his mind, Hal wondered exactly how that boat had gotten so far up on that gravel bar. *Dad must have been pouring the coals to it.* After two more times, they had it back far enough so that the back end of it had come down into the water enough to cover the prop, and the angle of tilt had corrected itself some. It took coaching for Sue, but she was finally able to get the motor started. Hal was quietly proud of his little wife for her ability to do what she needed to do in times of emergency, and he told her so.

She crossed her fingers and sighed. "Okay, let's give it a try."

"As soon as I yell shift, you cut the throttle and shift to forward then give it enough gas to maintain position against the current. I'll try and back up enough to untie the rope," Hal instructed her again. "I'll have to do that while backing against the current, so that may be tricky. I'll get out of your way then, and you can move on back some. You'll have to check in the bottom of the boat for any water seeping in. I couldn't tell if there were any holes ripped in the bottom from the gravel. I don't think there was, but we need to be sure. If there is, just gun the motor and drive it back up on the bar. We'll have to get if off later."

He had Sue engage the reverse mode on the controls and told her to give it more throttle as he hit the end of the rope with his boat. After a couple of tries that way, the boat finally came clear of the gravel bar with a crunch of rocks and sand.

Hal yelled, "Shift!"

Sue quickly did as she was told, giving just enough gas to keep from drifting backwards in the current. It took some adjustment but soon she had things under control, holding the steering wheel steady. While she had been busy with that, Hal had been busy backing his own boat up enough to keep from pulling her on backwards. He had to watch that their directions of travel didn't suddenly reverse and their boats collide.

When he was convinced it was safe to do so, he told Sue, "I'm going to try and back up enough to untie the rope. When I get out of your way, let your boat come on back a little bit. The current will drift the rope back with you so that it won't get caught in your prop. Can you see any water in the bottom yet?"

"It looks okay so far, babe," she replied warily.

"Okay, here goes..." With that Hal increased the throttle, and his boat slowly backed up enough for him to release the rope. He had trouble trying to keep his boat steady in the current while he untied the rope but finally was able to succeed. He shifted the prop direction and maneuvered toward the island bank where Betty and the kids were watching and cheering them on. When he got out of his boat, he motioned for Sue to try to move on back and come along side of him with her boat. While she was attempting that, he quickly tied his anchor rope to a small shrub on the bank and waited to see if she was going to be able to do so. He knew they were going to need to put the kids back in the big boat to get them back to the dock. There just wasn't enough room in the little boat for all of them, and Hal knew he couldn't leave part of them behind. Sue made a circle out in the deeper water and came back around at an upstream angle to the island. She had to throttle up some to come through the swift current out from the bank as Hal had to do. As she eased in beside Hal's boat, she displayed a small smile of satisfaction at her accomplishment. It was quickly replaced with a look of concern as focus returned to the gravity of the situation. Hal reached out and secured the anchor rope to an adjoining sapling. They quickly checked the boat as well as they could. There were some scrapes and dents on the bottom ridge, but other than that, all seemed okay. Betty had the kids nearby by then, and they quickly got everyone loaded and seated. Sue took the wheel, and Hal had Betty pull the rope back into the boat and stow it under the rear seat bench. Then, as Sue started the motor, Hal pushed the boat off from the bank, and she drifted back and then turned and accelerated for the dock.

Hal could hear Eddie say, "Mommy, let's go home. I want to check on Grandpa!"

His thoughts suddenly returned to Vietnam and a time when those same sentiments went through his mind. He remembered the "hand" pointing him in that direction. He quickly untied and got his own rope in the boat and followed the others. Anxiety about his dad churned in his mind, and a prayer of hope fell from his lips. He saw Sue turn and give him a wave. How he loved that girl and those two precious children she had bore for him.

CHAPTER 23

Hal's oldest brother and his two sisters came into the hospital room together. They were all travel worn and worried about their dad. Dot was keeping a bedside vigil and got up to greet them with hugs and kisses. Leah and Peg had gotten to the ranch last evening after Hal had called them and told them of the morning's happenings. Hal and Sue had arrived back at the boat dock just before the ambulance crew had finished stabilizing C. D. and were there when he was taken away. He was only semi conscious, but some of the blue in his lips had receded as the oxygen level increased in his blood stream.

Hal stopped at the ranch house to get Dot and Audra and to tell Pete to shut RKO down for the day. The others would get all the other kids home, and the ranch hands would take care of the boats and the horses as well. Sue got Eddie and Audra into the car while Hal had taken care of all those details, and then they were off for the hospital in Mt. Home. The ambulance always stopped there first for these kinds of emergencies. Jimmy's mom, Joan, had been notified at her job and was at the hospital when they arrived. Jimmy had been transported on the same ambulance as C. D., so they were both there when Hal and Sue arrived. Sue took Eddie and Audra to the waiting room, while Hal and Dot rushed to the emergency room nurse's station to check on C. D. and Jimmy. They were informed that Jimmy was being examined and would be x-rayed before they would know if his arm was broken. Hal's dad was in the emergency room and was being given an EKG to determine what was going on with his heart. Blood tests were also being taken. IVs had been started as well as stabilizing medications.

While they were waiting, Joan joined them in the waiting room. Hal filled her in on all he knew about what had happened and brought her up to date on Jimmy. As she questioned a nurse, Hal was reminded of waking up in that hospital in Bangkok so long ago. A lot had happened in his life since then, but looking back, he had a renewed appreciation for the gift God had given to doctors and nurses. He knew many prayers were being said for his dad and Jimmy and knew from experience how prayer aided in the healing process. He was convinced prayer would be a powerful force in this situation as well. The thought struck him, *Without prayer, doctors and nurses wouldn't be as effective as they are.* What a motivation to become a better prayer warrior.

Joan had come back to them and said that Jimmy's X-rays had shown no breaks but just bruising and the contusion. His arm was being cleaned and medicated before being bandaged. He would be released shortly. Joan had questions about what exactly had happened, but she knew now was not the time to press for answers.

The next morning as Hal and Sue came into the room, they observed the scene before them and realized that there was going to be some hard questions from Hal's siblings. A. J. had always expressed his reservations about Christianity, and he thought Hal spent too much time away from the ranch on the RKO ministry. He had always felt that way about Hal and Stu when they were gone to rodeos too. Hal had thought many times that A. J. wasn't at the ranch at all anymore so what right did he have to complain? Leah and Peg were mostly noncommittal about it, but Hal knew they would all have something to say now that Dad had been involved in this boating accident.

After hugs and kisses and handshakes, Dot said, "Dr. Belton came in a while ago and said that the blood test confirmed what the EKG showed yesterday. Dad suffered a myocardial infarction. What that means is that a small blood vessel in the wall of the heart had become blocked, and the stress of yesterday morning caused the wall to become starved for oxygen, causing damage to that area of the heart chamber. He will need to be hospitalized for several days and kept under close observation. He should recover okay unless something else happens."

"Well, let's thank God for that!" A. J. exclaimed.

"I didn't think you believed in God, Bro," Hal replied sardonically.

His oldest brother gave him a hard look and continued, "What I'd like to know is what Dad was doing out there in that boat with those kids in first place."

"He was out there doing what he wanted to be doing," Hal shot back quickly, "but we are not going to get into that right now. We're going to rally around Dad and Mom and take care of first things first.

Dot took one look at her younger son's face and quickly interceded. "A. J., your dad has always had a mind of his own, and he loved helping out with the boat ministry. If you could have seen him and those kids together, you would not be questioning us about what he and, for that matter, all the rest of us have been doing. God called Hal to start this outreach, but he also called the rest of us to help with it. It just so happens that we love doing it!"

"That's right, Son," a weak voice from the bed entered in.

"Dad!" three voices exclaimed together. "How are you? We thought you were asleep."

Just then Stu came into the room, and the hugging and handshakes occurred again. He had just gotten back from one of his long sales rep trips for the agri-chem company he worked for. Hal had finally been able to contact him late the day before, and he had hurried home.

"Dad just woke up!" Dot exclaimed. She repeated what she had just told the others about the doctor's report.

While Stu considered that, Hal could sense that he felt somewhat like A. J. did. Hal determined that any further discussion about Dad and the boat was going to be taken care of away from his folks, or at least, away from his dad. He prayed a silent prayer about it as he and Sue exchanged a meaningful glance. She gave him a reassuring smile, and they joined the others around Dad. A calming from the Holy Spirit came over him, and he sensed the "hand" on his heart again. God was still in control!

CHAPTER 24

The next several weeks brought many changes to the lives of those involved in the RKO ministry. Jimmy's injuries were not serious, but Joan was reluctant to let him be involved in the boating anymore. She had called Bob in Korat, Thailand, where he was now stationed with the air force. He was concerned about his son, but he didn't think it was a good idea to not let Jimmy go out in the boat again. He felt as Hal did; if you got thrown off a horse, you got up and got back on again just to prove to yourself that you were man enough to do it! Don't let fear take control of your life. Joan kind of agreed, but she wanted Jimmy to heal up and to have some time to think about it.

Hal's family had finally come to agree that C. D. had probably started having a heart attack before he ran the boat aground. He was fuzzy on the memory of what had happened, but he pretty well confirmed their suspicions when he told them he felt a pain in his chest. He said he knew he needed to get them all back to the dock. He was unaware of the gravel bar running out into the river where they had hit it. He admitted that he was probably going too fast as he turned the boat around to go back to the dock but he just knew he had to hurry. Some of the church people understood, but some felt that he should not have been allowed to lead the boat ministry because of his age. Hal's siblings agreed with that, which left some strained feelings. Hal and Sue talked about it and decided they needed to call a meeting of all those involved in the ministry to discuss the future direc-

HAROLD SOUTHWICK

tion of the program. If God was using others outside the team to guide them in a new way of doing things, then they should give consideration to that. The boating part of the outreach had been put on hold, but everyone decided the rest of it should continue for the kids' sake. They needed to learn that accidents happen but that didn't need to interrupt God's involvement in their learning experiences. Hal, the pastor, and all the rest of the team saw this as a test of their resolve to continue doing God's will. It was also an opportunity to show these kids and even the skeptics that there was a way around roadblocks and adversity. Life is not always smooth sailing, but it still goes on; how we react to the events that God allows to come our way determines, for the most part, how we end up at the end of the road!

The meeting was convened on the ranch house porch and a good deal of time was spent in prayer at the beginning. Prayers of thanksgiving were offered for the fact that no one's life had been lost, that C. D. was mending, and that much had been learned about the actual use of their emergency resources. No one was cheering because this whole event had come about, but all of them, as well as those outside the program, saw that the steps they had put in place to deal with emergencies worked. They discussed things they could do to refine the procedures, but for the most part they all agreed that it had turned into a teaching and learning experience. If you had a good emergency program in place and everyone followed it and did their part, then the situation could be contained and the needs met. They knew they could only do so much and that ultimately God was in control of all that came into their lives and that prayer was the key to seeing and reacting accordingly. Hal was reminded of his military training. They had all been trained to be responsible for each other and to look out for fellow soldiers. That had been ground into each of them in training, and it had become a vital part of their survival in Vietnam, especially in combat situations. He thought of Bob and their experiences on that day in the mud when they both needed others to survive. That training had proven to be invaluable in preparing this ministry on how to function as well.

We really are our brother's keeper, he thought. *That is part of God's way of maintaining connection and community between people. Wow, God surely does love us, doesn't he?* Hal felt humbled again by the privilege of being used by God. He was being strongly led of the Spirit to widen the outreach of this ministry with these kids and the team. The "heavenly hand" was tapping on his shoulder again.

In the back of his mind, however, as this meeting progressed, he had a feeling that the boat would play a significant role in the lives of his family somewhere in the future. If he could only have known, but only God can see the future and still let it advance for his own purposes.

Agreement was reached to continue with the original focus of the ministry for now, with emphasis on the horse training part. Hal also revealed his desire to start training a team of youngsters to eventually go to Thailand and do a two-week mission outreach project in connection with Leslie Davis's work with the homeless kids in Bangkok. Hal had been corresponding with Leslie about the possibility and feasibility of doing this. She was very receptive and had promised to research just how to set something like this up. She would let him know and also try to determine when would be a good time to do it. Hal knew it would take time to get these young kids ready to do something like this. It would also take some time and much prayer to get the parents to come alongside and be willing to help raise the funds necessary. They would also need chaperons to go with the team. By the time the meeting ended, he sensed that the idea was starting to take hold with some of the people

---

With that idea planted, Hal knew he had to have help to get this off the ground. He suddenly remembered that Betty Bourne's husband, Larry, had been a missionary for a while before they got married. Maybe God was already giving a sense of direction to follow. Eddie was just barely seven years old, and most of the other kids were around that age. Sue and Hal agreed that the

HAROLD SOUTHWICK

kids should be at least ten years old before they would be mature enough to try something like this. It was agreed that the kids' parents would be the best for chaperons, if at all possible for them to go. They knew that the first mission trip would be a learning experience and therefore it would be wise to keep the number of kids small. The next step was to contact Bet's husband, Larry. He proved to be a good choice to be the coordinator and trainer for the project, and soon it was taking shape. As more things fell into place, the idea began to take on an energy all its own, and several people began to work toward not only raising money for the kids but to begin training so they could go along.

CHAPTER 25

Larry showed just how valuable experience was as he began laying out the groundwork for the mission project Hal had in mind. He first suggested that he and Leslie Davis correspond and get to know each other. Then he pointed out it would be good if she could work up a plan for what she would like to accomplish with the help of a group like they wanted to bring. After that, they could devise a training program, which he could structure and get on paper so they could all study together. When they felt comfortable with the mission objective and with how it should work, they could set up some mission trips with churches in neighboring states and gain hands-on experience. They all felt they would need the three years before most of the kids reached ten years of age to accomplish enough in-states mission trips for adequate training experience before going to Bangkok. They felt they should be able to do at least three mission trips in the time-frame with time in between trips to evaluate and fine-tune their techniques and objectives.

Hal began to feel a sense of expectancy and could see it in Sue and others as well as the plan began to take shape. The rest of the outreach was continuing, and there was still enthusiasm for all of that; but the bond formed in the group over the time they had been together had prepared them for something else. God had been preparing them for much, much more, and they were ready to get started!

Larry brought some pictures and slides of some of his own

mission trips to Hal and Sue and asked them to review them. He wanted to compile them into a slide presentation so that he could hold a teaching seminar and present the pictures to the kids and the adults. This would give all of them some visual connection with those in other cultures and economic settings. Larry knew from experience that the Holy Spirit would then begin to work on each one's heart to see these people's needs, not only spiritually, but physically as well. Leslie had sent slides of her work in Thailand, and he wanted them incorporated into the presentation toward the end. He prayed the effect of the pictures would focus their minds and hearts in that direction. That was the ultimate goal of this outreach effort, so all the prior endeavors should point in that direction.

"Can you believe that God is letting us be involved in something like this?" Hal asked Sue one evening after they had been working on the slide presentation.

"What amazes me is that God seems to be wanting to use so many of our experiences from the past to make us aware of areas of need where he can use our desire to serve him!" she replied.

Hal had been thinking about one particular area of the country where he had participated in an Indian rodeo and roping contest. He asked Sue, "What is God laying on your heart, babe?"

"Well, I remember when you took Eddie and me with you to St. John, Arizona, to that rodeo. Do you remember when we visited the Zuni Indian Reservation on our way to see the Petrified Forest National Park? Remember those missionaries we talked to in that restaurant that day and how we were touched by what they were doing?" she asked, her eyes filling with tears. "That's where I think we're supposed to go first."

Hal felt goose bumps spread all over his body as he listened to her! That was where he thought God was leading them to also!

"You're right on, babe. That's where I think God wants us to go first too!"

"Do you remember how Eddie was so fascinated with the little Indian boys? He still talks about wanting to go back there someday."

"I know. I saw him looking at his picture scrap book of that trip the other day. Let's go ask him if he would like to go tell those kids about Jesus," Hal responded.

"I remember when our church sent several boxes of clothes to the Baptist Indian mission in Page, Arizona, years ago. There's another place we could probably help out for a few days also. I think those are Navajo Indians there. We need to educate ourselves about each of these tribes and their particular backgrounds so that we can relate to them better if we are going to minister to them," Sue replied. "Maybe that could be done on our way down to the Zuni Indian mission. We need to have Larry go through the Home Mission Board to see if we still have missionaries there and have them help us set up a mission trip to those areas."

Hal smiled. "I don't think God would be laying these places on our hearts if he didn't still need our services there."

"Right you are!" She grinned.

CHAPTER 26

Thus began the planning for that trip. Larry had indeed already been to that area once before and had actually preached at that little mission. He knew the missionaries there, and he was excited to see that God wanted them to go there: both places, in fact! He made contact with the area director of missions, who then coordinated with those on the field and had them contact him with specifics about what they were doing and how a missions group could be of help to them. Pictures were sent of the areas, and goals were shared. Language training programs were sent, and soon everyone was becoming deeply committed and willingly involved in getting ready for this trip. Since they were moving into late fall now, they decided that the following June would be the best time to go do the trip. That way school would be out, people could use vacation time to commit to this, and the weather still wouldn't be so hot down there. That set the course for the major emphasis for the rest of the year.

Training continued on a weekly basis, and local mission projects were planned and executed that gave everyone experience in what worked and what didn't seem to. They also gained exposure to different people's reactions to them and what they were attempting to do. Those reactions were as varied as the number of people they met, so they had great opportunity to learn how to deal with many different personality types. They all soon found out that they had a lot of growing to do in their own attitudes and reactions if they wanted to be good ambassadors for Christ.

The time seemed to fly by, and before everyone was quite ready for it, the time had come for them to leave on this first God-inspired adventure away from their own general area of service! A medium-size bus had been chartered by one of their sponsors. Hal and the other men had installed a tow hitch on it, and a good-sized enclosed trailer was being used to transport many boxes of donated clothing as well as vacation bible school literature and other materials. That barely left room for their luggage. Much discussion and cajoling went into that particular part of the getting ready, since women seemed to need so many more changes of clothes than men. The kids didn't seem to care one way or the other. They just wanted to get going.

On the last night before they left home, as Hal and Sue lay in bed, she surprised him by turning to him and saying, "I have some news for you. I hope you think it is good news!"

He looked down at her big blue eyes and upturned face. He thought, *She is more beautiful today than when I first met her.* He finally asked, "Well, how will I know it's good news or bad if you don't let me know what it is?"

"You're going to be a daddy again! I just found out this morning. The doctor called and told me. I told you last week that I hadn't been feeling well at times, and that's why I made the doctor's appointment. I suspected it, but now I know, and I'm excited about it, I think! I won't be sure until I know you are too!" She kept her eyes pinned on his and waited anxiously for his reaction. "I love you!"

Hal burst out laughing at her expression of concern. "Of course I'll be excited about it just as soon as I can get my breath back. I had no idea, but I don't reckon you got this way all by yourself, did you?" He grinned as he gave her a big bear hug. "I love you too! I'm sure Eddie and Audi will love this baby as much as we will."

Audra was being left at home with Grandma Dot and Grandpa C. D. because of her age, and Sue was struggling with having to be away from her for that period of time. Hal secretly was too since they never had been parted for more than a day or two.

HAROLD SOUTHWICK

Now, at least, they had something, or more appropriately, someone else to think about that might ease that concern a little bit.

"Sweetheart, only time will tell. I believe God's grace will be sufficient for the need like it always seems to be," Hal reminded her gently.

At the time, Sue had quietly thought that it was great to have Hal as spiritual leader of this precious family of hers. God knew what he was doing.

"What do we want this time?" he wondered out loud.

"I think whatever God wants to give us, don't you think?"

"You're so practical sometimes—I emphasize *sometimes*—that you astound me." He laughed. "I still want a little girl that looks like you and has your beautiful blond hair."

"I guess we'll see." She smiled. "I want another little boy with your dark hair."

CHAPTER 27

Larry had set it up for the group to travel to Salt Lake City, Utah, the first day and do some sightseeing, put on a short skit at a local church that evening, and then "camp out" in the youth center that night. That was accomplished with a great deal of enthusiasm and also some learning to accommodate each other. The next morning they were fed a wonderful breakfast by the good ladies at the church fellowship hall, and soon they were on their way south to Page, Arizona, where they were scheduled to help the Baptist mission there conduct Vacation Bible School for three days.

The drive was not all that many miles from Salt Lake, so several stops were made at some very spectacular natural scenic areas. All agreed that southern Utah could certainly boast about its great scenic beauty. When they arrived at the Glenn Canyon Dam, just north of Page, they were met by the mission pastor and his wife who led them on a tour of the visitor center and then the viewing area overlooking the beautiful gorge below. Hal thought of the Snake River Canyon at Twin Falls and Shoshone Falls back in Idaho. *God sure made a beautiful country for us to enjoy.*

The next three days were spent in conducting VBS classes in the morning with a good number of Indian children. In the afternoon after a long lunch break, they broke up into groups of two adults and two kids and went out to the various places where

HAROLD SOUTHWICK

the Navajo lived. They took tracts, which were supplied by the mission church, which they handed out and then invited more children to come to the vacation bible school classes. They also invited the adults to come to the evening worship services, where Larry preached. Although it was somewhat daunting, they had fun trying to communicate in the Navajo dialect, although the folks spoke good English. The Indian folks had as much fun trying to teach them their language as well. After the natural shyness wore off, the kids just seemed to take to each other. The RKO kids had brought Idaho potato buttons and other trinkets, which they passed out. They in return received bead necklaces, belt buckles, and other gifts from the Navajo children that reflected their own culture. Several children made professions of faith at the close of the three days of VBS, and a number of adults who had not already been ministered to by the mission expressed interest in Christ. All in all, everyone felt that it was a successful start to their trip

After many prayers and promises to correspond with each other, good-byes were said, and they were on their way. New friendships had been formed, and a new awareness of these folks' unique culture and their own particular needs had been implanted in everyone's heart. Hal shared with them how he had been impacted in a similar way by his exposure to the Vietnam children and people; that and his getting to know Leslie Davis in Bangkok. Her work with the less fortunate had been the impetus to start this very ministry. A new wonder and awe was dawning in these kids and in some adults as well. Hal was secretly thrilled more than he was willing to express to anyone except Sue.

On the way on down to St. John, Arizona, and the Zuni Indian mission, they went over to the south side of the Grand Canyon west of Desert View so everyone could enjoy the splendor of it. That took up the rest of the morning, so they had lunch and then headed on to Flagstaff, then east to Holbrook before leaving I-40 and taking SH 180 down to St. John. They passed close by the

Zuni Reservation near Hunt, Arizona, and got a firsthand peek of the area where the first half of the work down there would be conducted. By the time they arrived in St. John, it was late evening, and everyone was ready for a shower and a good night's rest. Accommodations had been arranged for them by the missionaries, Dewey and Annie Brewer. The rest could stay in the fellowship hall or camp out in their tents if they wanted. Because it was late, they all decided they would sack out on the floor in their sleeping bags. The kids all thought this was great fun, but the adults knew that by morning their own bodies would be protesting the hard floor! *Oh, to be young again*, Sue thought. That thought was followed by realizing that she was approaching thirty. *That's not old.*

A big pot of chili had been prepared by the mission folks. As they sat to eat, a young Indian boy came into the circle where they sat, carrying a large sack with wonderful aromas coming from it. He presented the sack to Hal with a shy bow and then backed away with downcast eyes.

Eddie suddenly stood up excitedly and said, "Mommy, it's him, it's him!"

The other children were suddenly asking, "It's who, it's who?"

The little boy was shyly looking at Eddie, and a smile of recognition registered on his face. Slowly, he nodded and then ran from the circle of curious adults and kids. Hal opened the sack to find it filled with loaves of a special Indian bread.

He smiled in anticipation and asked, "Eddie, is he who I think he is?"

"Daddy, it's that little boy I met in the restaurant that time we came down to the rodeo!" Eddie cried. "I want to go find him."

"Let's eat while this is still warm, and then we'll go find him."

Sue quickly rose and went to her son, "Love, I think God is in all of this in a special way; so we'll find him, and you'll get to know him. I just know it! Trust me! I think the two of you will become great friends."

HAROLD SOUTHWICK

Hal gave her a wink and nodded his head. They all felt some special working of the Holy Spirit.

After eating, while the ladies cleaned up and started getting the sleeping bags sorted out, Hal took Eddie and left to find Dewey. As they came around the corner of the little mission, they saw the little Indian boy sitting quietly on the old wooden steps. He looked up with a startled expression just as Dewey and Annie came out the door. He stood quickly and started to leave.

Eddie came swiftly to the bottom of the steps and exclaimed, "Please don't leave! I want to get to know you."

"What's going on?" Annie quickly asked.

"I saw him in the restaurant two years ago when we were down here for that rodeo," Eddie explained. He slowly extended his hand to the shy little boy and stepped forward. "My name is Eddie. What's yours?"

With a shy smile, his eyes downcast, he slowly came down the steps. As he reached the bottom, he suddenly smiled, raised his right hand, and said, "How. Me Hopi!"

Eddie raised his own right hand, and they did a high five. Just then Jimmy came running around the corner of the mission and joined them.

"Eddie, who's this?" he asked curiously.

"This is Hopi, Jimmy. You remember me telling you about him? Isn't this just great? Now we can get to know him," Eddie exclaimed. More high fives were exchanged, and off the three boys went as fast their legs could carry them.

Thus began what was to become a lifelong bond of friendship and caring between these three little boys. They would become known as "The Three Musket-eaters" by the time this occasion would end. In large part, that was because they were so close and they all loved to eat.

The other five kids from RKO were soon introduced to other children from the mission and the reservation. Other friendships were soon formed as well, and by the time the VBS classes and the other events that had been planned were implemented, each one of them had new pen pals to stay in touch with.

CHAPTER 28

Many contacts were made with the adult Indian population on the reservation, some of them over into western New Mexico. Christian tracts were handed out, and they were able to get some of these folks to come to the worship service at the mission on the last night of the campaign. Hal had brought his old guitar with him at Sue's insistence. Hal and Dewey, who played the harmonica, teamed up and played while everyone else sang along. Soon a couple of Indian fellows began playing drums they had found somewhere. A few of them began to do an Indian dance. It wasn't long before some of the kids were trying to dance along with them. Before long, everyone was trying to learn the rhythm. By the time Larry was ready to preach, a presence had descended on the group, and Hal could tell something very special was happening. He knew that all of them were experiencing something supernatural. He and Sue had talked about whether Eddie might be ready to take Christ as his Savior, but they were soon to stand in awe as God showered his love and mercy down on everyone there!

Larry preached on Christ calling the twelve disciples to come follow him. As he preached, Dewey translated his words into the Zuni dialect so that everyone would be sure to understand. As the message unfolded, Larry shared how Christ and his twelve disciples traveled around in the countryside and how Jesus went about doing miracles and telling people about God's goodness. As he brought the narrative along to the events in the garden of Gethsemane, the capture of Jesus, and the ensuing trial followed by his scourging before being taken to Golgotha, Eddie's parents began to realize something special was going on in the heart of their son. He was sitting with Jimmy and Hopi, and each of their faces were riveted on Larry. Soon, tears were beginning to run down the cheeks of many in attendance as the Holy Spirit came upon them. Larry brought the message to a close with Christ's death on the cross, his burial, and his resurrection; he related that it was all done so that all might have eternal life. Before he could even give an invitation to come to Christ, Eddie was up and moving down to the front of the gathering. He had no more than reached the little altar when first Jimmy, then Hopi came running down to join him. Soon others were coming forward. Larry quickly signaled for Hal and Sue and Betty to join him and Dewey down front to help receive them. Because of her Bible school training, Hal was quick to tell Sue to speak to Eddie, Jimmy and Hopi. As he listened to her lead the boys into the reality of what Christ had done for them, he was reminded again of the time when his friend Bob had come to him and asked him to explain the gospel to him and the others before they went into battle. It was really at that time, he now knew, when the reality of Christ's atoning work on the cross and what it meant for him personally set in and he "really" started believing.

In just a very short while, these three boys had become not only friends, but brothers in Christ! Before the evening ended, a couple of adults had made commitments, and some other children were close. Two of the girls in the RKO group would accept Christ before the trip home ended. This had turned out to be even more than they had hoped it would be.

By the time they reached home, they were already looking forward to the next mission project. Discussion of the trip revealed that most thought they should pick a city where there were a lot of homeless and abandoned children to minister to since that was primarily who they would be working with in Thailand. Through his many contacts, Larry was appointed to bring the names of the most likely cities to set up the next trip in.

HAROLD SOUTHWICK

CHAPTER 29

The months following the team's return to Glenn's Cove brought changes. Bob Johnston had been rotated back to Mt. Home AFB two weeks after their return. Hal's dad was having heart problems again, and Hal had to insist that he just back off from trying to do so much on the ranch. That required Hal to spend much more time involved in the day-to-day ranch operations, so he sometimes had to skip his previous commitments to the RKO training day. Since Bob was back and could arrange to get that day off from his duties at the air base, he began to take some of the load for Hal. It wasn't long after his return that Joan announced that they were going to be adding to their family as well.

Sue started experiencing some severe lower back pain in the late summer, and upon further exams by the doctor, they determined she was carrying twins. However, she wasn't convinced that was the total problem. She didn't let on, but Hal could tell this pregnancy was different from the one with Audra. He hadn't been around when she carried Eddie because of Vietnam, so he didn't have firsthand experience with that one. She acted like she was carrying a burden. She didn't know what it was, but she shared that with her mom and Dot. Hal noticed the three of them praying together more than usual, so he began to question her about it. She finally shared her concerns with him and said that she hadn't wanted to burden him if it was only her imagination.

"Darn it, sweetheart, I'm a part of this family. Don't you think

I have a right to know if you're not doing well? You're my wife and what happens to you happens to me. Don't keep things like this from me. If we need to do something different, I need to know so I can make it happen," he complained.

"It's a woman thing," she shot back.

"It's *not* a woman thing, it's a family thing. By golly, it's *our* family thing. Don't leave me out!" he said as he went to her and wrapped his arms around her tenderly.

He thought, *what's going on here, Lord? This is certainly different from the last time.* He didn't press the issue anymore but decided that he would pray more and he would try to not let her be overloaded with too many outside involvements.

――――――――――――――

Eddie was now eight years old, and Audra was four. Hal was quietly very proud of them. Eddie was starting to stretch up in height, and Audra was becoming a beautiful little girl. Her big blue eyes and her long dark hair set off her face, and her quick smile could melt his heart in a second. She was a daddy's girl, and everyone knew it. Sue recognized this and was pleased they had that kind of a relationship. She shared the very same kind of relationship with Eddie. She knew that Hal and Eddie were very close in the father-son, masculine sense and that Eddie was secure in that. Every once in a while, however, she noticed Eddie standing quietly at a distance watching Hal and Audra as they interacted together. She wondered what exactly was going through his mind. She found he would come to her, needing her special attention at times like that, and it always warmed her heart; she was his special refuge. That had grown into the close relationship mothers and sons naturally share a lot of the time. She also intuitively knew that was how Hal and Audra's relationship was structured.

Eddie mimicked his dad, but she was his refuge and pal. Audra mimicked her, but her daddy was her refuge and pal. Eddie adored his grandpa, and everyone could tell that his grandpa felt the same way. Grandpa took him fishing often. Hal determined he was going to insist the two of them spend more time doing that very thing, instead of his dad feeling he had to be so involved in the day-to-day things on the ranch. They both tried to include Eddie in the ranch activities that were appropriate for his age because they wanted to pass this heritage along to him. Besides, it would be an anchor for him as it had been for each of them, that basic need for a man to provide for those he loved. It enabled them to share the overflow with others also. Grandma proudly spent a great deal of time with Audra, teaching her things she had done as a little girl: cooking, sewing, and making little dolls and skipping rope. Audra adored her grandma, and the feeling was mutual. The kids were close to Sue's mom as well, but they didn't get to spend as much time with her because of her job at the King Hill Post Office.

At night as they lay in bed and prayed together before going to sleep, they often discussed the balancing act of shared family love. They prayed that God would help them become better at it.

———————

As the time for the twins to be born drew nearer, Sue was experiencing much increasing lower back pain and was limited in what she could do. Her younger sister, Kathy, would come over and help her out as much as she could. That helped where Audra was concerned and gave Dot more time to care for C. D.'s growing needs. Eddie spent most of his time either in school or with Hal, so he was no problem.

Christmas was spent with the whole family gathered in the family tradition at the ranch. The kids all loved the huge Christmas tree that stood in front of the big window looking out toward the Bennett Mountain range. Though everyone had a great time, there was an underlying concern for grandpa. He laughed and carried on with the grandkids and never let on that he was anything other than he had always been. Hal, Stu, and Leah shared with each other the last evening together they could see how tired he looked; he would sit by the fireplace and watch the rest of them more than he normally did. Peg, Leah, Stu and A.J. all promised to come home more often. Hal wondered if that would really happen but didn't say so. Mom was still doing great for her age, and she never let on about her own health, which seemed to be good. But she wanted the other kids to spend as much time with Dad as possible while they still had him. They both talked again with Peg and A. J. concerning their need for Christ as Savior, with no apparent effect. That left both of them concerned and disappointed.

One night in the second week of January, Sue woke Hal up as she came back into the bedroom from the bathroom. He looked over at the alarm clock and noted that it read three-thirty a.m. He groaned, and then, looking at Sue's face, he leaped out of bed and raced to her. She was doubled over with pain and grimacing.

When she could get her breath, she said, "Call Mom and Dot and have them get here now! It's time, and we need to hurry. It's snowing outside."

Hal raced to the phone and dialed his mom first, "Mom, Sue says it's time to get to the hospital! I'll run over in the truck and get you."

He then called Sue's mom and then ran out to the garage and started the four-wheel-drive pickup. He hurriedly backed out and went up the lane to get his mom. When they got back to the ranch house, Sue had Eddie and Audra both clinging to her as she waited for Hal. She hugged them and told them they would soon have a new baby or two to play with. The kids were concerned about their mommy, and that didn't seem to register much. Hal quickly kissed them and told them to mind Grandma.

Dot said, "Go on and get her to the hospital! And be careful on those roads."

As they were loading Sue in the truck cab, her mom arrived, and Hal had her get in with Sue so she could care for her while he drove. Hal had driven many miles on slick roads and was a very good driver, but this was the first time he had driven those thirty miles to Mt. Home on slick roads with a wife that was close to having a baby. They arrived safely, but by the time he got there he was wishing he had called for the ambulance.

The hospital had been alerted that Sue was in heavy labor and Hal was on his way with her. Dr. Belton quickly responded to the call to come. A nurse met them at the door of the hospital with a wheelchair. After much effort to get her out of the high truck, he had them step back.

"Here, let me do this. We have to get her in there to the doctor!" With that, he reached in, put one arm under her legs and the other around her back, and simply lifted her out and sat her in the wheelchair. She was quickly wheeled to the delivery room and placed on the exam table. The head nurse told Hal to leave them so she could do what she had to do. Hal grumbled that he wanted to stay with Sue to no avail. As he left the room, Dr. Belton came hurrying up the hallway.

"Hal, is she doing okay, do you think?"

"Doc, she's in a whole lot of pain. But she's had an uneasy feeling about this whole pregnancy that she didn't have the last time. I don't know exactly what's going on."

"I know that, Hal. She's told me about that. We'll soon see if her concern is legitimate." He patted Hal on the arm and hurried into the delivery room.

Sue's mom came out and led Hal to the waiting room close by.

She said, "Hal, you're a prayer warrior, so let's just let God know we trust him." She led them in a heartwarming prayer, and a calming began to invade his heart.

While they were sitting there, Pastor Don and Larry and Betty Bourne came hurrying into the waiting room. Hal was consumed with a sense of gratitude. *God's family is great,* he thought.

Larry had a great sense of humor and soon had them all laughing about some silly thing. Hal knew Larry did that to bring things into perspective, but Hal still wanted to be in there with his wife.

They sat there for what seemed like hours with nurses hurrying in and out of the room. In reality, it had only been little more than an hour when Dr. Belton came out and summoned Hal and Sue's mom to come aside with him. Hal's heart skipped a beat, and he choked back a sob.

Sue's mom Alice, said, "Hal, you remember our prayer."

Dr. Belton put his hand on Hal's shoulder as he said, "Hal, Sue is doing fine now. We have her slightly sedated because of the severe pain. She experienced some bleeding that isn't normal, but we have that under control. You are the father of a set of twins: one little boy and one little girl. The baby boy is just fine and has coal black hair, but the baby girl is having respiratory problems, and we are assisting her breathing efforts. There is something else that I'm not sure about yet, so I'm not going to know what it is for sure until we do some more evaluations. You can come in and see Sue in just a little while. The nurses are finishing up with her right now and with the little boy. The little girl has been placed in an incubator for right now. She is being constantly monitored by a nurse specialist. You can all come observe her through the window if you would like. Hal, Sue wants you to come see her for just a minute before you go to see your little girl. The rest of you can go down that hall and around the corner. A nurse there will take you to the baby."

"Is Sue aware of baby Angela's condition?" Hal asked.

"Not yet. I want you in there when I tell her. She knows something isn't right, and she asked for you," Dr. Belton said, gently squeezing his arm. "Is that what you've named her? Have you named the little boy yet?"

"Well, we weren't sure what they were going to be, but I think we're going to name him Joseph. Doctor, please tell me before we go in there to see Sue. What do you think is baby Angela's problem?" Hal asked with a tremor in his voice.

"She appears to have a condition known as Down's syndrome. A lot of research has been, and is being done on this. I'm familiar enough with it to recognize it, and I'm doing some extensive research on the subject because I suspected something like this may have been present because of Sue's problems with this pregnancy. Angela's facial appearance hints at that right now, although it is hard to tell this soon after birth. Her preliminary reaction analysis points to the condition though. We'll have to do more testing to be completely sure. Let's go talk to Sue now." Dr. Belton quickly turned and entered the room with Hal anxiously in tow.

Sue had Little Joe in her arms and looked up with a drawn and tired smile as Hal came to her side. "Here's that little dark-haired boy you wanted, babe! He's so cute." She looked at Dr. Belton with a saddened expression. "Where's our baby girl, doctor?"

Hal knelt down by her bedside and took her free hand as he reached over and touched Little Joe's head. "Sweetheart, I know you've suspected something was not quite normal about this pregnancy from the start. Dr. Belton wants to explain to us what he believes is baby Angela's situation."

Dr. Belton sat on the edge of the bed and quietly repeated what he had already shared with Hal before. As Sue listened, tears welled up in her eyes, and she clutched baby Joe to her breast with a sob. Hal leaned over and caressed her forehead as tears fell from his own eyes.

As they fell on Sue's face, he heard her murmur, "We love her anyway, don't we, baby Joe?" She looked at Hal then and saw him nodding his agreement.

———————————

The rest of that day had become a blur for both of them. The news of the babies' birth and then the updates concerning Little Angela had brought first joy and then concern for the parents as well as the little girl. The church prayer team had been alerted, and much prayer was offered up to God for all the family, especially baby Angela. Hal and Sue had shared their heartache with their families. Dot and C. D. had brought Eddie and Audra up to the hospital later, and they had gotten to see their mommy and their new baby brother, which thrilled them. Hal had noticed Eddie's puzzled expression as he looked at his little brother.

Sue noticed it too and handed the baby off to her mom and

said, "Eddie, you and Audi knew we were expecting two babies, didn't you?"

"Uh huh," they both murmured.

Hal pulled them both up on the bed beside him and Sue as she continued, tears running down her cheeks. "Your daddy and I have to tell you about your baby sister. God has special children in heaven, waiting for families he can give them to who will take special care of them. Your baby sister is one of those special children, and she is going to need all of us to help care for her. She is going to look different from you and other kids, and she will probably act different at times; but she will also be a lot like you in many ways. God has given her to us because he feels we as a family can give her that very special care she will need. Your grandparents have all agreed they will help us every way they can. Do you think we can do it, kids?"

Everyone in the room was wiping tears from their eyes by then, and Hal was so proud of his wife.

Eddie lay down beside his mommy as Audi hugged her daddy. They looked at their folks and then each other, and Eddie answered for both of them, "If you think we can do it and God thinks we can do it, then we think we can do it too! Isn't that right, Audi?"

Audi nodded as they all hugged. Hal pushed up from the bed and opened the door. A nurse had been waiting for his signal, and now she brought baby Angela into the room and handed her to her daddy. Hal turned and slowly crossed over to the bed and sat down close to Sue. As he did so, Eddie and Audi huddled up close with wide, curious eyes. Hal pulled the blanket back from the baby's face and turned to watch the children's reaction. The rest of the family crowded around close also, as they hadn't seen her yet either. Sue and Hal watched breathlessly as Eddie and Audi looked at this new little girl and studied her face. Eddie slowly reached out and touched her cheek.

Turning to his mommy, he said, "She's beautiful!" Audi smiled and nodded her head.

Just then Little Joe squealed as if to let them know he was

there also. They all laughed. An awareness and awe settled on them that none could have then explained. Hal sighed and looked at Sue. They both knew that somehow God was in control of this new challenge in their lives.

Suddenly Audi spoke up and said, "We'll give little Joe special care too, won't we?"

Hal looked at her with a big smile and answered, "I think Little Joe is going to become Little Angela's very special side-kick, and we'll be very careful to give him special love and care too!"

CHAPTER 30

The following weeks were a stressful time for Hal. He had his dad and the one hired hand they kept in the wintertime to help with the ranch and livestock, but his dad's health wouldn't let him do much. Eddie had school, and Audra spent the days with Grandma; so that part was taken care of, but Sue had not recovered from having the babies as quickly as they had hoped. Little Angela had to be kept in the hospital for a longer period of time to be sure her lungs were going to be all right, so Sue had to stay longer than she might have because she insisted on breast feeding the twins. Little Joe was doing great, however, and was a constant joy to everyone. Hal, his folks, and Sue's mom and sister were all trying to learn as much as they could about Down's syndrome so they would be able to help Sue care for Angela better. The weather had stayed cold and snowy into late February, and that had not made driving to Mt. Home every evening any easier. Finally, after three weeks in the hospital, they were able to bring Sue and the babies home. The grandmas, Eddie, and Audi had spent a couple of evenings decorating the little nursery room for the babies and the living room for Sue's homecoming. Church people had all helped with meals while Sue had been gone, and Hal was grateful for all of the help. The doctor and hospital bills had mounted, and that was a concern for him. But he figured that somehow God would provide. He missed his wife and wanted her and the babies home. Life was very hectic as they settled into the job of caring for two more little ones while

HAROLD SOUTHWICK

still meeting the two older kids' needs. It was a juggling act and would not have been possible without their families' help.

At first, Angela's syndrome was not too noticeable, but as time went along and Little Joe began to change and take on a normal little boy's nature and character, it became more evident that she was not going to be a normal child. There was one very special and wonderfully evident characteristic she had, however: her disposition! She hardly ever cried, and she had the most beautiful smile. Her eyes sparkled, and she won everyone's heart in no time. The whole family had adjusted to her needs, and there was no way they were ever going to put her in an institution. Little Joe was an easygoing little guy as well, and the bond between him and his twin sister was very evident. Eddie and Audi didn't get near the attention they were accustomed to before, but they were included in the twins' care, and that was a big help in the transition. Audi was soon helping change diapers and whatever else they would let her do. Sue thought at times she was more help than was needed, but Hal insisted they not let her know that!

As the months went along, Eddie, who had always been a very sensitive boy, became more and more protective of Angela. He loved to play with Little Joe while Audi would be the little mother hen to Angela, but he would bristle if anyone made a comment about her being different, especially anyone outside the family. While this pleased Hal and Sue, they began to be concerned. They didn't want him to develop a complex about it. They prayed together and finally sat down and talked with him about it. His response was a quiet intensity.

He said, "Mommy and Daddy, I believe God wants me to look out for her. I love her, so I have to do it."

He had watched some other kids as they had mistreated a less fortunate boy at school, and it had left him sad and confused. He had determined in his heart that no one would treat his little sister that way. Hal told him his feelings were the right way to be but to not let the situation take all the fun out of his young life.

CHAPTER 31

The spring months were busy with all the ranch activities and the new babies. The RKO group was busy preparing for an inner-city mission trip to Seattle to work with the homeless and abandoned street kids. There was a downtown Baptist Church that had set up a shelter for young girls and women who were hooked on drugs, had become pregnant, were abused, left out, or had chosen to drop out of the mainstream of life. This shelter was set up in a huge underground complex that was adjacent to the church. It was a separate complex from the church and was staffed by women who were church trained in that type of ministry. Women who had been rescued from that lifestyle also were part of the staff. A few of the ladies in RKO wanted to go and observe and learn about that kind of ministry, and others wanted to go minister to the homeless street kids, so with Larry's contacts again, it was arranged through Downtown Baptist Church to come work with them.

Because of the twins' age and Angela's special needs, Sue was not able to go on this trip. She sorely wanted to be a part of it; but the babies were her first priority, and Hal agreed. Eddie, of course, was eager to go, as were the other kids. The pastor's wife took on the responsibilities of keeping the kids on track in Sue's place. Joan Johnston's pregnancy was going to keep her from going on this trip as well. They all had an idea of what the environment would be like there, but Hal knew from his exposure

HAROLD SOUTHWICK

to downtown Seattle before and to similar conditions in Saigon, Vietnam, that they were in for a wake-up call.

When they arrived, they were filled with enthusiasm and bright expectations. By the end of the first week, they were subdued and filled with sadness at the scope of the need they were faced with. The depravity and rejection of so many, the feelings of despair and hopelessness of these young girls and the homeless kids seemed overwhelming. The group as a whole was amazed at the commitment of that church to even attempt this kind of an outreach. It caused all of them to reexamine their own lives and commitment to God. By the time they were to leave and go home, they all agreed with the motto of the shelter program: *one life at a time, one day at a time, for the good of the lives they could touch, all for God's glory.* It was a sobering experience as well as a great learning tool in preparation for their upcoming mission to Bangkok, Thailand, the following summer.

Bangkok was well documented as a major supplier of sex slaves for major cities in the US and other cities around the world. The kids had been exposed to conditions they had never experienced or even known about. That concerned the adults, but as they talked about what they had seen and had been able to share with the homeless kids, it was obvious to the adults that God was working in these young lives in very special ways. They were becoming less self-centered and more concerned with kids and others in need of the essentials of life. Hal could see more evidence every day of the importance of what God was having them do. It gave him great satisfaction that God had trusted him enough to use him to initiate this outreach. All in all, it had been a great learning and growing time for all of them.

CHAPTER 32

Dr. Belton had been doing a lot of research on the Down's syndrome disorder. He kept Sue informed of his findings, and as a result of that, they had worked out a daily routine to use with baby Angela. It consisted of exercises to try to stimulate the brain and motor skills that would also help develop her weak, underdeveloping limbs. Sue was animated in her commitment to this project, and she soon had Hal, Eddie, and Audi completely dedicated to the effort as well. Little Joe was not forgotten in the process either, and he was soon a vital part of it. They soon learned that Little Joe was Angela's link to the normal. As Hal and Sue had learned to watch the two of them together, they noticed that she lay and watched him and seemed fascinated by the things he did. An idea was forming in their minds that God wanted them to use Joe to help them help Angela.

One morning during the daily routine of rattling keys in her face to stimulate eye movement and promote the reaction to reach for them, Eddie suddenly said, "Mommy, Angie watched Joey reach for the keys, and now she's trying to reach them!"

Sue suddenly experienced goose bumps all over her body, and she knew they were on to something that was going to work. When Hal came in for lunch at noon that day, she shared the news with him.

His reply was, "Well, there you go! He's our link to her inner being, and I'll bet Audi and Eddie can help do the same thing too!"

HAROLD SOUTHWICK

The kids were taught how to exercise her arms and legs by flexing and extending them and to push her feet against their hands to develop strength. They used the same techniques on Little Joe while she watched, and after much coaching, she learned to attempt the same things. As a result of all these efforts, a sacrificial bond of love and care grew in all of them. This was especially true where Eddie was concerned. With Audi at her age, it was kind of like playing house. With Eddie, because of his sensitivity and caring nature, it filled his spare time after school and chores with a total focus. His energy concerning their goal to help this precious gift from God amazed and motivated his parents. When they seemed at the end of their own efforts, they would watch his steadfast efforts and devotion as he just went about helping his little sister. That never failed to reenergize them and made then realize that he was a very special nine-year-old. He was also setting a great example for Audra as she tried her best to do everything he did. Sue said to Hal one day, "These twins are the most precious gift God could have ever given this family. Just look how close we've become just because of our binding together to help Angie. Little Joe seems to even sense his part in helping her, and it just wouldn't be possible to do this if it weren't for the other kids. I wouldn't have her any other way!"

Hal nodded in agreement and smiled. "Neither would the rest of us. I think that also includes the grandparents."

CHAPTER 33

The preparations for the trip to Thailand were moving along smoothly. Others in the outreach group had stepped up and taken much of the load of training off Hal and Sue. They all reviewed what had worked in Seattle and what hadn't. After consultation with Leslie Davis in Bangkok and reviewing the photos and other information, they began to work out a plan of ministry for over there. They let Leslie know who all would be coming and gave her each person's area of interest. They decided to let her use each one where she thought best. Sue wanted very much to go but didn't feel it was possible with the babies, especially considering Angela, but she had looked forward to meeting Leslie for many years now. She secretly felt cheated out of something she had longed to help with. Hal knew this, so he contacted Leslie and shared this with her. Leslie decided that she could use the babies in some way to attract little Thai kids to come see what was going on, just out of curiosity. After much prayer by the group, they approached Sue with the idea. At first, she didn't think it was a good thing to do because of the extra care Angela required. Besides, the long plane ride would be too much for her. But the whole family had looked forward to this trip for several years, and she didn't want to miss it. Hal's mom and Sue's mom both said they would arrange to go along and help with the babies if Hal could get Stu to come help his dad with the ranch. By the time for the trip arrived, the babies would be seventeen months old, so after much prayer and prodding by the whole team, Sue finally agreed to give it a go!

Another winter passed, and Eddie and Jimmy had kept in touch with Hopi. They finally were able to persuade their parents to ask Hopi's family if he could come to Idaho for a couple of weeks' training and then go on to Thailand with them. They became more excited as the time for him to come to Glenn's Cove approached.

The whole adventure was going to require a lot of money to finance it. They still had those who had been faithful sponsors of the previous trips that were a large part of making it happen, and that was greatly appreciated. But Hal knew they needed a much wider support group.

One night while he was praying about it, he suddenly thought of Bob Green over in Jackson Hole, Wyoming. They had called each other a few times over the years. They still had great respect for each other. Bob had never been able to go back on active duty because of his war injuries, so he stayed in Jackson Hole and started a business with his wife. Hal knew they had done very well. They had told Hal to let them know if they could ever be of help to Hal and his family.

After talking to Sue about it, he decided to call Bob and tell him their need of financial help for the mission trip and that it would be to help the dear lady who had been such an inspiration to both of them while they had been in the hospital in Bangkok some ten years ago.

The phone rang for some time before being picked up. Finally, a breathless voice answered, "Hello."

"Hey, Captain, how are those old wounds doing? This is a voice from your past."

"Hal, hey, it's good to hear your voice! What's up with you these days?" Bob asked.

They exchanged family news and talked about their time in Bangkok, and that led into what Hal had called for.

"Bob, you know that Sue and I started a ministry for kids here in our area and we have spread our wings, so to speak. We've made a mission trip to two Indian reservations in Arizona and one to Seattle to work with the abused women and street kids in the last two years, as you probably remember. Now we have a trip planned to go to Bangkok and work with Leslie Davis and her street kids ministry for two weeks. Do you remember her?"

"I sure do remember her. She played a big part in my recovery with her prayers and encouragement." Bob then asked, "So how can we help? You know I owe you a lot and I promised I would help you whenever you needed help."

"Well, Bob, I don't feel you owe me anything; but I do have a large need, and that is some financial help to get the team over there and support them while we're there. We have our regular sponsors; and each of us has kicked in as much as we can, but there are some of the kids whose parents don't have the money to pay their way. So I wondered if you might have some ideas."

"How soon do you need to have the money, and do you have any idea how much you're going to need?" Bob inquired.

"I do know about how much we're going to need, but as Sue and I were praying about this, we decided we wouldn't name an amount. We felt we should trust God with the amount. So whatever God enables you to give will be what God wants us to have, and I reckon he'll make it meet the need!"

"Let me see what I can do. I have some people who might be interested in helping also," Bob replied.

They chatted about getting together as families someday soon and then hung up. Hal suddenly felt that old sensation of the "hand" on his shoulder; and the load of concern lifted, and he smiled.

Sue noticed and asked, "So, what was his answer?"

"He'll help! How much will be up to God, but I know it will be enough."

With less than a month to go before they were to leave for Thailand, Sue returned from the mailbox and met Hal at the ranch shop. When she handed him an envelope, he observed her smiling expression.

"Well, let's see how God has answered our prayers."

He tore open the envelope from Bob Green and withdrew a short note that had a check enfolded in it. Sue watched anxiously as he read the note and then opened the check. His big smile was all she needed to see to know their prayers had been answered!

"Their church helped them out, and what we felt we needed is exactly what they've sent us, babe!" Hal beamed. "$8000.00, that's a lot of money."

"Oh my, that's a load off our shoulders," Sue breathed a sigh of relief.

CHAPTER 34

Eddie's little buddy, Hopi, came into Boise a few days prior to their departure for Bangkok. His plane flight from Flagstaff, Arizona, was a new experience for him, and he was wide-eyed with wonder as Hal and Eddie met him in the air terminal. The boys' excitement as they greeted each other was heartwarming for Hal. He was glad they had decided to let Eddie invite Hopi to come with them. He knew Jimmy was anxiously waiting at home to see Hopi again. It was going to be well worth the extra expense. God had already taken care of that through the generous check from Bob Green.

The next few days were filled with activity as the final preparations were completed. Stu and Leah came down to the ranch to be with C. D. while Hal, Sue, and Dot were going to be gone. Hal was grateful; he knew things would be okay at home. They could focus on the mission trip now. This would also give his siblings some quality time with their dad in the old home setting.

The long, long flight to Bangkok took them from Boise, to San Francisco, to Seoul, Korea, and then on to Thailand. With layovers and flight time, it took twenty-seven hours. By the time they arrived in Bangkok, the twins and Audi were flat out tired of riding on an airplane, even though it had been an adventure. The other kids did quite well because the flight attendants had tried to make the trip an adventure for them. The twins had become little celebrities with the other passengers, and that had helped keep them occupied. With wide-eyed wonder, Audra watched the attendants, completely fascinated. Hal wondered what was going through her mind.

———————————

The airport in Bangkok seemed as large as the whole city of Boise, and extra care was taken to make sure no one got lost. As they exited the plane and came into the terminal, Hal kept noticing Sue's eager searching of all the faces in the waiting area. He suddenly realized that her biggest thrill of this whole trip was to finally get to meet the lady who had meant so much to Hal when he lay wounded in that army hospital and she was unable to be there to comfort him. He could hardly believe that it had been ten years ago already. Would he be able to recognize Leslie; or for that matter, would Leslie be able to recognize him?

As they reached the end of the long hallway ramp and entered the large waiting area, Hal spied a slender, silver-haired lady standing to one side with a quiet smile on her face, her head slightly tilted to one side, looking intently at him. As she started to move toward him, Hal was aware of Sue watching first Leslie and then him.

"There she is," he whispered to Sue.

Leslie came to him and gave him a long, warm embrace and then turned to Sue.

"Hello, young lady! I've looked forward to meeting you for such a long time," Leslie said as she embraced Sue. "You're just as lovely as your dear husband said you were way back when I first got to know him. These must be those precious little ones I've heard so much about over the years!"

"I'm not little anymore," Eddie quickly informed her.

"I am," piped up Audi, "and so are my baby brother and sister!"

Leslie laughed, her eyes dancing. Sue felt an attachment to her immediately; she had no problem understanding why Hal and Bob had such high regards for her. She just seemed to exude a down-to-earth sincerity and warmth that drew people to her.

The kids all smiled shyly as she hugged each one of them. It was obvious she loved children.

Hal smiled and introduced each of the adults and then the other children as they gathered around Leslie. Then a two-seat stroller was set up for the twins, and soon they were off to airport currency exchange so everyone could get some Thai money for personal items, gifts, etc. When that was taken care of, they went through customs and then on to baggage claim, which seemed like a mile from the gate they had come through to the lounge. By the time all the luggage was loaded on the bus Leslie had waiting for them, they were very tired and hungry. In spite of being tired, everyone was intent on their surroundings as the bus took them to their hotel on the outskirts of Bangkok. Rather than go through the rigor of eating at a restaurant, they decided to eat snacks they had in their carry packs and get to bed. Tomorrow was another day.

The next day was Saturday, and Leslie had scheduled a bus trip to tour all around Bangkok and outlying areas for the day. With the time differential, this day had been extremely long; by the time everyone had been settled into their own rooms, they were dead on their feet. Soon all were asleep except Hal. He had memories flooding back in his mind, scenes of those traumatic events that had led to his being brought to Bangkok. He couldn't seem to turn off the switch in his mind. Finally, he resorted to the one thing that never failed him; he got up and knelt by the bedside and began to pray. He soon sensed movement by his side and realized that Sue was kneeling next to him. Emotions seized him, and he began to cry tears of gratitude to the God who had led him back to this place. He felt Sue's arm go around him and heard her quiet crying there beside him. He knew a divine appointment was in the process of being fulfilled. Their prayers finished, they were soon back in bed and sound asleep. Their four dear children slept blissfully next to their bed on cots set up for them.

CHAPTER 35

The next day started off with breakfast in the hotel cafeteria where everyone had the option of a traditional American-style meal or they could choose to eat what the Thai people usually ate. Since this was the first time for most of them to be in a foreign country, there was the normal curiosity concerning the Thai food. Some tried a little bit of it; others ate only traditional American food ,and a couple went completely for the Thai menu. Hal remembered that he liked some of the local diet but not all of it, so he ate a combination of both, telling Sue and his kids what he thought they might like. Leslie met them in the dining room with much advice for all concerning stomachs that were not accustomed to the hot spices much of the Tai food contained. Larry, who seemed to have a cast-iron stomach, ate strictly Thai and chided the others good-naturedly, "When in Rome, eat what the Romans eat."

Many answered, "This ain't Rome!"

After the meal was finished amid much laughter and joshing, they loaded up and left on the tour. As the day progressed, they were all amazed at the size of Bangkok, its beauty, and its impoverishment. They spotted a Buddhist temple in the distance that garnered a lot of attention because nobody in the group had seen one before. The most frightening stop of all was watching men fight with deadly snakes for a large crowd; the women didn't want to stick around to see the winner. The tour guide had to hurry every one along so they could stay on schedule. The stop at a woodcarving establishment was especially fascinating as they watched men and women do their amazing work. The morning's sight-seeing ended with a tour of a coconut farm. The kids were greatly interested to learn that this was where those coconuts they loved to eat came from. One of the workers opened coconuts so they could drink the delicious milk from inside them. For lunch, Leslie had arranged for them to eat at The Royal Gardens outdoor café located on the banks of a large river, where they had opportunity to try many more Thai dishes. That proved to be another fun experience.

The Royal Gardens consisted of large areas of the most beautiful roses and other flowers, culture displays, and exhibits, an area where elephants were shown doing things they had been trained to do and then could be ridden. At the close of all that time, they were taken to a large cultural arena where young Thai men and women put on a historical Thai culture presentation that was not only informative but was orchestrated with great beauty and technique!

A young Thai lady who had become a Christian and a young Thai man whose dad was the pastor of Promise Baptist Church in Bangkok accompanied them and Leslie for the whole day and kept up a running dialogue as they progressed on the tour. By the time they returned to the hotel, they were completely worn out, but absolutely delighted with the day of touring.

Leslie had also included in the tour areas of downtown Bangkok and outlying places where street children and the less fortunate, the drop-outs and the depraved side of life was evident. She and Hal had decided to do this in preparation for what the group was going to be encountering. Hal had shared all of this with the team in preparation training, but he knew that words themselves didn't convey what their own eyes would to their hearts. This certainly proved to be the case. On Sunday morning, they attended services at Promise Baptist Church, where they got to hear the message in Thai by the pastor and then again in English for their benefit by Num, the pastor's son. It was a very moving occasion, after which they were served a traditional church fellowship meal. Hal had to smile as he thought about how Baptists loved to eat and share meals no matter where they were located in the world.

CHAPTER 36

Both of the grandmas decided to work out a schedule where one of them would take care of the twins one day and the other the next day. There was an area at the hotel where they could be entertained, and, since Leslie had obtained a van for Hal to use to transport those ministering downtown on the streets, he planned on stopping in at the hotel at least once a day to check on them. Since there were sixteen people in the group, there might be one of them who didn't feel up to going out to minister every day who could lend a hand in caring for the little ones. Leslie planned to have them come to Abba House, where they met daily to hold Bible classes and do crafts with street and slum kids. She hoped that with the entire team helping a visible presence of God's love for them might help them see the reality of a family who loved them for the first time since they had been abandoned.

This little house was in the outer area of Bangkok where the poverty was terrible. Leslie and Num had named it Abba House with reference to the holy God, and had been restoring it when they had the funds to work on it. One of the main objectives of the men in the group was to work on Abba House in the mornings when the oppressive heat wasn't so intense and then go hand out tracts in the evening to people on the streets and in shops or anywhere they had opportunity to do so. The women and girls would help with the classes and craft projects in the afternoons and then visit hospitals in the evenings, handing out tracts as well. In the mornings, they were going to be allowed to go to the public schools and teach English classes and put on Bible skits. The boys would be getting to teach the Thai boys how to play baseball and football. Sports equipment to play these games had been included in the things brought with them on the trip.

On Friday and Saturday evenings during the two weeks they would be there, Larry was scheduled to preach the Gospel at Promise Baptist Church in an evangelistic outreach. Part of the objective of handing out gospel tracts printed in Thai was to also invite people to come to these services. Other missionaries who worked in Bangkok were included in these events, and as a result, the campaign covered a large part of the city.

"Okay, gang, listen up," Hal called as everyone assembled out in front of the hotel after breakfast. "We're going to split up into the groups we talked about last night. Jake will take the men out to Abba House and meet with Num there. He will show you what they want to accomplish in the house while we are here. There's some removal to be done in some of the rooms, and a new roof needs to be installed. Leslie says the shingles are stacked behind the building. You have some tools you'll need with you, and others are available out there. Jake, you can take the boys with you to be your helpers, okay?"

He turned to the ladies and continued. "I'll take Sue, the ladies and the girls around with Leslie this morning to the first school they're scheduled to visit. This first day will just be to get acquainted and set up plans for classes for tomorrow and skits for the girls and ball games for the boys. The plan is to spend two days at each school. They eat lunch late around here; so I'll have the ladies out at Abba House by two p.m., and we will eat our sack lunches then.

"After that, while the ladies and girls are helping with Bible classes and crafts, we men will hold a prayer time and then go with Num to see if we can get some more kids who live in those little shanties to come join in the activities at Abba House. After supper back at the hotel about six p.m., we will head out to do our evening outreach; women and girls to visit hospitals with Leslie and the men and boys to go hand out tracts with Num and me. That will last for an hour or two, depending on how well it goes. Is everyone set?"

When they all nodded their assent, he had them bow their heads as he led them in prayer. They all set off with high expectations and no little amount of anxiety!

Thus began a very busy and increasingly rewarding effort. They learned as they went along, and each night after they returned to the hotel, Hal and Larry called a hallway conference where everyone sat on the floor to share their day's experiences. They used this time to make suggestions and ask for opinions on how they could become more efficient in what they were doing. These critic times had been perfected in their previous mission trips and had proven to be very helpful for everyone. Hal had become more at ease in leading them and had gradually learned how to help everyone feel free to air frustrations and ask questions and get answers and still keep everything in focus. They had all come to look forward to these times together where they critiqued and complimented each other; it was fun and gratifying. Leslie and Num attended the first meeting and told Hal and Sue later how impressed they were with the process. They added their observations about what might work better and what worked well, and that gave everyone focus for the next day's effort.

By the end of the day their first Friday there, they had doubled the number of children attending classes at Abba House, the new roof had been finished, and they were ready to start putting in the new walls and tile down on the floor in two of the rooms. The classes at the two schools they had worked at had gone well after everyone got over their anxiety, and the skits had provoked a lot of questions amongst the Thai children. The school staff also opened up and started asking questions, which really pleased the ladies. The boys had a great deal of fun teaching baseball and football. Eddie, Jimmy, and Hopi soon found themselves the center of attention as these young boys wanted to find out all about life in Idaho and the US.

A large tent had been set up on an open area adjacent to Promise Baptist Church for the gospel preaching services. A lot of tracts had been handed out, and a lot of people had been invited to come hear about Jesus Christ. The team handing out tracts and invitations had met some resistance from a number of young men. There seemed to be an undercurrent of hostility toward the group from these people, although most of the people they had contact with were very courteous.

As the song service began on Friday night, a large crowd started to assemble. However, Hal and others in the group noticed some of those who had opposed them on the streets hanging around the fringes of the crowd. When Larry started preaching with Num interpreting for him, some of that crowd started heckling and trying to interrupt the services. Hal quickly had the women in the group begin to pray while they all made sure the kids were seated with the adults assigned to them.

They had been heckled by a few rowdies on the downtown streets in Seattle, but it had been nothing like this was becoming. As a result, the children and some of the ladies were increasingly concerned for their safety. Num's father decided he better call the police to send someone to disperse those causing the disturbance. As the police cars began to arrive, the agitators slipped away, and the services were able to go on. When the invitation was given, a good number of people went forward to find out more about this Christ they had never heard about before. By the time the evening came to a close, several made decisions to accept Christ as their Savior. That was cause for much rejoicing by the team and those from the church.

Saturday was a day of rest, shopping, and sightseeing. At one very large outdoor flea market, while the group was gathering to get back on the bus, rocks were suddenly being thrown from behind an old building on the far side of the street. One of the rocks hit

Hopi on the shoulder with a loud thud. He cried out as Eddie and Jimmy ran to help him. Soon they were being pelted too. Hal and Jake ran toward the building to try to stop the assault, if possible. When they rounded the side of the building, they saw several scraggly looking young men disappearing into the under-brush bordering the space behind the building. Hal knew it was no use to pursue them, so they returned to the group to help get them all on the bus and away from there. He found Sue and the two grandmas crowded around the twins' stroller. He could hear Angela crying as he came up to them. She had been hit on the head by a rock and was bleeding. Little Joe was hugging his sister and sobbing. Hal looked around for Eddie and Audra and the other kids. He saw they were being tended to by other ladies in the group. As he came to them he saw Hopi lying on the ground with blood on the side of his face. Eddie and Jimmy both had welts on their heads and arms. Hal struggled with a feeling of anger. He noticed Eddie wasn't crying; he was flat out ready to do damage to those responsible for this.

"Daddy, they've hurt our friend! Why?" he cried.

Hal put his arms around him saying, "They hurt your little sister, also, pal."

Eddie jumped up to go see Angela as Hal reached out and caught him and said, "Let me take a look at you first, buddy. You've got some lumps yourself."

"I'm all right, Dad! I've got to see if Angela is okay! Help Hopi and Jimmy for me, please." With that, he raced to his mom and the twins. As he came up to them, Sue could see that he had fire in his eyes. She had known that this oldest son of hers felt a strong sense of protection for Audra and the twins, but until now she hadn't known how intense that feeling really was. *Nor had Hal,* she thought. She suddenly wondered if Eddie had known the depth of that feeling himself.

"Angela is going to be okay, love. The rock bounced off Little Joe and hit her, but he's okay too. Are the others all right?" she asked, looking around. "Where is Audi?"

Just then her seven-year-old daughter pushed through those

HAROLD SOUTHWICK

around the stroller and hugged her momma's legs, her eyes filled with tears and fright.

"Mommy, why did someone throw rocks at us? We weren't hurting anyone."

Sue quickly knelt beside her daughter and hugged her, "Sweetheart, sometimes when we're doing the Lord's work, it upsets others. The devil doesn't like for Christians to share about God's love and mercy with those who are lost. I think that is why what happened last night and again today took place. We have to not let things like this keep us from doing what God wants us to do, okay?"

"You're right, honey," Hal said as he knelt beside them. "Now we need to get everyone on the bus and get back to the hotel."

Just then a police van pulled up and stopped beside the bus. Num and Hal along with the other men went to talk with them as Sue and Leslie helped the other adults get the kids loaded on the bus. The bus driver had gotten a first-aid kit from the bus, which they had used to tend to Hopi's head. As he was putting it away, Sue could tell he was still pretty shook up. Hopi was calming down now, but Hal told Sue and Eddie to keep an eye on him. They would have a doctor look at him after they got back to the hotel. He wanted to get everyone off the street right now and felt that Hopi was okay to move. He didn't want the rest of their time in Bangkok going sour on them; he needed to get them all calmed down and to praying.

After answering questions for the policemen, they were told there had been a lot of trouble with gangs of rebels out of Cambodia and Vietnam. They hated Americans and anyone who had been allies with them during the Vietnam War. They had been committing acts of violence and vandalism in southern Thailand since the end of the war. The police thought this was probably more of that. Hal and Bob Johnston thought it was probably part that but that there was more to it than that; these attacks were by the devil and his disciples against them because they were here to serve God. Leslie and Num agreed with that assessment later at the hotel.

A poll was taken concerning going ahead with the evangelism services that evening. The response was unanimous. They weren't going to let the devil stop them from doing what God had sent them here to do! They were going to go on with everything they felt God had laid out for them! With God being for them, how could they fail, even if they had to suffer some in doing it?

Privately, Sue and Hal and the two grandmas shared a fierce determination that these little ones of theirs had better not be hurt again. None of them realized at the time the depth of turmoil Eddie was experiencing concerning all of this. He was having a great deal of trouble with why God would let things like this happen, not only to his little sister who needed so much extra care and protection, but also to his two friends. Each of them was only trying to do good things for him! If she had understood him better, Sue would have been motivated to go to greater lengths to help him avoid some reactions that were to alter the course of his life later on.

The rest of their time in Thailand went as planned except for a window being broken out of Abba House one night the following week. Police patrols were stepped up, and a few of the perpetrators were arrested. Hal and Num and the other men in the group went with Leslie to try to witness to these young men in jail. For the most part, their hostility was untouchable, but one of them finally took a tract from Num as he tried to share about Christ with them. After leaving the jail, they joined hands out on the street and prayed that by the power of the Holy Spirit the tract would begin to break down the walls of hate and misunderstanding that kept so many from Christ's love for them. Hal joked somberly that they really hadn't intended for this trip to include jailhouse evangelism along with all the other efforts.

"But our God works in mysterious ways, does he not?" Num's accented English and the portent of his words brought smiles to their faces as they got in the van to return to the hotel.

The bonds that had been formed between all the members of

the RKO team and Leslie, Num, and Promise Baptist Church, and the helpers at Abba House were all the more special because of this persecution. But what was even more so were the friendships between the little homeless kids being ministered to at Abba House and the team kids. Those bonds were worth the cost of the whole trip. Leslie and Num choked with emotion and gratitude as they observed how the entire team came to care deeply about the ongoing welfare of these poor, deprived children. The promises of continuing financial assistance warmed their hearts and helped them to know they would be able to sustain the ministry and to even expand it. The good-byes were tearful and heartfelt.

As they boarded the plane to return home, Hal knew deep in his heart that they had just completed a major portion of the ministry God had started laying on his heart back when he had been confined to that hospital bed and being visited and encouraged by his dear friend Leslie. He also knew that Sue now had a much better perspective of why he had felt so strongly about what they had set out to accomplish. As they bowed in prayer before bidding Leslie and Num good-bye, they all agreed that these two weeks had been one of the best times of their lives, in spite of the opposition. The long trip home seemed much shorter because of the sense of accomplishment they all shared!

CHAPTER 37

The months following the return from Thailand were very busy. Hal had fallen behind in his ranch work simply because his dad couldn't keep up with things anymore. That required him spending more time making a living. It soon became apparent that the RKO ministry would either have to be turned over to others or put on hold for a while. At Sue's insistence they decided to concentrate on the ranch and spend more time dealing with Angela's needs.

Sue and Hal were talking one evening after supper about the challenge she presented for them.

"I'm just exhausted so much of the time. It's not so much the effort required, it's not knowing for sure if I'm doing all I should be, or if what we're doing is the right thing."

Hal was understanding, but didn't know why Sue worried so much. Angela was doing much better than many of those who had been placed in an institution. Their doctor had told him that. "It is something we have to learn as we go. Don't you think you should trust the Lord a little more, rather than wear yourself out worrying?" he asked his wife. "Let Eddie and Audi help more. They're big enough to be doing that."

Eddie happened to hear his mom and dad having this discussion and it left him troubled. He loved his mom very much and didn't want anything to hurt her. He was a very sensitive young boy and was beginning to question a lot of things about life a boy his age normally didn't think much about. He still couldn't understand why the incident in Thailand had been allowed to happen. Because of his nature, he decided he needed to do more to help with his little sister. She had to be protected. He and Audra had already heard other kids making fun of her at school. There was a festering beginning in him that needed some attention. It wasn't long after the discussion Sue had with Hal that she began to notice a subtle change in her son. He was starting to take things too seriously.

A few months later Hal and his dad were coming back from a livestock auction. His dad had taken Eddie fishing a few days earlier and Hal and he had been talking about the experience.

C.D. was quiet for a while and then asked, "Son, have you and Sue noticed anything different about Eddie lately?"

"Yes, we've talked about it a few times. Why? Has he said something to you?" Hal wanted to know.

"He was asking a lot of questions the other day when we were out in the boat. He likes to talk to me about a lot of things. I guess he thinks I have all the answers. I wish that was true. He wanted to know why God lets bad things happen. I told him I'd like to know the answer to that sometimes myself. I don't think that satisfied him. He's a pretty deep thinker; I guess he gets that from his mom," C.D. mused.

"She would argue that with you."

"I know; she already has. He's more complex than most kids his age and I think we probably should learn to channel his thinking in the right direction if we can. I can tell he worries about me a lot. I guess you know we're pretty close."

Hal smiled as he noted the emotion in his dad's voice, "We couldn't really tell that, Dad … No, Sue and I both think that's great."

CHAPTER 38

In the following years Eddie and Jimmy became interested in the Bible studies the church provided for kids their age. They received a great deal of encouragement from home, but Sue could tell by the questions Eddie asked her at times that he was puzzled about some of the precepts he was being taught.

It was in his freshman year in high school that he asked, "Mom, what does it mean that we are saved by grace? God tells us to do good things. I know; I've read it in my Bible."

Sue was delighted that her son was interested in what the bible had to say, but she knew by his expression that what she had to say about this very important question was pivotal in his outlook on life.

"Son, you know the Bible says we can't earn the right to go to heaven by doing good works. We're all imperfect people, and the works we do are imperfect. God's grace makes it possible for us to go to heaven," Sue silently prayed that what she was saying would make sense to him.

"Okay, but I know we're supposed to do good works. I just think God might get angry at us if we don't. Look at what he let happen to the Israelites."

She started to answer him, but he jumped up and said, "I've got to go practice baseball with Jimmy. Thanks for talking to me."

She knew somehow that she hadn't altered his thinking with the answers she had given. She devoted herself to prayer about it, hoping that the Holy Spirit would begin to reveal the truth to Eddie concerning these questions he seemed to be preoccupied about.

Eddie had become interested in football and made the starting team in his sophomore year at wide receiver. The family became great fans and went to as many games as they could. In his junior year he became the backup quarterback. As a result of those extra skill requirements he had to stay after school for additional practice.

It was on one of those evenings that Audra came home with news that disturbed her mother greatly. "Mom, I know you're going to hear about this from someone at church so I'm going to tell you first."

"You're going to tell me what?" Sue asked with alarm.

"Some high school boys were making fun of Angela when they were outside at recess. Someone went and told Eddie about it."

"Lord have mercy, what did he do?" her mom demanded.

"He hunted 'em down after classes let out before football prac-tice," Audi finally volunteered, not wanting to get her brother into any more trouble.

"And?"

"Well, Mom, he told them they better apologize and then leave her alone. They wouldn't do that so he just punched 'em out. He's pretty tough; did you know that?" Audi said with pride.

"He's pretty mixed up about some things too," her mom mut-tered. "We're supposed to turn the other cheek!"

"Mom, Eddie and I believe we need to *watch out* for Angela," her daughter said angrily.

"You do, but you can't solve all the problems by fighting."

"Well, Mom, Eddie doesn't agree with you. He feels God holds him responsible for me and Angela and Joe when we are all away from you and Dad. I'm proud of him and I love him. I feel safe when he's around." She watched her mom go huffing off to the kitchen. She knew Eddie would catch holy you-know-what when he got home. She figured she better go let Dad know so he would be ready to calm Mom down.

The family discussion following supper that evening involved no small amount of heated opinion sharing. Hal attempted to moderate, but it was obvious that mother and son who were so much alike were butting heads. Eddie loved his mom and she knew it, but he was becoming an independent thinker and his mom was having trouble adjusting. Her son was growing up and away from her apron strings and she didn't like it. It left her feeling lost in that area of her life.

By the time Eddie entered his senior year he had reached five-foot eleven-inches and was starting to fill out. He worked out in the weight room and did all the team exercises. In addition to that, he worked hard on the ranch handling hay bales, wrestling calves for branding and doctoring, etc., and was in very good shape. The girls were attracted to him, but you wouldn't have known it from his reaction. He was a shy individual when it came to the opposite sex and that pleased his mom just fine. . He was much too young as far as she was concerned. She had drilled what the bible said about how to treat the opposite sex into both Eddie and Audra and they never questioned her stand. Some thought of him as a momma's boy, but those who really knew him knew he could stand up to the best of those who were considered tough.

What Eddie was going through was no different than what any healthy lad his age experienced. He was beginning to declare his independence. Hal knew that was part of the plan of life. He had been through it himself. Although he had concerns for Eddie because of the load he put on himself, he knew that Eddie would excel at whatever he attempted. He guessed his son couldn't help being who he was.

PART TWO

THE JOURNEY …
AWAY … AND BACK

CHAPTER 1

The lights shone brightly on the football field, and bugs and fireflies could be seen buzzing around them behind the Glenn's Cove High School building cluster as the noisy crowd waited for the start of the game. This game was not just another football game for this bunch of boys and their young coach; this one was for the right to compete in the State High School A3 Championship game! They had come so close the last two seasons, and most of these kids would be playing their last high school game on this home field. More than that, this would be their last chance to bring home the coveted trophy that had eluded the little school for so long. Expectations were high because they were undefeated. However, those expectations were fringed with much anxiety because the starting quarterback, Billy Jones, had been injured in the previous playoff game. He wouldn't be able to play tonight. That left the starting wide receiver and backup quarterback to try to fill this most important role. He had played as quarterback in part of each game this year when the game was "in the books," so to speak. But he had not had to face the task of leading the team through a whole game, and he was very nervous about it.

That lean, broad-shouldered young man was no other than Eddie Edwards. He was a senior this year and was considered a fierce competitor and a very good wide receiver. In fact, several colleges were scouting him and Billy, as well as Jimmy Johnston, for their college teams! Jimmy was not as tall as Eddie, but he was solidly built and just plain tough, so he was the starting half-back. If you needed a tough couple of yards for a first down, you gave the ball to Jimmy and watched his powerful legs propel him through those big bodies in his way! The linemen were big kids as well and had given the quarterback good protection to get his plays off all year, so the coach had used that for an encouragement for Eddie to just trust his teammates

––––––––––––––––––

They had played some very good teams to get to this game and had come from behind on several occasions to win, but the caliber of the team they were facing tonight was a notch above anyone they had played so far. This was the same team that had beaten these kids out of playing in the championship game the year before. Revenge was a motivator, but Coach, as they all called him, had told them in practices and again in the locker room before coming on the field to just play their game and trust each other, to not let other factors cloud their minds. If they did that, then they could be proud of what they accomplished whether they won or not. He reminded them, however, that losing was not an attractive option. They already knew that and the disappointment that went with it. They just wanted to experience the other side of the coin this one time while they had this last opportunity!

"Okay, guys, let's go play the game and have some fun. We each know what we have to do. Eddie, remember the first two plays will be running plays, so relax and hand off cleanly! Jimmy, you be sure you have the ball in your hands before you make your break off left tackle, okay? And you guys up front remember you're going to have to give Eddie a little more time until he feels comfortable back there. Okay, let's go kick some butt!" Coach said as he led them out on the field to the cheering of the large crowd.

The band struck up their fight song as they came onto the field, and the adrenalin was flowing like a river! Eddie had dreamed about something like this happening to him, but he had no idea it would ever come about. Now that it had, he just hoped he didn't mess things up for his teammates. His intense personality wouldn't let him "just relax," so he knew he would have to depend on the Lord to help keep him calmed down. His dad had told him to look up in the stands when he needed assurance; his family would all be up there praying for him. Jimmy's family would be setting right there next to his family. That always pleased Jimmy and Eddie. They both got encouragement from both families.

Eddie had noticed recently that Jimmy was becoming attracted to his sister since she had entered ninth grade. That pleased him. If he was going to lose his best friend to some girl, better it be to his sister. He knew Jimmy shared the same values that he and Audra shared. Eddie himself was too shy to get involved much with girls, although he liked to be around them. Jimmy was always telling him that some girl in class wanted a date with him. He always said he was too busy. The truth was he was just too shy, although they did double date sometimes. It secretly pleased his mom that he wasn't interested in girls. She wasn't ready to give this handsome young son up to some other "female" just yet. Hal watched it all with amused detachment and remembered his own youth. He had had the father-son talk with Eddie, and he trusted Eddie's wisdom because of his relationship with Christ. He knew to just keep an eye on things and let his son grow into being the man God wanted him to become. Hal knew he needed to watch Eddie's fierce dedication to his siblings, though, so it didn't get out of hand.

The Glenn's Cove Pioneers lost the coin toss and kicked off to the opposing team. Eddie was glad of that. He could get into the game on defense first. He played linebacker on defense, splitting plays with a teammate. That helped him break a sweat and burn off some pent-up energy.

The Paladin Panthers tried a quarterback option on the first play, but the Pioneers front line penetrated and knocked the quarterback down as he tried to cut around the right end. The next play was a run between the guard and tackle on the left. As he broke through the line, Eddie hit him low and stopped him for a two-yard gain. The next play was a pass over the middle, which went incomplete. *Now it's our turn!* Eddie thought. The tackle he had made helped him relax, and he was ready to see if he could get the job done.

As he ran off the field to wait for Paladin to punt, he looked up in the stands where his family was sitting. They were all there, including Grandpa. Man, that made him feel good! Gramps was really having some health issues, and Eddie was very concerned for him. To see him here to watch his grandson play this last home game meant everything to him. They had shared so much over his short life. His dad gave him a thumbs-up, his mom blew him a kiss, and the twins waved excitedly. He knew he was Little Joe's hero, and Little Angela was his special project to watch out for. Audra was down with the cheerleaders where she was a rookie.

Jeb Dillon took the punt and broke for the left sideline. He picked up his blockers and was able to get the ball out to the thirty-five yard line before being leveled by a defender.

Coach grabbed Eddie's arm as he sent him onto the field, "Remember, halfback right off tackle on two. Keep it cool! Go!"

Eddie felt as though he were going to swallow his tongue! As he entered the huddle, he looked at each of his teammates and saw they were looking to him to lead the way. He called the play, and Jimmy gave him a big wink.

"Let's show them what we can do, tiger!" He grinned confidently.

As his team lined up, Eddie looked over the defense to see what their set was. He handed the snap off to Jimmy and watched as his buddy was leveled at the line of scrimmage. *Well, that didn't work*, he thought. He knew the next play was a quarterback keeper on the left side.

HAROLD SOUTHWICK

As he called the play in the huddle, he looked at Jimmy and said, "Make a hole for me, buddy. I'll be right on your heels."

Eddie took the snap and faked the handoff to Jimmy as he went by Eddie. Eddie broke to his left to avoid the linebacker bearing down on him and ran head-on into the defensive end. He picked himself up and thought, *Well, that didn't work either!*

The coach sent in another wide receiver for the next play, and Eddie dropped back and threw a long pass toward the left corner. His man slipped just as the ball was coming to him, and the defender intercepted the pass. Eddie raced to the sideline and was in on the tackle. His disappointment was evident as he came to the sideline.

Coach slapped him on the back and said, "Not your fault. Shake it off."

The Panthers finally worked the ball down to the nineteen yard line and settled for a field goal. The score stayed that way through the rest of the first half with both teams making some good drives partway down the field only to be stopped by strong defensive plays. Eddie had settled down and was beginning to feel comfortable at quarterback by halftime. He had started finding his receivers better and was making better decisions, not trying to force the ball. Coach had started noticing this. He decided their running game wasn't going to work if they couldn't get more out of the passing game.

In the locker room before talking to the team, Coach and his assistants decided to trust their quarterback and open up the passing game more. They laid out their plans to the team and huddled up and prayed before going back out on the field.

Eddie had noticed Billy Jones staring at him with resentment in the locker room. He wondered what that was all about. He knew that Jones thought he was kind of a sissy because he believed in Christ, but he had never been openly hostile before. As they were going back out to the field, Billy came up beside him and pulled Eddie's head over to him.

"If you sc … up and lose this game, I'll break your neck, you hear me? I need a win to secure my scholarship to Boise State," he threatened in a whisper.

Eddie pulled violently away from him. As he ran on ahead, he looked back and shook his head. *You idiot, I'm trying to do my best,* he thought. His competitive nature kicked in, and he decided to not let Jones distract him. As Eddie waited on the sidelines for the kickoff, he noticed Coach had Billy over by the bench with his nose in Billy's face, talking earnestly. They both looked at Eddie, and Coach gave Eddie a thumbs-up as he came over to him.

"You just go play the game the way I tell you to, and don't let him bother you, okay?"

Dillon took the kickoff at the two-yard-line and ran down the middle before cutting to the left side line. He made it to the forty-six yard line before being knocked out of bounds. Coach called for a pass out to the right flat to the wideout. Eddie was then to cut to the left side line and run downfield. The right wide receiver was to cut back toward the middle behind the fullback and throw the ball downfield to Eddie as he sprinted toward the goal line. Eddie looked back for the ball as he neared the twenty yard line. He saw the ball in a perfect spiral coming toward him, but he knew he would have to leap to catch it. He timed his leap and gathered it in on his fingertips at the sixteen yard line. He was stretched out in the air, and the defender hit him hard on his way down. He clung desperately to the ball and landed hard. He felt the wind go out of himself, and he lay stunned for a moment. Suddenly, his teammates were pulling him to his feet and slapping him on the back. It was then he realized he had hung onto the ball! He shook his head to clear it as he returned to the huddle. On the way, he glanced up in the stands and saw his dad give him that thumbs-up sign. A burst of adrenalin surged through him as he nodded to his dad. He was ready for the next play! On that next play, Eddie rolled out to the right, stopped suddenly, and threw the ball back to Jimmy in the backfield. The opposing line had shifted toward Eddie and had left a hole to the left side. Jimmy cut that way as he caught the ball and powered his way

HAROLD SOUTHWICK

down to the three yard line. Next, Eddie took the ball from center and ran left. Seeing Dillon open in the end zone, he lobbed a soft pass over the top, which Dillon caught and danced out of the end zone with a big grin. The try for the extra point was good, and the Pioneers were on top. The crowd was going crazy! Eddie saw his grandpa on his feet clapping with the rest of them, and he felt charged to the limit!

The Panthers took the ensuing kickoff and ran it back for a touchdown. Just like that, they were in the lead again. The crowd let out a loud groan, and people were sitting on their hands again, anxiety in every expression.

The Pioneers ran the ball back to midfield and started the next series of plays from there. On the first play from scrimmage, Eddie dropped back and threw for the end zone. His receiver and the defender went up for the ball together. It was knocked up in the air and came down in the field of play, and a Pioneer came down with it on the four yard line. Eddie lined his team up and handed off to Jimmy. Jim was stopped for a two-yard loss. A groan went up from the crowd. That just didn't happen to Jimmy! The next play was to the right corner of the end zone, which went incomplete. On third down, Jimmy was stopped again for no gain. Coach called for a field goal attempt. Eddie usually did the kicking for field goal attempts. Billy Jones always held for him. As Jones came on the field, he growled at Eddie.

"You better not miss this, hotshot!"

Eddie walked up to him, stuck his face in Billy's face, and muttered, "You hold the ball right and I'll kick it through, tough guy." The attempt was good, and suddenly they were tied again.

The teams fought back and forth between the twenty-yard lines for the remainder of the third quarter. It continued that way until the clock showed two minutes remaining in the game. The Panthers were driving, and things looked grim. Eddie looked up at his dad and saw him give a hand over his heart sign. Eddie knew what that meant, and suddenly he felt as though a "hand" had been placed on his shoulder! Calmness came over him, and he realized he was having the most fun. This was what this game should be like. The next play was a pass in his direction. He leaped as high as he could and tipped the ball away from the receiver. His teammate, the defensive end, dove for the ball and caught it just off the grass! They had the ball again, but the end zone looked a long way away! They had the ball again on their own twenty-nine yard line.

Coach called a time-out and had everyone come to the side-line. He knew they weren't going to be able to gain enough yards to get in field-goal range in the remaining time by running the ball. He instructed them to run the ball up the middle on the ground on the next play. Jimmy picked up eight yards on the attempt, so he decided to go for the first down on the ground on the next play. Jimmy hit the line on the left side and broke through for three yards.

They were still in business; but the clock was winding down. Coach called for one more running play to set up a pass play to follow. It went for no gain, and they were still out of reach of a field goal by a long way. The clock read thirty seconds remaining. Coach called his last time-out and told the team there was still plenty of time. This was what they had played for all season! He called for a reverse, with the left wide receiver cutting back across behind Eddie and taking the ball to the right side. The right wide receiver was to come around behind to meet him and take the handoff from him behind the protecting linemen. While this was going on, Eddie was to run down the left side line with Jimmy following him. Eddie was then to take a long pass from the right wide receiver, with Jimmy hopefully being there to protect him from any defenders covering him.

As they went to huddle, Eddie said in a calm voice and a smile on his face, "Okay, guys, we know what we have to do. Let's say a quick prayer and go do it!"

They each bowed their heads and prayed silently and broke the huddle. There wasn't a sound in the stadium as Eddie called the play. His mom could hear his voice loud and clear. She clutched Hal's hand and felt goose bumps all over her body.

HAROLD SOUTHWICK

Hal grinned at her and said, "He's got it, babe!" The twins were spellbound, as were the grandparents.

The play worked just as they had practiced it so many times. Eddie took the pass and raced for the end zone. He thought he was going to make it! These Panthers were the state champions and they weren't about to quit. As Eddie dove for the goal, he saw the defensive linebacker flying through the air at him. He tried to shift the ball to his other side, but as he did so, he was crushed by the defensive linebacker. He groaned as the ball flew out of his hands into the end zone. Both he and the defender were stunned by the collision but were trying to scramble for the ball. Suddenly, a body hurtled over both of them and landed on the ball in the end zone. Jimmy had saved the game! Eddie knew he had just about blown it, but he could not have been happier for Jimmy. His running game hadn't worked well tonight, but he was in the right place at the right time to recover the ball.

The extra point attempt was good. The clock ran out on the following kickoff, and the Pioneers were headed for the championship game at Holt Arena in Pocatello the next Saturday afternoon. Jimmy was carried off the field on his teammates' shoulders. Before they cleared the field, he jumped down and hoisted Eddie up.

"This guy deserves a lot of credit, too!" he shouted.

Everyone agreed—everyone, except one.

The locker room was a madhouse while the team showered and dressed. Coach yelled at everyone, "Don't leave until we talk. We still have the most important game of the season to play."

When they had all gathered in the gymnasium, Coach stepped out in front of them and thanked his staff for their help in getting the team ready for this game. Then his face lit up with a big smile, and he raised both hands into the air, "Great game, guys! You all did your job and played together and stayed focused. The win is the result of that. We can enjoy this win tonight, but tomorrow we have to focus on next week's game. I personally feel we have already beaten the better of the two teams. But if we go into that game with the big head, we will beat ourselves! Everyone be home in bed by midnight tonight. Remember, don't break training rules, okay?"

As Eddie started to leave the gym, Coach took him aside and said, "Eddie, you played a great game tonight under a lot of pressure. I know you could lead the team next week and get the job done. But Billy has been our starting quarterback all season. If he is ready to play, he will start next Saturday. If he doesn't appear to be up to leading the team, I will put you in and see how you do."

Eddie had expected that announcement and knew it was the fair thing to happen. That still didn't stop his tinge of disappointment. He just thanked God for helping him play well. He was thrilled with the win and that was what was important in the long run.

CHAPTER 2

The following week was filled with before-school strategy sessions and intense afternoon practices. They studied game reports of the Sheldon Rams' style of play and planned accordingly. By week's end they felt they were ready. Billy Jones had recovered sufficiently, so he would be the quarterback. Eddie accepted that and was determined to do his job as wide receiver and linebacker the best he could.

He was becoming irked, however, at Jones' cocky attitude. He also noticed Billy making embarrassing remarks to Audra, and that bothered him a lot. He knew if that continued he would have to do something about it. Jimmy and he had talked about it, and Jimmy was upset about it too. They didn't want anything to distract from the need to concentrate on the upcoming championship game, so they decided they would wait to challenge Billy. If Audra complained to either of them about it, though, they would have to act. Eddie knew he had to talk to his folks about the matter,. They both promised to pray about it and cautioned Eddie to not do anything rash. Hal decided that he needed to make Coach aware of the situation and did so.

Holt Arena in Pocatello was packed to overflow for the game. Sheldon was in the eastern part of the state, which drew a lot of fan support. Glenn's Cove was about 170 miles west, but with this being their first chance to win a state football title in a long time, almost everyone went to the game. The teams were announced, and the Pioneers won the coin toss. They elected to kick off to start the game; they wanted to get into the game with some hits to relieve nervous tension. It had worked last week. Hopefully it would this week as well.

The defense held on the first series of downs, and the Pioneers took over on their own twenty-eight yard line. Billy led the team downfield in methodical fashion, and they scored a touchdown on a pass over the middle to the tight end. Pioneers seven, Rams zero! The teams went scoreless until just before halftime when the Rams made a field goal to make it seven to three. In the locker room at halftime, Coach encouraged them all to keep playing their game; things were going well.

Eddie went to get a drink of water before going back on the field. As he straightened up, Billy Jones shoved up against him and muttered, "Watch my smoke, wimp!" With a sneer, he ran from the building.

Eddie stood there just shaking his head. He'd had about enough of this kind of treatment. He thought, *God, why are you letting this happen?*

The Pioneers took the kickoff and quickly moved the ball to the nine yard line on two quick passes: one to Eddie down the right sideline and the other to Jeb Dillon over the middle. On the next play from scrimmage, Jones scored on a quarterback option.

As he ran by Eddie in the end zone, he taunted, "See how it's done, pretty boy?"

Eddie ignored him and headed over to the sidelines. Coach had noticed what went on and came to Eddie, "Don't react, Eddie. Just play your game. You're doing fine."

The Rams took the ensuing kickoff, ran it back for a touchdown, and were right back in the game. Coverage by the Pioneers had been lax, and Coach called them over and told them to get their heads in the game.

He went to Billy and said, "Concentrate on football and quit showing off, or I'll pull you so fast it'll make your head swim! Do you understand me?"

The Rams kicked off, and Glenn's Cove ran it back to mid-field. On the very first play from scrimmage, Jones threw into triple coverage over the middle and was intercepted. In four quick plays, the Rams moved the ball to the fifteen yard line, where they stalled and settled for a field goal. Just that quickly, the game was tied. Coach pulled Eddie aside and told him to get ready. He was going to go in at quarterback on the next series of downs. The ball was kicked into the end zone and was brought out to the twenty yard line to start play for the Pioneers.

As Billy started to go onto the field, Coach said, "Stay here. Edwards is going to run this series of downs. I want you to go over on the bench and think about what's important to you!"

Eddie engineered a beautiful drive downfield with a mix of runs and passes. Jimmy took a handoff at the eight yard line and waltzed into the end zone untouched. That touchdown proved to be the last score of the game, and the Pioneers had their state football championship trophy! Everyone was jubilant, but Eddie knew that a confrontation with Billy Jones in the near future was going to be hard to avoid. He didn't tell anyone this, but he was about ready for it to happen.

CHAPTER 3

That confrontation wouldn't come about until the following summer. Over the last three summers, Hal had been teaching Eddie the techniques of team roping. Eddie seemed to have a knack for it, which pleased his dad. He had enjoyed the sport so much! They both knew that Hopi, Eddie's Indian buddy, was a good team roper, so that summer following graduation, Hal had agreed to let Eddie and Hopi do some roping at area rodeos, even going so far as to take them down to compete in rodeos in Hopi's part of the country for a couple of weeks. Sue and the other kids decided that would be a great way to spend their vacation time that year. It could be part of Eddie's graduation present. The RKO activities had been curtailed to a large part because the kids had wanted to spend time doing other things. The adults had kind of grown weary also and decided to suspend it for a while. Hal and Sue had mixed feelings about it, but their work load had increased since Dot and C. D. were no longer able to help with ranch activities and certainly not with the ranch ministry any longer.

Eddie had received a football scholarship from the University of Idaho in Moscow for the following fall. He was excited about that, but his folks had wanted him to attend a Bible school first. He knew if he did that he wouldn't receive his scholarship, so he finally convinced them to let him play football and study engi-

HAROLD SOUTHWICK

neering at Idaho next fall. Billy Jones and Jimmy Johnston had received scholarships to attend Boise State and play football. That bummed Eddie out because he would be playing against his best friend, Boise State and Idaho being arch rivals. However, he looked forward to confronting Jones on the field.

Hopi had received a used pickup in pretty good condition from his folks for his graduation present. He had talked his dad into letting him borrow the horse trailer to transport his beautiful roping horse and come to Idaho to compete with Eddie. They spent a couple of weeks practicing their skills under the tutelage of Hal and decided to enter the Hailey rodeo for their first event. In the first go around, they were over eager and didn't place. On the second night, they did a little better and started to get over the "jitters." By the time they had competed on Saturday night, they felt they were getting the hang of competing and decided they loved what they were doing! They competed in three more rodeos before the Elmore County Rodeo was scheduled and were excited to compete before the hometown crowd. Audra had entered as a queen contestant, and she was all excited about that. Little Joe and Angela were nine years old now and loved everything their older brother and sister loved; hence, they couldn't wait for the fair and rodeo as well. Mom and Dad were pretty excited about it too! After all, that was where this whole family affair had begun. They couldn't believe that had been twenty-two years ago already.

Angela still had the typical disabilities associated with Down's syndrome, but with the way her family and most other people had attended to her needs, she had come a long way. She was mobile, could talk well enough to express most things she wanted to convey, and attended public school along side of Little Joe. Even though she had the typical Down's syndrome appearance, hardly anyone even noticed that anymore. Her family accepted her as a normal and equal part of them and wouldn't have had her any other way. She and Little Joe were special mostly because of the way they were with each other. They both adored their big brother and mimicked him constantly. Audra looked up to Eddie almost as much, and even though she was starting to establish her own identity, she still looked to Eddie for a sense of security out in the school and social setting. Of course, she enjoyed similar attention from Jimmy! Billy Jones was another matter altogether. He made suggestive comments to her when others weren't nearby and couldn't keep his hands to himself. Eddie hadn't actually seen him do these things, but he sensed it and had questioned her about it. She had talked to her mom about it, and they were praying about it. Sue didn't want Eddie to get in a fight over it either. She didn't think that was the Christian way to solve the problem. They both knew Eddie wouldn't let that stop him from confronting Jones. Sue had talked to Hal about it, and they decided to see if God would take care of the problem. Although they weren't friends with Billy's family, they wanted to avoid controversy with them.

CHAPTER 4

The fair began on a Thursday afternoon with the rodeo starting that evening. The fairgrounds always featured animal displays and judging, as well as produce, arts, and crafts and other things of interest. The grand champion in each of the animal categories was auctioned off, and the kids who had owned them usually used that money for college later on. Audra had helped Little Joe and Angela raise a steer for this year's judging contest. That turned into a family focus project, and they were excited about showing their animal. The judging took place the first afternoon, and their steer won a blue ribbon. That brought proud smiles all around. By rodeo time, they were all anxious to see how Eddie and Hopi would do. Eddie always roped the head, and Hopi was the "heeler." He seemed to be able to get both legs into the loop better than Eddie. They wanted to do their best for the family. Hal wanted them to do well for their self-confidence and his pride of course. He secretly wished his body would still let him do some roping. Where had his youth gone?

The saddle-bronc riding led off the rodeo, and Hal helped at the chutes. He hadn't ridden a bucking bronc since before he went to Vietnam, but he still loved being around the action. The bareback riding was next, and then came the calf roping. That was finally followed by the team roping. As that got underway, the twins were excitedly looking for Eddie and Hopi. Hopi had come to mean a great deal to Hal's whole family, not just Eddie. Soon they were to compete next. Sue thought, *What a handsome young man our son has become. I'm so proud of him. He makes me think of his daddy when he rode here way back when!*

The boys backed their horses in behind the barriers on each side of the steer chute, and the barrier rope was fastened. As the steer burst from the lifted gate, Eddie spurred his horse and made a clean start. Quickly he twirled his rope and let it sail. It settled over those horns, and he brought his pony around and pulled the steer backward so Hopi could throw his rope down under and in front of the hind legs of the steer. As Eddie's pony pulled the steer forward a step, one side of the loop slid in under the hoofs, and Hopi tightened his rope and backed his horse up to stretch the calf out, being careful to not upset the animal. The judge brought his flag down, and this go-around was in the books for them. They waited for their time to be announced and were quietly pleased to find themselves in fourth place for the night. They coiled their ropes, rode stirrup to stirrup and slapped their hats together, then waved to the crowd, and exited the arena. It had been a lot of fun. Audra had placed as an attendant in the queen contest which wasn't bad for a first try for that honor.

The next two days and nights were filled with similar results. On Saturday night after the rodeo was over, Eddie and Hopi met his family at the fairgrounds after caring for their horses. They wanted to do some of the rides with the twins and Jimmy and Audra. They did that for a while, and then Hal took them over to the food booths, where they all got burgers and drinks. There was a dance going on at the entertainment pad, so they went to watch that while eating their meals. Hal and Sue didn't forbid the kids to dance, but because of their Christian beliefs, they wanted them to be modest and not compromise those beliefs. They understood the pressure the worldly culture put on kids who wanted to follow Christ. They had been young once themselves. While Hopi, Audra, and Jimmy were chatting with the family, Eddie wandered over to the bandstand to talk with the guitar player, Kurt. He liked to mess around with his dad's old guitar and had learned to play some. While they were discussing techniques of chording and picking, Eddie felt someone brush by

HAROLD SOUTHWICK

his shoulder. He moved aside without looking up and continued talking to Kurt, the guitarist. He saw Kurt glance up, and he became aware the person who had brushed past him had stopped and turned around and was looking at him. When he followed Kurt's glance, his eyes fell on the most beautiful face he could ever remember seeing. Before him stood a young girl about his own age with big brown eyes with long, dark lashes. Her slender face was lined with long, black hair that fell below her shoulders in ringlets. He was aware of Kurt glancing back and forth between the girl and him, but he felt himself drowning in those big eyes. They held him captive with their curious smile, one eyebrow slightly raised questioningly.

"Well, Kurt, aren't you going to introduce us?" she asked.

Kurt stood up with a smile, "This is my sister Katy, Eddie. Kat, this is Eddie Edwards. He team ropes with his buddy, Hopi."

"I know he does. I saw them out in the arena!" She reached to take Eddie's hand. "Hi! I was one of the barrel racers."

"You're that beautiful girl on that palomino mare!" Eddie stood blushing. "You won tonight!"

"You noticed?"

"I think every cowboy out there noticed," Eddie returned then dropped his head and kicked the ground with a sheepish grin.

"Well, when they start playing again, can I have a dance?" She cocked her head to one side with a challenge in her eyes.

Eddie glanced over where his family stood watching him. His dad had an amused smile on his face. Eddie couldn't quite discern his mom's look, and he saw Audra and Jimmy nodding at him and smiling. Jimmy suddenly gave him the thumbs-up sign. With that, he turned back to Katy. "I don't know how to dance very well. Do you think I'm too old to learn?"

"If you can throw a rope like you did tonight, you can learn to dance! I'll be back in a little while," she said with a dazzling smile.

Eddie watched her slender figure as she walked away with a graceful sway. In that moment, he felt a surge of emotions he had never experienced before. He stood in confusion and excitement that left him speechless.

Kurt said with an amused grin, "She has that effect on a man. Walk with caution, my young friend!"

Eddie returned to his family with some feelings he had no idea how to express. His mom was looking at him with an intensity he had never seen in her eyes before. His dad looked at him as though he knew exactly what his son was feeling. The twins were looking at him and then their folks with looks that said, *What's going on?* Audra and Jimmy stood back and observed with grins on their faces. The young "centerpiece" of the family had just experienced a profound confrontation with the realities of his young manhood. As a girl, Audra sensed some of his turmoil, while Jimmy knew exactly how he felt. He was experiencing some of those same emotions in his own life.

"Mom, she wants me to dance with her after a while. Will that be okay?"

"Well, just who is she?" Sue asked, somewhat mother like.

Hal reached over and touched her arm.

She turned to him with a protective yet questioning look. "What?"

"We were young once. He knows what, or rather who, guides our reactions in life. He is not our little boy anymore. We have to let him take a step into manhood." Hal felt a catch in his own throat as he watched Sue react to his counsel.

"Well, you just behave yourself and remember who you are! I love you, Son." She had to turn away and wipe tears from her eyes.

Audra watched all of this and knew she would probably never be able to untie Mom's apron strings. Her next thought was, *But Daddy is my buddy, so…*

Soon the band started playing again. Eddie looked around to find Katy, but he couldn't see her. Disappointment swept through him. He wanted to hold her and talk to her some more. What was going on inside him? He had never felt this way about any girl before.

HAROLD SOUTHWICK

He started to walk away when Hopi came over to him and said, "Friend, you are sad? Be patient. She'll come back!"

They walked around for a while and returned to the dance pad. As Eddie stepped up by his little sister, he felt a hand on his arm.

When he turned around, Katy said, "Are you going to dance with me, cowboy?"

Eddie could only nod his head. He was a nervous wreck. He didn't know how to dance, and he didn't want to make a fool of himself. But he knew he had to try.

"Just let me lead." She smiled at him. "It's easier than you think. Don't be afraid of me. I won't bite you, and I sure won't break!"

She showed Eddie how to hold her right hand and where to place his right hand on her back. Soon they were moving around the dance floor, and Eddie felt as if he were on a cloud! She kept looking at him and smiling.

"Well, what do you think? Are you having fun yet?"

"Yup! I've never been this close to someone as pretty as you! I can't believe I'm doing this!" He gulped.

"Believe it, mister! I'm real, and I'm having fun too!"

They danced several more times before the band stopped playing. Eddie then introduced her to his parents and was pleased that she chatted with them freely. He watched his mom and could tell she was starting to loosen up a little bit. His dad was just his quiet, gentle self, and Eddie was pleased. He watched Katy's face when he introduced the twins to her. Little Joe had taken a fancy to her already, and Angela clung to his arm and looked shyly up at her from lowered eyes. Katy didn't know it then, and Eddie's family wasn't conscious of it, but her reaction to Angela would go a long way in how she was perceived by the family.

She smiled and held her hand out. "Hi, I'm Katy. What's your name?"

"Her name is Angela," Little Joe interjected eagerly. "I'm Joe, Little Joe. She's my twin sister."

"Hi, I'll bet she can tell me herself," Katy said as she knelt in front of the shy little girl. Katy noticed that Little Joe stood a good six inches taller than his twin.

"I … uh … I'm … uh, Angela," she responded so low she could hardly be heard.

"That's a beautiful name! I like it very much! Would you like some cotton candy?" Katy asked as she looked up at Sue to see if that would be okay.

Sue smiled and nodded her head. They all watched as Katy took Angela's hand and marched off to the cotton candy booth.

Hal put his arm around Sue and gave her a hug. She responded by laying her head against his chest.

"Well! She sure passed that test with flying colors," Jimmy said out of the blue.

"Yeah, isn't she great," Eddie beamed. An expression suddenly furrowed his brow. "What test?"

"I wanted some cotton candy too!" Little Joe exclaimed plaintively.

"Let's go get some then," Eddie replied as he grabbed his little brother's hand and followed after that beautiful young girl who had suddenly entered his family circle.

HAROLD SOUTHWICK

CHAPTER 5

The following weekend was rodeo time down in St. John, Arizona, Hopi's home town. Hal had committed to taking the family down there for their vacation time, but he was reluctant to leave the ranch right then. His dad was getting very frail, and his mom was having health problems as well. He finally was able to get Leah and Stu to come spend time with them and kind of look after the hired help. Eddie wasn't very happy about being away from Katy for two weeks

She just smiled at him and said, "Oh well. We'll just have to see what happens!"

Eddie didn't understand just what she meant by that, but he shrugged his shoulders and didn't ask. His family had invited Kurt and Katy to a Sunday-afternoon barbecue at the ranch following the fair and rodeo. They were sitting in the front-porch swing seat. He wanted to hold her hand but was too bashful to do so. His dad and mom were on the front lawn where his dad was cranking the old two-gallon homemade ice cream freezer while his mom sat on it to hold it down. Eddie sat there remembering watching Gramps and Grams do that. His face suddenly clouded with sadness.

"What's wrong?" Katy was watching him closely.

Eddie glanced at her quickly and said, "I was just remembering. My grandparents used to do that for barbecues when I was little. Now he's sick all the time. I don't get to go fishing with him much anymore like we used to do."

"You have a very close family, don't you?" Katy said as she reached and patted his arm. "I like them! I'll go fishing with you sometime if you wouldn't mind a girl showing you how to catch the really big ones!"

"Ha! You're on." He grinned. "I think my family likes you too."

Just then Jimmy, Audi, Kurt, and Hopi came around the corner of the house laughing and joking. They had just returned from a horseback ride and were ready for some homemade ice cream.

Audra came up the steps, dramatically put her hands on her hips, and said, "Well, aren't you two just cozy?"

"Now I need a girlfriend too!" Hopi lamented.

"They'll just spend your money," Jimmy joked.

Audra poked him in the ribs and laughed.

As they ate ice cream and visited, Eddie's family asked about Kurt and Katy's family. Their dad was retired air force. He was now director of civilian personnel on base, and their mom was director of nursing at the Mt. Home Air Base Hospital. They were originally from the Flagstaff, Arizona, area, where Bill Parker had grown up on a cattle ranch. They had purchased a small ranch north of Mt. Home so that Katy could have a horse and pursue her barrel-racing activities. Kurt was attending Boise State on a music scholarship with a minor in computer science. Katy planned on attending Boise State next fall as well. She wasn't sure what she wanted to study yet.

As Jimmy listened to them talk about their dad's career in the air force, he suddenly asked, "Did you say your dad is Colonel Bill Parker?"

"Yes, why?" Katy asked.

"My dad served twice in the air force. His squadron commander was a Colonel Bill Parker."

"Really? Did your dad spend time in Thailand near Korat?" Kurt asked with a smile. "Their fighter squadron flew air-support missions for the ground war in Vietnam out of Korat."

"He did! Dad has talked about it some ... Uncle Hal was one

of the first US soldiers to fight in Vietnam," Jimmy replied as he glanced at Hal.

They all looked at Hal as he shook his head and replied, "We can talk about that some other time. That's a whole other story. I'm just enjoying listening to you young folks visit."

Eddie looked at his dad with pride, "Dad's story is very special to our family!"

"It sure is," agreed Sue as Hal looked down and away.

Katy wondered at the pain and something else she saw on his face. She would have to ask Eddie about it, if he would share with her.

CHAPTER 6

Plans had been made to leave for Arizona Tuesday morning with Hopi. The boys needed a couple of days to work their horses in preparation for the rodeo in St. John, which would open Friday evening. Eddie and Little Joe and Hopi would ride together in Hopi's pickup pulling his horse trailer. Hal, Sue, Audra, and Angela would ride in Hal's one-ton truck pulling their stock trailer carrying Eddie's horse. They planned to take two days for travel time. That would get them into St. John Wednesday evening. The St. John rodeo would end on Saturday night with horse racing, greased-pig catching, and a large cookout on Sunday afternoon. Eddie's family and Hopi would go on to Flagstaff the following week for the rodeo there before Eddie and his family would return home.

When Eddie had shared those plans with Katy, she seemed mysterious to him. He realized he didn't know her well enough to interpret her demeanor.

When she hugged him good-bye Sunday evening, she said, "I'll be seeing you!"

Eddie looked at her questioningly. "When will that be?"

"Oh, we'll see." She tilted her head, smiled, and waltzed away.

———

Monday evening, after supper, Eddie and Hopi decided to take Hopi's truck into town to fuel it up for the trip home. Audra wanted to go with them so she could tell Jimmy good-bye again before leaving for two weeks. They were planning on meeting him at the little hamburger joint next to the highway on the west side of town. All the young people hung out there in the evenings during the summer. When they arrived there after fueling Hopi's truck they looked for Jimmy, but he hadn't arrived yet. As they stood talking to some friends from school, Jimmy drove into the parking lot. Eddie turned to watch him get out of his old pickup and come toward them. He heard some voices behind them and turned to see who it was. He felt a body shove him aside roughly.

Billy Jones stepped up to Hopi and said, "Get out of my way, reservation rat." He gave Hopi a shoulder in the face and then turned to Audra. Grabbing her ,he swung her around and then patted her on the backside as he looked at Jimmy accelerating toward them.

"Why don't you pick a real man to hang out with, baby?" he sneered as his two companions laughed, lewdly starring at her.

Eddie gathered himself, grabbed Jones by the arm, and spun him around, saying, "Keep your filthy hands to yourself and your loud mouth shut, you arrogant jerk!"

Billy started to retort as Eddie threw a hard right-handed punch to Billy's jaw, knocking him off his feet.

Billy's two buddies moved to interfere but were grabbed by Jimmy and Hopi and shoved aside.

"Stay out of this if you want to stay healthy! This hotshot has been asking for a fight for a long time. Now he's found it, and you will too if you don't stay back!" Jimmy threatened.

"Would you like to find out what a 'reservation rat' knows about the hard knocks of life?" Hopi asked quietly from a crouch, ready to swing into action.

Billy rolled over and put a hand to his mouth. It came away bloody, and he came off the ground wildly.

"Why, you two-bit Goody Two-shoes, I'm going to rip your head off!" he screamed.

He lunged at Eddie, swinging wildly as he charged. Eddie slipped on a piece of gravel as he stepped aside and lost his balance just as Billy rammed into him. He fell heavily with Jones landing on top of him. Eddie wasn't as tall as or quite as heavy as Billy, but his pent-up feelings toward his opponent gave him strength beyond himself. He was in great shape because of hard work, but he knew he was going to have his hands full now that this had finally come to a head. A vague feeling of regret crossed his mind coupled with a sense of guilt. As he struggled to throw Billy off, he thought, *God, why have you let this happen?*

Billy hit him in the face as he was coming to his feet. As he fell backwards, Audra ran to keep Jones from kicking him. As she did so, Billy threw her aside and kicked at Eddie's ribs. Eddie saw the kick coming and grabbed his foot, twisting as he came to his feet. Jones was thrown off his feet, which gave Eddie time to clear his head and step back. He glanced at Audra as she got up from where she had fallen. A surge of anger coursed through him; as Billy came to his feet, Eddie began to rain blows on him with a fury. Suddenly hands grabbed him from behind. He struggled to free himself as Billy came at him swinging. Eddie raised his foot and caught him in the midsection and pushed as hard as he could. The wind went out of Jones with a whoosh, and he fell in defeat. Eddie struggled to stand and gather himself. He hung his head as he experienced a feeling of disappointment with himself and his reaction.

"What are you doing, Eddie?" asked Jack Henley, the city policeman. "I'm surprised by your behavior."

"What are you doing here?" Eddie asked.

"I'm doing my job. I was called to respond to a fight out here. I sure didn't expect to find you involved. What are your folks going to say about this?"

"He was defending me, Officer!" Audra said, coming to her brother's defense.

As the policeman went about questioning everyone, Eddie began to feel a sense of resentment that he was being held accountable for the altercation; at least he felt he was. He knew his mom and dad would want to know why he had acted as he had. How could he get across to them his sense of responsibility for his younger siblings? In the back of his mind, though, he knew he had been wanting to fight Billy. He underwent a pang of guilt, but just as quickly, he rejected that feeling.

Audra, Hopi, and Jimmy finally were able to get Eddie away from the crowd and start toward Hopi's pickup.

As they were leaving, Billy yelled, "This isn't the end of anything," as he cursed at Eddie.

Hopi and Jimmy held Eddie's arms as he just shook his head. "Let's get out of here. Jimmy, you and Audi follow us out to the ranch so you can help explain all of this to Mom and Dad Edwards!" Hopi counseled.

By the time the kids arrived home, the police department had already phoned Hal and Sue to inform them of the events at the West End Stop. They were seated on the front porch as Eddie and Hopi drove in, followed by Jimmy and Audi. Eddie looked at them sitting there together and thought about how that scene had always cheered him. This time, however, it left him apprehensive and unsure of himself.

Audra ran ahead of Eddie up on the porch and exclaimed, "First of all, let me tell you what started it all. You already know about the fight, don't you? Eddie was standing up for me, and I'm proud of him! You should be too!"

Sue started to reply, but Hal said, "Let her tell us what she has to say, Mom. Then we'll know more how to respond."

"Thanks, Dad!" Audra related the entire incident rapidly, hardly pausing to take a breath. When she finished, she placed her hands on her hips the way she always did and said, "There you have it, and that's the way it happened!"

Sue looked at Eddie and asked, "Are you okay, sweetheart?" She wiped tears from her eyes.

She saw that his face was scratched and he acted as though his ribs hurt when he breathed. She and Hal could both sense the anger still doing a slow burn inside him. Hal was amazed again at Eddie's grit and determination to look out for his younger sisters and brother.

"I know everyone thinks I shouldn't have reacted the way I did, but Billy Jones thinks he doesn't have to show respect for anyone. My talking to him has never done any good. When he treated Audi the way he did, I couldn't help myself. And I'm not going to apologize for it either, Mom! If God wants to be mad at me, then he can just be mad!" Eddie fumed. "The police think I started the whole thing. This started a long time ago."

Hal got up and went to his son. "Calm down, Son! We know you have a high sense of what's right and wrong, and no, you are not wrong in feeling that way. But we also know that you need to be careful in how you pursue justice to right those kinds of wrongs. If you go overboard, it could bring you much grief. Come on. Let's go in and get you cleaned up. We've got a trip to get ready for. Audi, thank you for defending your big brother's actions. You're fortunate to have him looking out for you. And thank you too, Jimmy and Hopi. I guess we'll just call you guys the three 'fighting' musketeers!"

"Well, is that all you have to say, Dad?" Sue seemed disappointed with Hal.

"We'll talk about it more later, babe," Hal said lowly and went inside.

Sue seemed gripped by some sense of foreboding as she followed him; at the time she couldn't define it.

Audra asked Jimmy and Hopi to stay out on the porch with her for a bit. She said, "We need to pray for my big brother. He's hurting inside, and I think he feels bad about fighting. Mom gets on him about his temper some times. But he needs our support right now. Jimmy, will you lead us, please?"

They sat on the porch swing and held hands as Jimmy prayed. Hal and Sue had turned to see what they were doing and noticed the poignant scene. They could hear the prayer through the screen door and were touched. The look they gave each other spoke volumes. They knew these kids were good kids, and they thanked God for that. Hal wondered what he could do to try to reach Billy Jones in his need. He wondered if Billy's parents were aware of their son's attitudes and actions.

CHAPTER 7

The next day began long before daylight. Chores had to be completed and last-minute instructions concerning the ranch work had to be gone over with Stu and Leah. Hal left written instructions for the two ranch hands, along with phone numbers and an itinerary of where they should be each day they were away. After the luggage was loaded in the camper on Hal's truck and the horses were loaded into the two trailers, they all gathered on the front porch for prayer before leaving. Eddie had been quiet and somewhat withdrawn all morning, and Sue had the feeling he was pulling away from her. She was having a struggle with the changes she could tell were taking place in her son. She felt the Holy Spirit restraining her from saying any more to him just yet. She didn't feel she knew exactly what to say anyway. She hoped Hal and she could get time to talk about him soon.

The trip south went without problems, and everyone began to relax and enjoy the beautiful scenery. Little Joe was thrilled beyond words to be riding with his big brother and Hopi. He was almost ten years old now, and to be able to spend time with these two special people and listen to their talk opened new avenues of wonder and interest for him. The more he studied Eddie and listened to him, the more he realized his big brother seemed different somehow. He noticed Hopi glancing at Eddie during lulls in their conversation. Eddie just seemed preoccupied, which was not his normal behavior. Stops to check the horses and use bathrooms occurred every two hours or so. Meals were prepared in the camper and eaten standing around the rigs. The kids were glad to get a few minutes to stretch legs and jaw at each other. The one night on the road, the boys all slept in sleeping bags on the grass alongside the trucks, while Hal , Sue and the two girls all sacked out in the camper. By the time they arrived at Hopi's home in St. John, everyone was tired but looking forward to their time there.

Hopi's dad and mom's greetings to Hopi amused Hal. His mom hugged and kissed him just as any mom would do, but his dad walked up to him, put his hand on Hopi's shoulder, and looked him up and down. Then he took hold of Hopi's arm and kind of shook it, all the time shaking his head up and down and smiling. His eyes were full of pride, and he grunted approvingly. They turned to Hal and Sue and greeted them in the traditional Indian fashion. They then looked at their children and nodded and smiled, their lined faces showing pleasure in seeing these dear friends again. These two families knew their relationship was unusual and special; they also knew it existed because of the uniting power of the Lord Jesus Christ.

The missionaries who had been there when the Edwards had been there several years ago for their summer outreach were no longer here. Hopi's family had the new missionaries join them for supper. That began a wonderful time of sharing and fun as they took in the rodeo and the Indian festivities.

Eddie and Hopi were still not skilled enough to win their team roping event, but they were improving and were having fun competing in front of their families and friends. Hal was invited to help down in the chutes alongside Hopi's dad, and just like always, he wished he were young enough to ride those broncs again.

The week ended on Sunday evening with a worship service at the mission. Eddie and Hal were asked to play their guitars together as everyone else sang along. They all joined in on old traditional hymns and then shared an Indian-style meal before saying good-bye. Promises were made once again to get together in the future.

Eddie and Hopi planned to do some rodeos again next year, but that was a long time away. Hopi silently wondered if that would happen; he knew Eddie was very fond of another certain person. They still had one more rodeo to compete in this year, though, and they would meet in Flagstaff the following Wednesday afternoon. Hopi's folks planned to join them there if at all possible. Hal was going to take his family to visit the Grand Canyon again the first part of the week. Eddie was wishing Katy was with them so he could show her the canyon. He was experiencing a longing he didn't understand. *Is this how girls affect every young man?* he wondered.

CHAPTER 8

The trip to see the Grand Canyon was a great family time. Hal, Sue, Eddie, and Audra had been there before, but the twins hadn't. Little Joe was naturally curious and enthusiastic about almost anything, and he was no different in this case. The look of wonder on Angela's face as she stared over the rim into the vast depths below was worth more than words could tell. She clung to Eddie's hand and then had him pick her up as she questioned him excitedly in her soft, unique way, looking and pointing at features below and then turning to Eddie as he answered her. Hal and Sue were blessed by that as much as by the scenery. Audra had taken Little Joe and was walking along the viewing fence, excitedly pointing out the features below. Hal suggested they sign up and take a helicopter tour of the canyon. That got everyone excited in a hurry. It was expensive, but Hal thought it was worth it this one time. Sue agreed; their kids wouldn't be with them forever. They had to split up and go in two choppers; so Sue took Eddie and Little Joe, and Hal took Audra and Angela. The kids squealed with fright and excitement as the chopper swooped down into the gorge. The way a person's perception of the awesome rock formations changed as they descended took their breath away. God sure had made some beautiful places on this earth. Only he could do something as awesome as this.

They arrived back in Flagstaff late Wednesday evening and checked into a motel close to the fair and rodeo grounds. The town was all a bustle in preparation for the yearly celebration. At breakfast in the little country-style restaurant next to the motel, they listened with interest to the excited chatter concerning the day's planned events. Hopi was to meet them at the rodeo arena around noon. After they met up, the two of them took their horses and worked them out to get them ready for the night's action. They were able to do some practice roping to sharpen their skills as well. They were beginning to feel the jitters that went with competing; every athlete experienced that nervous energy. It put him or her on their toes and motivated them. Eddie wished Kat was here.

The rodeo began with the traditional introduction of the rodeo queen, who led the procession into the arena carrying the American flag, followed by her three attendants, then the pickup men and other arena helpers and dignitaries. The crowd all stood as the national anthem was played and acknowledgments were made to some local military veterans who had distinguished themselves in combat.

The saddle-bronc riding followed, and then the bareback riding took place. While the calf roping was getting underway, Eddie and Hopi were riding their horses around outside the arena activities to get them warmed up and over being skittish. Eddie had glanced around as some of the lady barrel racers were getting their horses warmed up over in another area. As he watched through the dust being stirred up, he thought he recognized one of the horses and caught a glimpse of long dark hair beneath a hat just before the rider disappeared behind a horse barn. He thought, *Could it be; surely not, clear down here.*

He and Hopi were the third team up to rope, and they were aware of the crowd noise and were pumped up. This was the biggest crowd they had performed in front of, and they really wanted to do well. His horse broke fast and broke the barrier, which cost them a ten second penalty, and then Eddie missed his first loop and had to try with his second rope. He was able to catch the steer with it. Now it was Hopi's turn to try for the hind legs, and he missed. They looked at each other with disappointment and decided to not waste everyone's time by trying with the second loop. They were out of the money for this go-around.

Hopi said, "We better practice tomorrow, right?"

"Yeah, I guess we better if we hope to win any money!"

The barrel racers were being announced as they went to put their horses in their holding pens. Eddie decided to go watch a few of the cowgirls compete so he would have a shared interest to talk with Katy about the next time he saw her. Hopi went along with him; maybe he would see some girl that would interest him. The event had already begun by the time they returned to watch from the roping end of the arena. Two girls had already finished their race, and the third girl was being announced as she broke from the lane under the announcer's platform.

Eddie was watching as the girl and her horse emerged; he stood with his mouth open, not hearing the announcer as he called the girl's name.

"That's Katy," he exclaimed. "What is she doing here?"

"Well, partner, it looks like she's barrel racing," Hopi drawled as he slapped Eddie on the back.

"I thought I saw her horse earlier, when we were warming up our horses," Eddie replied. "I just thought it was wishful thinking, so I didn't say anything."

They stood amazed as Katy made her run. She handled her horse with skill and grace, and Eddie felt a surge of pride that he knew her. Why hadn't she told him she would be here? She finished her run with a sprint to the finish line and disappeared under the platform. Eddie turned to Hopi excitedly.

"I've got to go find her! I'll catch up with you later where we told Mom and Dad we'd meet 'em." He jumped over the fence and ran for the back of the chutes.

Katy was tending to her horse in the assembly area behind the chutes, looking expectantly over her shoulder as Eddie came running up to her.

"How'd you get down here? Why didn't you let me know you were going to race here? I can't believe you're here!" Eddie blurted. He skidded to a stop in front of her as she turned and planted her hands on her hips and beamed at him, her eyes dancing with excitement.

"I told you I'd be seeing you!" she exclaimed as she threw her arms around his neck and hugged him.

He picked her up and swung her in a circle, her horse snorting and stepping back at the sudden movement. He put her down as quickly as he had picked her up and kicked at the ground bashfully, his face turning crimson.

"I talked my dad into bringing me down for the rodeo. My uncle lives here in Flagstaff, you know, so Dad and Mom decided to come visit them and bring me so I could compete here. Are you glad?" She took his hand as she led her horse to its holding pen.

"Can't you tell?" Eddie asked as he looked down on her upturned face.

Impulsively, he reached around her waist and gave her a quick hug. "I can't believe this! Let's put your horse away and go find my folks. Is your family here?"

"They're all up in the stands. Where's Hopi? Your family is up in the stands too, right?" Katy said as she led her horse into the corral and Eddie unsaddled the little mare for her.

"Thanks," she murmured as he finished. "Let's just walk around a little while before we go find them. I'm so happy to see you!"

As she turned to look up at him with those big brown eyes, Eddie observed a serious contemplation mingling with her smile. In that moment, he became aware of a depth of feeling and attachment and longing he had never experienced before. If he had been asked to explain his feelings, he would have been at a loss for words. This was new and compelling territory for him. Somehow, he sensed a similar feeling in Katy. He breathed a silent prayer of thanks to the Lord for her.

"What's that bruise on your cheek from, big guy?" Katy asked, reaching up and brushing the fading blue spot.

Like a kiss from an angel, her touch erased his suppressed frustration and embarrassment concerning that whole ordeal. As he reluctantly told of his fight with Billy Jones and what had caused it, she was aware again that this handsome young man was like no other who had shown an interest in her. She knew he went to church with his family, and she wanted to know about that. She had so much she wanted to talk to him about. As they walked hand in hand, contentment with each other began to radiate from them. People glanced at them as they passed and smiled. They looked so young and innocent and alive. Little did the two of them know the memories they evoked in some of those grownups who smiled at them.

A short time later they returned to the stands and went in search of Katy's folks. Eddie spied Audra and the twins coming down an aisle to intercept him. The twins were surprised and excited to see Katy with Eddie. Katy gave each of them a hug as they ran up to her.

Audra gave each of them a questioning look and said, "Well, where have you been hiding her, big brother? We saw her do her barrel race. I didn't know she was going to compete here. Did you?"

Eddie explained everything and then asked, "Where's Mom and Dad? Is Hopi with them?"

Audra gave Katy a hug as she replied, "Hopi's folks showed up, and they're all down on the far end of the stands."

Just then a tall, slender man with wide shoulders and a military bearing came down the steps from the upper seats, a dark-haired, nice-looking lady following him. As he approached, Katy

HAROLD SOUTHWICK

exclaimed, "Mom and Dad, this is Eddie Edwards. He's the one I wanted you to meet!"

As she introduced Audra and the twins, Eddie felt the lady studying him.

He smiled as he removed his hat and spoke, "I'm pleased to meet you, ma'am, and you also, sir." He felt the power in Katy's dad's grip as they shook hands. Her dad returned Eddie's steady gaze, surveying this young friend of his daughter.

"Hello, young man. I'm Bill Parker and this is my wife, Katherine. We saw you and your friend try your hand at roping a while ago," he said with a smile.

As Katy's mom shook his hand, she exclaimed, "So you're the one who has captivated our girl's every waking thought?"

Eddie saw his own family approaching then, followed by Hopi and his folks. Introductions were made, and the rest of the rodeo was forgotten as they got acquainted. They made their way to the concession booths for refreshments, commenting about having to travel all that way to get acquainted. Eddie and Katy managed to fall in behind the rest of them on the way to the booth.

"Is that true, what your mom said to me, Kat?" he asked, his heart thumping. "Can I call you Kat?"

Katy looked up at him as they walked along, then dropped her head and murmured, "Yep!" and then, glancing up at him with a tear in her eyes, she reached and grasped his hand tightly. "Yes, it is!"

The next two days of the rodeo were a blur for Eddie. He and Hopi did okay in roping, although they didn't win any money. Katy, however, won second place in the barrel racing, and everyone heartily congratulated her. She was fast winning Eddie's family's affection, and Hopi's family thought she was quite the cowgirl. The three families were becoming good friends, finding they shared much in common. This thrilled Katy and Eddie a lot. Eddie felt vaguely aware that he was not spending as much time with Hopi as he should be. They would be saying good-bye for several months in just a few hours. After their final event on Saturday night, he talked to Hopi about that, assuring him that he would always be one of his two best friends. They prayed together and asked God to always keep them close and to be there for each other, no matter what happened in their lives.

They all went to the local steak house for a final meal together after the rodeo on Saturday night. Hopi's mom and dad finally agreed they could find their way to Idaho the following summer, so plans were made for all to get together for a big barbecue at the Parker place. While all those discussions were going on, Katy and Eddie wondered off for some time together before they had to part. They both agreed they had something special between them and wanted to see much more of each other. Before returning to the group, Eddie finally worked up the courage and turned Katy to face him. She waited with expectation.

With his hands on her shoulders, he stammered, "Would it be ... uh ... could I ... uh ... I want to kiss you, er, well ... if that would be all right?"

"I was afraid you wouldn't ask me before you left, you being the gentleman you are! Yes, you can kiss me!" She blushed, reaching to embrace him.

Their first kiss was the shy kiss of innocence, and it left them amazed in the wonder of it. Without a word, they returned to the group, the eyes of Katy's mom on their faces.

In that moment, she turned to Sue and asked, "Do you sense what I sense?"

"I sensed it the first night they met. Do you remember those days back when?" As Katherine nodded, Sue thought again of the rodeo arena at home.

Hal decided he had better call home to check on things before they went to sleep for the night. As he quickly returned to the table, Sue could tell he was deeply disturbed.

"What's wrong, Dad?" she asked.

"Dad must be having another heart attack. Leah said they had just called the ambulance for him. He was having trouble breathing and was having chest pains again. We better get loaded up and head home," Hal replied grimly.

Prayers were offered, and good-byes were quickly said. Katy knew how close Eddie was to his grandpa and felt his pain. She assured him she would get home as quickly as possible and would call him.

The next two hours were a blur as everyone helped get Eddie's horse in the trailer and they loaded everything and prepared to leave. It would be crowded in Hal's truck for the whole family going home, but they could do it. They would take turns driving with Hal first, then Sue, and finally Eddie would take a turn. They would sleep as best they could, between driving times. Again, good-byes were said and condolences and encouragement offered. Katy gave Eddie one last tearful hug and a quick kiss, and then they were gone.

The long drive north to Page, Arizona, seemed to take forever. Hal wouldn't give up the driving and sat grimly praying as the others dozed fitfully. They stopped in Page to fuel up, and while Eddie filled the tank, Hal went to call home again. He was unable to get an answer at home, so he called the hospital in Mt. Home. Stu finally came to the phone in the lobby and told Hal the sad news. Dad had gone into cardiac arrest in the ambulance on the way to the hospital. The EMTs had been unable to revive him, but efforts had continued at the hospital until a short time ago. He had been declared dead at one fifteen a.m. The family had all been notified, and they were waiting now for the undertaker to come get his body. Hal said they would be home tomorrow evening and expressed his sorrow that he had not been there for his mom. He could not believe he would never see his dad in this world and hear his assuring voice again. He broke down as he returned to the truck. They all cried together as he told them the news. After venting their grief for a while, they decided to press on toward home. Sue was able to convince Hal to let her drive for a while. He finally dozed for a while. Eddie seemed shell-shocked; his folks had worried about this moment. C. D. and Eddie had always been inseparable; he was Eddie's fishing buddy, his biggest fan in football and roping, and his confidant when Eddie needed someone other than Dad or Mom to ask for advice. Eddie felt cheated that he hadn't been there with his grandpa in his last moments of on earth. The rest of the long trip home was spent reminiscing and crying. This was a new experience for the four children, and they clung together for support.

Angela helped all of them gain a measure of comfort when she suddenly said, "Grandpa with Jesus now, right?"

Eddie started to comment, then abruptly stopped, frowning.

Sue replied with amazement, "Out of the mouth of babes! Thank you, dear Lord, for that assurance."

She was reliving the death of her own father as a young girl and realizing again that the pain never completely went away.

"What were you going to say, Son?"

Eddie shook his head and didn't answer; his thoughts would just upset his family. He was beginning to feel resentment toward God for taking his grandpa away from him just when he needed him the most. He had wanted to talk to Gramps about his feelings for Katy. He knew he needed an older man's perspective, and he knew Gramps would understand and be able to help him. He broke down and sobbed as he thought about the times he had listened to Gramps as he talked to him quietly while they sat on a creek bank fishing. He would never get to do that again! Gramps' words to him after the barbecue that evening at home returned to his mind, *She's a right pretty young filly, sonny. Treat her right. Ya' know what I mean?"*

HAROLD SOUTHWICK

CHAPTER 9

Hal's mom met them on the front porch late Sunday evening as they arrived home. They were totally exhausted, and it was obvious that Dot was too. Leah and Stu came to join them as they embraced and quietly cried together.

"Mom, I'm so sorry I wasn't here with you. I'm glad these two were here, though," Hal said as he held his mom. "Dad wanted Eddie to go do those rodeos, though."

"Your being here wouldn't have changed anything. God has his own timing and doesn't make mistakes, so don't let the devil cause you undue heartache. Dad's in a better place now, and we just have to wait our turn to get to see him again!" Dot patted his back as she turned to Eddie, "Come here, sonny. I know this is tearing you apart. Gramps whispered to me to tell you how much he loved you just before he went into a coma. He loved all you kids so much!"

Eddie towered over his grandma now, but she cradled him in her arms as she had done all of his life and let him pour out his grief. As she turned to the other children, Eddie left the porch and returned to the horse trailer to unload his pony and put him in the corral. His uncle Stu followed him from the porch and, without a word, helped him.

As they walked the horse toward the barn, Stu put his arm around his young nephew and said, "Dad used to take Hal and me fishing when we were little too. He always knew when we needed some time and encouragement. When we grew up and didn't have time for things like that, Mom said he would some-times express his longing for those times again. When you came along, it was like he got a new lease on what was most important to him. I guess that was why that kids' ministry thing your dad and mom had going those years was so important to him."

Eddie looked at his uncle, nodded, and muttered, "Thanks, but I still need him."

"I do too! It just seems like our anchor has come loose from the boat!"

The following morning A. J. and his family arrived from Washington, followed shortly afterward by Peg and one of her daughters from Montana. The church family and neighbors had been bringing in food and offers of help, as always. Hal's sib-lings weren't believers, but they were very favorably impressed with these expressions of love and support. Sue and Hal quietly prayed together that this might influence them toward Christ.

The funeral services were held in the little Baptist church on Thursday afternoon. The turnout was huge, and they wished they had chosen the veteran's hall for the funeral. The family was overwhelmed. Pastor Don preached a simple gospel mes-sage, which was what Dot had wanted. Betty played the organ, and Joan Johnston sang, followed by Hal on his guitar, singing an old country ballad his dad had always wanted sung around a campfire in Hal's youth. Tears were flowing down his cheeks by the time he finished, and there wasn't a dry eye in the place.

Sue became increasingly concerned about her oldest son as the service came to a close. He had sat with his head down and seemed present in body only. As the mourners filed by to view the open casket, she felt a hand on her shoulder. She turned to see Jimmy and closely behind him Katy looking at Eddie with tears in her eyes. Sue reached for Eddie's arm to get his attention.

As he turned to her, he noticed his friend and then Katy, and he sat up and nodded his head before dropping his gaze again.

On the way to the cemetery, Sue spoke to Hal. "Eddie feels everything so much more intensely than others. I'm afraid for him!"

"I know. I'll take him aside tonight at home and see if I can't help him let go of some of his grief and let me have it. What I'm afraid of, though, is something else. I'll talk to you about it later, okay?" Hal heaved a deep sigh, "Let's hope Katy can lift his spirits some."

"She is hurting for him and so is Jimmy, but I'm not sure they know how to approach him. Audra doesn't want to let Grandma out of her sight, and the twins need their big brother to comfort them. He just puts his arms around them and doesn't say much. We need to gather on the porch tonight as a family and pray through all of this, don't you think?"

After the graveside services, Eddie stood up and wondered off by himself. Katy watched him go and tried to decide if she should follow. As she tried to make up her mind, Hal walked over to her and put his arm around her.

When she looked up at him, he looked at Eddie and said, "Go to him, will you? I think maybe only you can touch his heart right now."

Katy squeezed his hand and nodded her head and gave him a tearful smile. Then she hurried to catch up with Eddie. As Hal stood watching, Sue came alongside and put her arm around him. They watched Katy as she reached out and took Eddie's hand and walked beside him. He glanced at her quickly, nodded his head, and kept walking. Hal and Sue kept looking for them but didn't see the two of them again until after the meal at the church was over. When they finally left the fellowship hall to return to the ranch, Hal saw the two of them sitting on the front steps of the church talking to Jimmy and Audra. Katy got up and came to them.

"Would it be okay if Jimmy and I came out to the ranch for a while? If not, we understand." She turned and looked at Eddie. "I think he's doing a little better, but he still isn't saying much."

"He's never been a big talker. Audi is the one who jabbers all the time." Hal smiled. "Of course you kids can come to the ranch. You're both like family anyway. As you get to know him better, you'll find Eddie's actions tell you more about him than what he might say."

"I'm beginning to see that." Katy gazed pensively at this young man who had impacted her so powerfully.

"You care for him a lot, don't you?" Hal asked as he studied her expression.

Katy gave him a quick glance and returned her eyes to Eddie. "Yes, sir, I do."

CHAPTER 10

The two weeks following his grandpa's funeral were filled with getting Eddie ready to report to the University of Idaho at Moscow for fall football drills; school would start two weeks later. Hal didn't want Eddie to have a vehicle the first year away in college because he didn't want that distraction for him. Other kids would be asking him to take them somewhere when he needed to be studying and concentrating on fulfilling his football scholarship commitment. Sue held a going-to-college party for Jimmy, Katy, and Eddie on Saturday evening at the ranch. Several other classmates and kids from the church who would also be going away to school were invited. She made it a point to send Billy Jones an invitation, although he failed to show up. She asked parents and Pastor Don to come as well.

After the barbecue was finished, the pastor spoke concerning the different setting college life confronted young people with. He stressed the temptations and opportunities they would face and reminded them to remember what their families had taught them about being responsible: last but not least, remember the Lord. The evening ended with the parents praying specifically for their own child. Hal then closed the prayer time by asking God to help each parent for strength and courage to release their child into God's care as they left home to go off to school. Tears were running freely by the time he finished.

Jeb Dillon was going to Idaho with Eddie. Jimmy and Katy and a couple of others were going to Boise State, and two were going to Idaho State. After the prayers ended, the kids all hugged, slapped each other on the back, and said good-bye, with jabs about the intrastate rivalries. Eddie and Katy promised to correspond by letters and call once in a while. They promised to get together whenever Eddie came home for holidays. They told each other it would be okay to date others if they wanted, but each of them silently hoped that wouldn't happen. Eddie walked her to her car, and after he opened her door, he embraced her and gave her a tender kiss.

As he released her, she put her hand to her lips and murmured, "Oh my, thanks!" He stood waving as she drove into the night.

There goes my heart, he thought, and he was filled with loneliness for her and for his grandpa.

CHAPTER 11

The family drove Eddie north to Moscow the following Monday and helped him get registered and settled into an on-campus dorm. They got to meet his football coach again and some of his teammates before doing some sightseeing and heading back home. It was a long way from Glenn's Cove to Moscow, Idaho, and Eddie had never been this far from home for an extended time by himself. Saying good-bye was difficult.

This was especially true for Sue. Coming days proved that it was very difficult for Angela also. She depended on her big brother more than the family had realized. While Eddie was eager for this new phase of his life, he dreaded being this far from the family he loved more than he would admit. Added to that, the loss of his grandpa and his concern for his grandma weighed on him. Hal knew all this and prayed for each of these concerns as they said good-bye.

Eddie's first year in college proved to be the hardest time thus far in his young life. He was red-shirted his freshman year on the football team, but had to participate in practice and inter-team games, as well as go with the team on road trips. He had always been fascinated about his dad's army service, so he joined the ROTC program on campus, which took much time. Keeping his grades up to maintain eligibility required a whole new discipline. He had always gotten good grades, but this was a lot different from high school. The transition from his previous life to this seemed overwhelming at best. His commitment to excel proved to be his anchor, however; being so busy kept him from wallowing in loneliness for family, friends, and that pretty little gal who had come to mean so much to him in such a short time. Katy, her very name gave new meaning to his life. *What does the future hold for us?* he wondered.

The football team played Boise State in Boise in early November, so he got to see his family then. Being a red-shirt, he didn't get to play in the game; he did get to see both Jimmy and Billy play sparingly for the Broncos. The night before the game, he got to see Katy for a short while, and again after the game when he was able to visit with his family briefly, she was there. They both looked forward to Christmas break!

He spent Thanksgiving on campus, another first away from family. He was glad when the football season ended. It gave him more time to hit the books. Besides, he had found out what so many good high-school athletes found out: when you start playing ball on the college level, everyone was as good as you, and many were a lot better. That was the reason for the red-shirt system, to have that first year to learn the higher level style of play before playing full time. Some kids were gifted enough to play their freshman year, but most were not.

ROTC training was proving to be fascinating for Eddie. He enjoyed the training and different disciplines, and he found he really liked marching. The precision and finesse of foot movement, along with the weapons maneuvers, just seemed to match his disposition. Their unit got to march in the Thanksgiving parade up in Spokane, Washington. That filled the holiday weekend for him.

Christmas break was a welcome time for him, allowing him to catch his breath from his new life away from home. The time spent with his family had a new significance for him. He had begun to realize that long periods at home would become fewer and further between. It was good to be able to attend church with them again, and Mom's home-cooked meals beat anything on campus, hands down. The time he got to spend with Katy was limited because of her family commitments, but they both realized their feelings were developing beyond being very good friends. They had a long road ahead in getting their education completed, so they were reluctant to verbalize too much; but the bond was developing between them, and it was obvious to their families. Hal and Sue were proud of the way Eddie showed respect for her, and his siblings loved her like a sister.

The rest of the school year passed with more of the same hard work and a growing sense of accomplishment. Eddie had attended church sparingly because of his busy schedule, and his mom chided him in letters to not neglect that important aspect of his life. He still hadn't come to terms completely with how he had felt when his grandpa died. He just wasn't comfortable in his relationship with God for some reason. He wondered at times if this was part of growing up and leaving the influence of the home environment. He was glad when summer break came, and he returned to spend the next three months on the ranch with his family.

CHAPTER 12

Eddie's summer was busy helping on the ranch, helping neighbors stack baled hay to make some money for college, and seeing Katy as often as he could. It was time for school again before he knew it. The only rodeo he got to participate in was the hometown fair and rodeo. Hopi wasn't able to come up, so Hal decided he would be his son's team partner. The time they got to spend together practicing was special for both of them, and although they didn't place in the team roping, they had fun participating together. Katy did the barrel racing again and did well. Her family came down to watch her, and the two families got together again for a barbecue.

Eddie and Katy spent time out in the boat fishing as often as they could, and Eddie learned to his delight that she was indeed, a good fisherman. They had great fun competing to see who could catch the biggest fish. Sometimes they took the twins; at other times, Audra and Jimmy would go with them. Eddie knew his future had to include Katy somewhere down the road. He knew he still had school to finish and some growing up to do, but he couldn't imagine life without her. She had become an important part of his entire family, and every member expected that someday they would become partners for life. She seemed to feel as he did, but Eddie never pressed for a commitment. It was too soon for that.

Eddie returned to campus for fall football drills in late August, and soon he was into his sophomore year of school. He was a full-

HAROLD SOUTHWICK

fledged member of the team this season and earned the starting position at wide receiver. His skills at the college level slowly developed with each game, and by the time the Boise State-Idaho game arrived in November, he felt he was ready to play in front of so many people he knew from home. The game was to be played in Boise this year. Idaho's football team had greatly improved over the last few years under their present coach, and they were tied for the league lead with Boise State. Both were undefeated. Eddie was excited about this game. Jimmy was splitting time in the backfield for the Broncos, and Billy Jones was getting to spend some time as quarterback for them. This would also be the first time Katy saw Eddie play a college game as a starter. His folks had been able to come to a couple of his games, but the ranch didn't allow that to happen often. Katy was in a quandary about whom to cheer for since she attended Boise State but the young man of her life was a player for the Vandals! She finally decided to cheer for Eddie on the plays featuring his position and cheer for the Broncos otherwise.

The game was a nail biter throughout. Eddie caught a pass for a touchdown but also fumbled the ball once after being hit hard. Jimmy Johnston scored a touchdown for the Broncos on a run up the middle late in the third quarter, and Billy Jones threw for a touchdown in the fourth quarter after their starting quarterback was shaken up on a broken play. All in all, the hometown Glenn's Cove boys had done well for their fans. That brought the game down to the last drive as time was running out. The Vandals scored on an option play with the quarterback rolling out to the right and throwing a touchdown back across to the opposite corner of the end zone.

As Eddie went up for the pass, he prayed, "God, please don't let me drop this pass in front of my family and Katy!"

He came down with the ball clutched tightly in both arms, and his teammates mobbed him.

Coach called a last timeout and told them, "This game isn't over, so quit celebrating and go finish the job. We're still behind by one. I want us to line up to kick the extra point, but I don't want to just tie it up. I want to win it now! Jack, you're the holder, so I want you to take the snap from center and run out to the left. Bobby, you're the kicker, so I want you to run outside Jack to the left, and as Jack nears the defender, I want him to pitch the ball to you on the outside of the line of play, hopefully, just like we've practiced all week. We can win this thing! Everybody got it? Let's go!"

The play was executed flawlessly, and the Broncos and their fans were stunned! The hated Vandals had defeated them on a trick play as time ran out, on their home field, in front of a packed stadium, and Vandal fans were going crazy!

The Vandals went on to play in the division playoffs and were defeated in the first round. But they all felt their season had been a rousing success; they had defeated Boise State on their own turf. Because Eddie and Jimmy were so close, their friendship was still intact, but Eddie received some caustic remarks from Billy when he was home on Christmas break.

Christmas was again a welcome break from school. Eddie was becoming accustomed to being away from family, but it was great to be back with them for a short time. His time with Katy was everything they wanted it to be, just too short. There was a worrisome aspect to his time at home, however. Angela's health was beginning to deteriorate. Sue told Eddie that Angela had developed a virus of some sort and had not been able to completely recover. Eddie remembered thinking when he saw them briefly at the football game in Boise that she hadn't looked or acted her normal, bouncy self. Doctors had told Hal and Sue that situations like this sometimes happened to children with Angela's condition around this stage of their lives. Because of his strong feelings concerning her, Eddie returned to school after the holidays with a new sense of worry. Before his next summer ended, his concerns would become grounded in reality.

CHAPTER 13

Eddie came home for summer break in late May and had two weeks at home before reporting for ROTC summer camp with an army National Guard unit for two weeks. They would be training at Ft. Lewis, Washington, doing armored personnel carrier and tank combat maneuvers in support of infantry operations. His mom was reluctant to see her son heading off to play war games. She still had memories of not knowing whether her young husband was alive or dead when he had been in Vietnam. Hal was proud of his son, but he too had unexpressed concerns for Eddie. His boy was growing up too fast. He just hoped Eddie wasn't growing away from his Lord, but he sensed otherwise.

Eddie invited Katy to come down for a weekend so they could take the boat out and do some fishing before he had to leave. After much begging by Little Joe and Angela, he finally agreed to take them along. They decided to take the boat up to Anderson Dam and fish for Kokanee salmon. Audra and Jimmy were still seeing each other, so they decided to come along. They set up camp at the Curlew camp grounds, one tent for the girls and one for the boys. The fishing proved to be great on Saturday evening, and they had a great time fixing fresh fish and fried potatoes and biscuits for supper. After everything was cleaned up, Eddie got out his guitar, and they sat around a big campfire, singing and telling stories about the past school year.

Sunday-morning breakfast consisted of leftovers from the previous evening along with scrambled eggs that Audra and Katy insisted on fixing. While they finished a last cup of coffee, plans were made to fish until noon or until they caught their limit and then do some water skiing after lunch. The fishing proved to be much slower than the night before, and storm clouds were drifting in, so they ate a hurried lunch and set out to do some skiing before the water got too rough. Katy and Jimmy were both good skiers, so they helped Audra and Little Joe learn how to ski for a while. Angela desperately wanted to try her luck at it, but Eddie was reluctant to let her try. Finally, the rest of the kids talked him into it. He was a fair skier himself, so he decided he would ski on one side of her with Katy on the other while Jimmy drove the boat. The boat wouldn't pull three of them very fast, but they didn't want to go fast anyway. Audra and Little Joe stood in the back of the boat, ready to alert Jimmy when to go, when to stop, etc. Angela was frightened but excited; she trusted her big brother completely. She desperately wanted to ski to make him proud of her and to show the others she wasn't completely helpless! Deep down in her heart, she wanted to be like Katy; she was so pretty and could do about anything. Angela could tell by watching her big brother around Katy that he adored and admired everything about her. She wanted to know that same feeling from him.

It took numerous tries before Angela was able to maintain her balance and keep her legs pointed forward and stiff enough while Jimmy accelerated the boat and could get her up on the water and skiing. Katy and Eddie had taken several tumbles themselves helping her. Eddie was a nervous wreck by then, and the wind was beginning to whip up waves. He knew they needed to get back to shore, but Angela and all the rest were so proud of her accomplishment he decided they would make one more circle out in the lake before heading into shore. A few people fishing on shore had been watching the kids, and when Angela finally was up and skiing, they started shouting and cheering her on.

As Jimmy brought the boat around toward the shore, she

noticed her audience and cried to Eddie, "One more turn, one more turn."

Eddie didn't have the heart to say no to her, so he said, "Okay, one more!"

Eddie could tell she was starting to tire out, and just as they made the turn toward the boat dock, a strong gust of wind whipped up waves on the water.

Katy yelled, "We're in trouble," as she guided in close to Angela.

Eddie was closing in from the other side just as the front of one of Angela's skis caught a wave and she went flying through the air. Both Katy and Eddie lunged for her as Audra and Little Joe screamed for Jimmy to stop the boat. Luckily, they were all wearing life jackets and quickly popped back to the surface, but Eddie couldn't tell if Angela was hurt as he reached her. He grabbed her in his arms just as Katy started swimming and pulling them to the boat. Those on board reached down to them and soon had the frightened little girl in the boat. While Katy retrieved their skis, Eddie climbed aboard and began examining his little sister. His heart raced as he silently condemned himself for being so stupid. Mom was going to ring his neck. He found no broken bones, but her right leg was extremely sore from the ski catching the wave the way it did. She had also swallowed some lake water and was coughing and having trouble getting her breath. Katy quickly climbed into the boat, and Jimmy started up and took them to the dock. With Audra's help, Eddie was trying to clear Angela's lungs of water by patting her on the back. As fast as possible, they got the boat loaded on the trailer and went back to their tents. While Katy and Audra rolled sleeping bags and put the cooking gear and coolers in the truck, Jimmy and Eddie broke down the tents and packed them. Little Joe was tending to Angela while all this was going on, and soon they were on their way home. They had to stop twice to help Angela recover from fits of coughing. By the time they pulled into the yard, all of them were worried sick about her. Eddie blamed himself for letting her ski, but the others reminded him they were the ones who had pleaded for her because she wanted to learn to ski so much. They were all at fault, and they would not let him shoulder all the blame, if there was any. He still felt responsible because he was the older brother and Mom and Dad had trusted him with all their welfare.

Sue heard the truck pull into the yard and went to meet them. "I didn't think you would be home this early. What's happened?" she asked, noticing each of their worried expressions.

Eddie started to explain, but Audra cut him off as Hal approached the truck. She went on to relate the events of the afternoon of skiing and what had led to Angela's being on the skis. As she told her story, they all got out of the truck, and Eddie took his little sister in his arms and started for the front porch.

Sue came alongside of him and opened the front door. "Here, lay her on the couch and let me check her out!"

Eddie put her down, and Sue took her in her arms. "Sweetheart, tell me how you're doing." As she did what a mother does at times like this, Hal joined them.

"What in the world were you thinking, letting her get on those darn skis, son?" Hal asked sternly.

The others had come around them by then, and Audra quickly came to Eddie's defense. "Daddy, big bro didn't want to let her try; but she wanted to so badly, and we all wanted her to be able to enjoy what we were having so much fun doing. So we finally talked him into it! You ought to have seen her! She was so proud when she finally got the hang of it! People on shore were cheering for her. Then that darn wind caused a wave, and she took her fall. We're all at fault, but God causes the wind to blow, doesn't he? So maybe it was just an accident, and no one is at fault!"

Eddie felt his mom's gaze and turned to look at her. He couldn't discern if she was blaming him or not, but with what his dad had just said he felt the stirring of an alienation. If he had been asked right then, he could not have told anyone if it was self-imposed or whether his folks were the cause of the feeling.

HAROLD SOUTHWICK

Hal asked his son again, "What in the world were you thinking, letting her get on those skis? You're the one who should have made the decision." He experienced a vague sadness and a feeling that God was somehow abandoning him. Deep down where his emotions lay, a festering feeling of unfairness began to take root. He slowly turned and left the house to go put the boat away.

Katy followed him out to the truck, "Eddie, I'm sorry! I shouldn't have helped talk you into letting Angela try to ski. I'll try to talk to your folks if you want me to."

Just then Jimmy came to help them, guiding Eddie as he backed the boat into the shed. "Looks like the dang boat is always a part of bad things happening, isn't it?" he muttered. "Let's just hope she'll be okay."

Eddie silently agreed with him. When they had stowed the camping gear and returned to the house, Angela had been put to bed, and Sue was tending to her. Hal was nowhere to be seen, and Little Joe and Audra were getting cleaned up.

Jimmy told Eddie good-bye and left. Eddie had to report to the National Guard unit in Boise the next afternoon, so Katy asked if she could come get him and take him to Boise.

That seemed good to him, so he gave her a quiet hug and kiss.

"Your little sister loved what you let her do. Don't be too hard on yourself, okay," she encouraged him as she got into her car and drove away.

The rest of the evening Eddie was busy getting his gear ready to leave for camp. He didn't see his folks again until they gathered for supper. After Hal had asked a blessing on the meal, the family ate with very little conversation. Eddie finished his meal and asked to be excused, announcing that he would be leaving right after breakfast in the morning to report for military training camp.

"Well, how are you getting up there?" his mom asked.

"Katy is coming down to get me."

"I thought your dad was going to take you. What changed that?" she asked with a sigh.

"Katy wanted to, and this way I don't have to bother you guys," Eddie replied as he turned and left for his room.

An unusual silence settled around the family table in his absence. For some unexplained reason, a family who always prayed about everything, failed to gather together and pray concerning this whole situation.

CHAPTER 14

Katy pulled her car into a parking space in front of the armory building south of the Boise airport and turned it off. Turning to Eddie in the passenger seat, she reached across and took his hand and put it to her lips. He had been quiet on the way here, and she didn't want him leaving without knowing how much he had come to mean to her. She sensed his strained feelings with his mom and dad, and she didn't want him leaving in that frame of mind.

"Eddie, I have to tell you this before you leave. I love you. You've become the center of all that matters to me. I know you're troubled about your folks and worried about Angela, but I don't want you leaving for camp without knowing that *I love you.* And no matter what happens, I know your folks love you too!"

She got out of the car and came around as he got out. He was struggling with his emotions, and she saw tears forming in his eyes. They embraced with elation, longing, and a touch of sadness, and then he bent to her upturned face and claimed her lips with his own.

Finally he pulled away. "I've wanted to tell you for a long time that I love you too, but I was afraid to. *I love you too!* We have a lot to talk about when I get back, but I have to go now. I'll call as soon as I get to Ft. Lewis and get a chance. Let me know how Angela is doing, okay."

Katy watched as he grabbed his duffle bag, gave her a wink, and walked to the door. As he turned and waved, she suddenly realized he was no longer a college boy going off to school. He had become a young man overnight going off to learn how to fight a war. The thought suddenly left her with an aching heart.

The long trip by convoy to Ft. Lewis began on Monday morning before daylight and didn't end until well after dark. The unit was billeted in the old barracks on base. Eddie remembered his dad telling about when he had been at Ft. Lewis prior to shipping out for Vietnam and then again at Madigan Army Hospital when he had been shipped home from Bangkok to finish his rehabilitation. He wondered where he had been on base. He felt a pang as he thought how close he had always been to his mom and dad. And now, well, he would just keep so busy he wouldn't have time to think too much.

The first week was spent in classroom sessions in the morning and after lunch with becoming more familiar with the inner workings of these huge war machines. Everything was becoming high-tech, and Eddie was fascinated with learning the mechanics of operating them.

They also spent long hours learning how to do emergency repairs, required maintenance, and becoming familiar with their capabilities. Other sessions dealt with support operations, logistics, and combat maneuver techniques. Emergency medical techniques were taught to equip each of them to care for critical first-response requirements they would most certainly be faced with in actual war situations.

Eddie had called Katy late the second day in camp and had learned that his folks had taken Angela to the doctor in Boise that same day. She had developed a fever, and the virus she had suffered from while he was away at school had apparently returned. He told Katy he would call his mom the next night if he had a chance. The conversation turned to their feelings for each other. There was a new depth of commitment and anticipation about their future in each of them, and they looked forward to exploring these anticipations together when he returned home.

He was able to call his mom the following evening and talk briefly with her. He learned that they had admitted Angela to the hospital in Boise to deal with her virus. She had made her mommy promise to tell big brother she loved him and missed him. When Sue relayed that to Eddie, she broke down and cried. She relayed the rest of the family's love and prayers and started to tell him something else but quickly stopped and said she had to answer another call. Eddie was left with the feeling she wasn't telling him everything. That left him feeling worried and vaguely guilty.

————————————

The rest of the week was so busy he had very little time for anything but what they were learning and sleeping when they finally got to bed. They finally got Saturday afternoon off, so he didn't get to call Katy again until then. They expressed their longings for each other, and when Eddie asked if she knew how Angela was doing, he was left with the feeling that she too wasn't telling him everything. All she would say was that Angela was still in the hospital but that she hadn't seen her. Before they said good-bye, Eddie told Katy they would be going by convoy to the Yakima Firing Range the next afternoon for the entire next week for actual field exercises. On the following Saturday, they would break camp and return to Boise, arriving late Sunday afternoon. There would be no access to phones while at the range, so he would be unable to call her again. They made plans for Katy to come to Boise and pick him up late Sunday evening to bring him back home. Before hanging up, Katy urged Eddie to call his mom and dad; they needed to talk to him.

Eddie called home as soon as he ended his call with Katy. He felt a sense of trepidation as he waited for someone to answer. His dad finally came on the phone sounding out of breath.

"Dad, what's going on down there?" Eddie asked after their hellos. "Is Mom there? Both she and Katy seem to be avoiding telling me everything about Angela. Kat says she's still in the hospital. Is that right?"

"Your mom and Little Joe are at the hospital right now, Son. Your little sister doesn't seem to be responding to the treatment she's getting for the virus. Mom hasn't wanted to worry you while you're concentrating on all you have to do. That's why she asked Katy to not give you all the details. Son, you left here feeling we were blaming you for her getting hurt up at the lake. We're sorry for the way we acted, but you know how we all try to protect her. You're more that way than any of the rest of us. We've had time to pray about it and finally listened to Audra and Little Joe. Besides, you're not the cause of this virus, although the doctor says the water she swallowed probably helped it flare up again. We miss you, Son! I'm trying to get the chores finished up so Audi and I can go up and see Angela. When will you be home?" As an afterthought, Hal asked, "By the way, how's camp going?"

"I'm really enjoying getting this training, and I'm looking forward to the field exercises we'll be doing at the firing range next week. We'll get back next Sunday afternoon. Katy will pick me up and bring me home. If Angela is still in the hospital, I'll go see her first. I miss all of you too, Dad. I want to talk to Audi before you hang up, Dad. Tell everyone I love 'em!"

Eddie talked to his sister for a while and finally asked her, "Sis, is Angela going to be all right?"

"Don't let Mom and Dad know I told you, but, no, she is not all right. I'll be glad when you get home. She keeps asking for you. Well, Dad's ready to leave now, so I have to go. Love you, big bro!" Audra blew him a kiss on the phone.

"Love ya too, Sis! Tell Jimmy hi for me. Bye."

HAROLD SOUTHWICK

CHAPTER 15

The next week was filled with the thrill of getting to put into practice what they had been learning in the classrooms. They were amazed with the noise of the big machines, the shock of the recoil as they fired at simulated targets, and the dust the activity kicked up. By week's end they had become very competitive with each other over the accuracy of target destruction. The sobering side to the exercise was that in war you would be on the receiving end as well as the giving end of this devastating power that these machines were capable of. Their instructors drilled that fact into them daily. Psychological warfare preparation was as important as the rest of the training.

––––––––––––

The return to armory headquarters in Boise went without a hitch. By the time the equipment was parked, everyone was glad to be home. After debriefing, they were released; full-time guard personnel would be cleaning the machines and preparing them for future exercises or for the real thing. Eddie left the armory and found Katy waiting for him in the visitor's parking area.

Katy's face was a mixture of joy at seeing him and sadness by what she had to share with him. As she came into his arms, she was acutely aware of the maturity taking place in his demeanor. He was becoming a strong and capable young man; she was thrilled and filled with pride. Her kiss conveyed that to him and filled him with wonder and awe that this beautiful young creature was his soul mate.

"Hi, pretty girl. I've missed you! Your eyes tell me you don't have good news," Eddie expressed wearily.

"I'm so glad you're home safely, sweetheart. We all need you. We need to get to the hospital. Angela is very sick, and she wants you with her," Katy explained as they loaded his duffle bag. As they hurried down Broadway to St. Luke's Regional, Eddie spoke of his week of field training and his emerging desire to pursue a career in the military.

Katy's response left a question in his mind. "I thought you might be leaning that way."

He gave her a weary smile but said no more about it. As they hurried into the waiting room at the hospital, Eddie's two grandmas got up and gave him hugs.

"You need to hurry up to Angie's room, hon!" Dot said.

He started to question her, but Katy took his hand and hurried him to the elevator. Kat stayed back as he entered the room and went to the bedside. Sue and Hal stood and came up behind him as he leaned down with a shocked expression on his face. His sister had never looked like a normal child, but now she lay there resembling a ghost.

He turned quickly to his mom, "How can she be like this in such a short time? Is this all because of her fall in the lake?"

Angela stirred as she heard his voice, and her sunken eyes fluttered open. He bent to her as her face lit up, "Bubba, you're here; you're here!" she whispered weakly.

Tears fell from his eyes onto her face as she reached to hug him. "I'm here, babe. I'm here now. He knelt and smothered her in his arms.

Little Joe, Audra, and Katy gathered around Sue and Hal and hugged each other as they witnessed the reunion before them, tears running down their cheeks. Sue looked around to find her mom and Dot sitting on the couch, holding hands with heads bowed in prayer.

Sue pulled Eddie to his feet and embraced him fiercely,

"Thank God you're back!" She stood trembling as sobs racked her body.

Hal put his arms around them both and said, "We've missed you, Son."

CHAPTER 16

Eddie spent as much of the next two weeks at Angela's bedside as possible, along with his family. They watched with aching hearts as she slowly lost her battle with the disease. Late on Friday night she sank into a coma. The family and Katy came to spend the last hours with her. Dawn was beginning to break in the east as she suddenly sat up in bed and said, "Eddie, Eddie, I go see Jesus. He called my name. I'll be whole like you!"

Eddie was first to her bedside and hugged her close, Sue right beside him. Then she gave each of them a radiant smile, and her eyes closed as peace came over her face.

The little Baptist church was overflowing, and chairs had been set up in the fellowship hall to handle the crowd. Speakers were quietly being set up in there so the services could be heard. Jimmy and Hopi, along with four other young men from the congregation, served as pallbearers. Hopi had flown in at Eddie's request to fill this honored position; he was like one of the family. The family had also insisted Katy sit with them in the reserved section. She had started to decline, but Sue took her aside and begged her to reconsider for Eddie's sake. He was devastated by his little sister's death, and Sue knew Katy would come closer to comforting him than any other.

Katy's family was in attendance, and her brother, Kurt, would be doing the two requested songs. Pastor Don, with Brother Larry

HAROLD SOUTHWICK

assisting, was conducting the service. Betty was at the organ as they entered the sanctuary, and the beauty of her playing gripped their hearts as they sat down. Hal's siblings sat behind them, and just before the service began, he felt a hand on his shoulder. Looking up, he was startled to see his old Vietnam team leader, Bob Green, standing with his hand outstretched.

As Hal started to rise, Bob said, "We'll talk later."

Eddie sat throughout the service with his face and eyes downcast, gripping Katy's hand so hard she finally lost feeling in it. She had closely watched the family in the five days since the center of their focus had left them. What she had seen and was seeing again now, during the service, was a source of inner strength she didn't quite understand. She had attended church with Eddie a few times, and they had talked about his faith; but she had never made any commitment. She had even been present when the twins were baptized after accepting Christ as Savior, but she had only been respectfully curious. Her family had never been church-goers, but she had nothing against it.

Now a longing to know more began to fill her heart as she wept with them in their loss. It was her loss too; she had become very attached to this special child. Angela truly was a special gift and had blessed everyone who knew her. Katy was coming to realize that Angela had become Eddie's own personal "spiritual project," and now she was gone. No wonder he seemed adrift in sorrow and loss. She vowed to do her best to console him. Little Joe needed some attention of his own too, especially since he had more or less been in the background from day one because of his sister's condition. Maybe she could help Eddie focus in that direction a little more. Although she was three years older than Audra, she was like the sister that Katy had never had. She thought about all this as the service progressed and longed for the day when she and Eddie would become one.

CHAPTER 17

Hal and Sue Edwards had always known their family had been given a "special" child by God. They didn't completely understand the reason for that, but each of them had learned so much about what was really important in life just by watching her deal with her struggles; things that most people never thought twice about. The entire family had identified with her struggles and also her triumphs, none more so that Eddie. So he was the one who, perhaps, felt the greatest sense of loss. The family's faith was the anchor that kept them pointed forward in life. Knowing that Angela was now with the Lord in heaven gave them comfort in their grief.

Hal and Sue were aware of Eddie's struggle with the world pulling one way and his Christian beliefs the other. Grandpa's death had rocked him, and they began to notice his reluctance to participate in church activities since then. Their concern now was that Angela's death would increase that trend. Sue was praying one evening not long after the funeral when Audra knelt beside her and began praying and crying. She put her arm around her daughter and pulled her close.

When they finished praying, she whispered, "Share with me, sweetheart. I know you miss your little sister, but it's more than that, isn't it?"

"Mom, Jimmy and I are worried about Eddie. He doesn't want to do anything with our college kids' group at church any more. Katy has started asking me questions about why we believe

HAROLD SOUTHWICK

the way we do, and she says Eddie just kind of grunts when she tries to talk to him about it. I'm surprised he hasn't told her about Christ yet, as close as they are! What do you think is going on?" Audra's concern for her brother touched her mother deeply.

Sue longed for insight as she answered her daughter. Audra would be a senior in high school the coming year and would soon be facing a lot of the same things Eddie was trying to deal with since leaving the nest. *How do I prepare her for the coming battle?* she wondered. She suddenly remembered a similar conversation her own mother had with her when she was dating Hal. She thought, *The battle hasn't changed, only the players, as they enter this stage of their lives. God is the same yesterday, today, and forever, so the answer has been, is, and will always be the same for each generation. Christ is God's answer to our every need. If he doesn't seem to be fulfilling our needs, then we have lost focus because of different pressures and temptations and are not looking to him daily for what will sustain us.* She quietly began sharing these insights with her beautiful young daughter and concluded with an explanation concerning her son that God had given her.

"You know Eddie's personality; everything is either black or white, and he seems to need to understand the reason why everything happens the way it does. God doesn't operate that way with us much of the time. He wants us to learn to trust him, and he allows us to be tested by events in our lives. Our reactions will reveal to us just where we are in our spiritual journey, if we only give it consideration. Grandpa was a pillar for Eddie, and that pillar was removed. God wants to be Eddie's pillar. Not that God wasn't pleased with Gramps being there for his grandson, but death happens, and it creates a new need that only God can take care of. Angela became even more of a focus for Eddie, and now she is gone. The devil does everything he can to pull us away from our focus on Christ. All these events can be building blocks to deeper trust in the Lord if we stay focused, but if we don't, they can cause us to doubt God's love for us and make us turn to other things or people. Many of these distractions are not bad in themselves, but if they keep us from what God wants for us, they hinder us and take away our sense of peace and direction."

Sue paused to catch her breath. *I can't believe I'm saying all of this. Where is it coming from?*

She continued, "Prayer for Eddie is our greatest resource right now. Dad and I are finding that out more and more, and we have always been a praying family. So you and Jimmy pray together for your big brother and remember we are praying for the two of you also. Honey, the next time Katy comes down and you get to talk to her alone, bring her to me, and we'll talk to her about Christ if she'll let us. I know she is concerned about Eddie because she's told Dad as much. Eddie isn't just dealing with these losses in his life. He's dealing with finishing college, with football, with his wanting a career in the military, and more than anything with his physical longings for more from Katy. Every young person goes through that. Your dad and I went through it too, but God was able to help us. It's a one-day-at-a-time thing, and you don't have to fight the battle alone. You'll face it too, if you haven't already, and I want you to know I'll be here anytime you need to talk to me. I understand what a young girl faces, and I know your daddy knows what Eddie is going through, even though his personality is not so intense. I'm not sure who Eddie got that intenseness from, but I think it must have been from his grandma."

"Oh, Mom, you're that way a lot more than you think! Thanks for talking to me like this. I needed it, and I think you could help Katy a lot by telling her some of these things too," Audra said as she wrapped her arms around Sue and squeezed her.

Hal's attempts to draw Eddie into conversation about his relationship with the Lord more or less fell on deaf ears. Eddie would start to ask a question and then suddenly say, "Dad, I just don't want to talk about that right now. I'm twenty years old, and I want to deal with this from my own perspective, okay? Mom and you don't need to worry about me. I just have a lot on my mind and a lot of things to deal with."

HAROLD SOUTHWICK

Hal understood he needed to let Eddie start being his own man and didn't want to push him away from Christ any further, so he didn't press the issue. The church held a back-to-college barbecue as the summer break came to a close. Audra invited Katy to attend after asking Eddie if he would mind. He didn't have any objections, and she finally talked him into bringing Katy to the event. Eddie didn't let on, but he was secretly glad his little sister was interested in Katy's spiritual needs. He hadn't said anything to Katy about accepting Christ because he didn't want her to think he was trying to push his beliefs on her. He believed if she was interested she would ask about it.

The barbecue was a good time for all the young people, and soon they were all off to school again. Their parents were all left wondering what all parents wonder: how had their little ones grown up so fast and moved into a life of their own so easily?

CHAPTER 18

Eddie's junior year as a starting wide receiver on the Vandal foot-ball team soon became his most satisfying and successful. He threw himself into fall practice determined to let the pain in his heart carry him as far as it was able. His hard work paid off, and he led the conference in pass receptions and was third in touch-downs for wide receivers. He had his best game against Boise State on the Blue Turf, in front of his family and many friends from home. Playing against Jimmy and Billy from his high-school-team days and doing well was its own reward! The short time he got to visit with his family and with Katy was welcome, but it reminded him again of the pain the family was still deal-ing with from losing Angela. Christmas break came and went quickly, as much of it spent with Katy as possible. It was becom-ing increasingly hard to say good-bye to her. He was thankful that school and ROTC (Reserve Officer Training Corp) kept him so busy he didn't have much time the rest of the school year to be homesick.

The summer months soon came, and he had two weeks at home before he left for a two-month officer training school in Georgia. Audra graduated from high school the weekend he returned home from college, and the family had a big get-together afterwards. The following week, Hopi came to Glenn's Cove, and he and Eddie team roped in a local rodeo. Katy participated in the barrel

HAROLD SOUTHWICK

racing. She was on the Boise State rodeo team and was going to spend much of the summer doing the rodeo circuit. That would fill her summer since Eddie was going to be away at military school. Those weeks passed quickly with Eddie completely convinced to become a military man by the time he returned home. Katy's longing was to be with him wherever he went.

Soon the summer was over, and it was time to return to college for the last year. Before leaving, Eddie invited Katy and Jimmy to accompany him and Audra for a weekend of camping at the cabin on Trinity Lake. Eddie knew the story of how special that place was to his mom and dad, and he had something very special to talk to Katy about. He wanted it to take place there.

After swimming in the lake, fishing, sitting around a campfire, and singing to Eddie's guitar, Eddie asked Katy to go for a walk down by the lake. He had told Audra he was going to give Katy an engagement ring, so she gave Jimmy a big smile as they got up to leave. Katy noticed the two of them grinning knowingly, and her heart began drumming in her ears. She was afraid Eddie could hear it. Was he finally going to pop the question to her? She had dreamed of this moment for so long!

They walked arm in arm down through the trees to lake's edge, Eddie glancing down at her often. Her eyes were like stars looking up at him, the moonlight reflecting from their dark depths. His throat was choked with emotion, and she could feel his heart thumping against her shoulder. As he turned to her, he reached into his pocket and withdrew a beautiful little box. As Katy looked up at his face, she was instantly taken back to the rodeo arena in Flagstaff, Arizona. He had the same look on his face now that he had when he had come hurrying behind the stands where she had been tending her horse, waiting for him. His face conveyed his love better than any words could ever do. She saw it then, and she was totally convinced again. She was eager and ready for this moment.

"Uh, Katy ... uhm, I'm uh, I don't know if I can ... uh, can get this said, but I...I love you so much." He drew her close and looked down into her eyes, and she could see glistening in his eyes. "Katy," the words burst from him, "I love you, and I want to spend the rest of my life proving that to you. I want to give you this engagement ring to seal my commitment to you, and I want to marry you next June after we graduate from college. So what do you think? Will you marry me?" He dropped to his knee and reached for her hand.

"Well, you big lug, would you stand up here and let me answer you. Yes, yes, I will marry you! I love you too. I've told you that!" she cried as she pulled his head down for a long, heartfelt kiss. "It seems like I've waited forever for you to ask me!"

"Really? I was always afraid you wouldn't want to! I don't know why, though. You've never given me any reason to feel that way."

"You fear losing the ones you love, don't you, sweetheart?" Katy asked with a God-given insight.

"I don't know, maybe. May I put this ring on your finger, babe?" he said with a shrug, diverting any more questions of that nature. "I want to come ask your dad if he will let you marry me tomorrow night."

"He better, or Mom and I will ring his neck! No, he will; he really likes you and your family also!" She was jumping up and down with excitement. "Let's go back! I want to tell Audi."

"She knew I was going to ask you. I wanted to find out if she thought you would accept. You know what she said to me. 'Are you crazy? She can't wait for you to ask her.' Have you two been talking?"

"You know we're pretty close. Of course, we talk about a lot of things," she teased him.

"Jimmy wants to ask her the same question, but he knows Mom and Dad want her to attend two years of Bible school first, just like Mom did before she could marry Dad."

As they entered the cabin, Katy ran to Audra, and the two of them started dancing around the room. "He asked me, Audi!"

"Well, and what was your answer, dear girl?" Audra asked as if she didn't already know.

Katy's beaming smile was all the answer she needed.

Jimmy gave Eddie a bear hug, "Congratulations, bro! When's the big day?"

"Sometime the first part of next June. She wants to work that out with her mom. Will you be my best man?"

The drive home the following morning was filled with laughter, planning, and anticipation. Eddie was a little intimidated about asking Katy's dad and mom if he could marry their daughter. The four of them joked about just what he should say, but Eddie's serious nature made him want to do it right.

When they made the announcement to Hal and Sue, Katy displayed some shy anxiety of her own. The exclamations of delight soon dispelled that, however.

Later that evening Eddie took Katy home filled with excitement and yet nervousness. Before leaving the car, Katy said, "Let me go in first and tell Mom and Dad you want to talk to them, okay? I think I should stay out of the room when you ask them, don't you?"

Eddie laughed nervously, "I've never done this before, so I don't know. You just do what you think is best. This is harder than asking you to marry me!"

"It's going to be okay, love. Uh, do you think we should pray first?" she surprised him by asking.

"Well, yeah, I guess so. Do you want to lead?"

"No, you lead us," she replied.

As they held hands and Eddie said a quick prayer, the thought ran through both their minds that this was the first time they had prayed together when they were alone. Eddie felt a twinge of guilt, while Katy wondered just why Eddie had never asked her to pray with him before. A vague concern registered briefly somewhere in her heart concerning that fact. She was going to have to talk to Audi about this sometime, if possible.

Eddie waited in the foyer while Kat went to speak with her parents. Soon she came to the door and motioned him to follow her. As he came into the room, her mom stood and said, "Kat, let's go fix something to drink while Eddie and your daddy talk. I think that's traditional, isn't it?" She gave her daughter a tearful smile as she put her arm around Katy and led her from the room.

"Mom, do you know? I'm a nervous wreck! Are we doing this right?"

Bill Parker motioned Eddie to a chair and said, "Well, young man, what's on your mind?"

"Sir, if you don't mind, I think I should stand … uh … out of respect for you." Eddie lifted his hands and let them drop.

"Suit yourself, son." Bill smiled as he watched Eddie fidget.

"Sir, I've known your daughter for three years now, and she's become the most important person in my life. We have talked about our future a lot, and we both want to spend it together. I, uh, well, I want to marry her. So, sir, I would like to ask for your permission to marry her. If you don't think that's the right thing for us to do, then I'll try to understand and try to live with it, but, sir, I sure do want to marry her!" Eddie ended with a gesture.

"Do you love her?" Bill asked sternly, remembering being asked that very same question.

"Oh, yes, sir! I do! I'd give my life for her!"

"That'll more than likely be a daily requirement," was the smiling response. "How do you plan to support her and a family, young man?"

"Well, sir, after I graduate from college this next spring, I'm committed to four years as an officer in the army. That's to fulfill my ROTC obligation. I'll have an engineering degree when I finish school, so if I don't want to stay in the army after that, I will explore that field, sir," Eddie replied confidently.

HAROLD SOUTHWICK

"Katy's mom and I have been expecting this, and I'm happy to be able to tell you we are very pleased you want to marry our daughter! So, yes, young man, you have my consent to marry my little girl! One word of advice though, young man; always treat her like a lady and never do wrong by her. She means the world to her mom and me; you understand what I'm saying, don't you?" Bill Parker said as he stood and offered his hand. "Aw heck, I want to hug my future son-in-law!"

With that, he threw his arms around Eddie and gave him a bear hug. "Come on back in here, little girl! Bring your mommy with you!" he yelled to be heard.

The two ladies must have been waiting just beyond the door because they immediately rushed into the room, Katy running to her daddy and hugging him, while her mom went to Eddie and embraced him.

"Whew! I'm glad that's over with!" Eddie murmured, wiping his forehead.

"That wasn't so bad, was it, babe?" Katy smiled as she came into his arms.

"I guess that depends on who was doing the asking. Thank you both so much for sharing your beautiful daughter with me! She's wonderful!" Eddie said with deep emotion as he hugged her and looked to her parents.

The rest of the evening was spent making preliminary plans. Late June was tentatively picked for the wedding to take place. They both would be graduating in early June. It was going to be interesting for both families to get to both graduations, one being in Boise and the other in Moscow, some three hundred miles north of Boise. Hopefully, the graduation exercises wouldn't be on the same day. Katy's mom assured Eddie they would get right to work on all the details. They would want his mom and sister to be a part of it. They would keep him up to date on progress.

Bill grinned at Eddie. "She's a whiz at this kind of thing. Plans for her daughter's wedding have been flying around in that head of hers for the last year or so. She's had this bet with me about when you would ask for Katy' hand. It looks like she was right too!"

HAROLD SOUTHWICK

CHAPTER 19

The following nine months couldn't go fast enough as far as Eddie was concerned. The last year of football was fun; and he played well, but it was no longer a major focus. He got to see Katy and her family when they came to the Boise State–Idaho game in Moscow. The Thanksgiving holiday was taken up by his ROTC unit marching in a holiday parade in Seattle, so he wasn't able to go home. Christmas came, filled with the usual church and family events and further planning for the wedding. At the Christmas Eve candlelight service at the church, Eddie noticed Katy in deep discussion with his mom and Audra when he was up helping light each person's candle. When he came back to his seat beside her, he saw tears on her cheeks and whispered, "What's going on, pretty girl?"

"I want to talk to your pastor after the service," she murmured quietly.

His mom and Audra were watching them, smiling and wiping tears, and it suddenly dawned on him what was happening. A thrill shot through him as he considered what her decision would be, followed closely by a brief, chilling apprehension. It was so sudden it left him confused and speechless. *What is God doing now?* he wondered. That feeling was to haunt him in the dark of the night for weeks, and he couldn't get a grip on it.

Sue, Audra, and Katy asked Pastor Don for a few moments after the closing prayer. As Hal and his two boys were visiting with friends, Eddie felt a hand on his arm and turned to find his mom there asking him to come to the front of the church. As they came forward, he watched the pastor and Katy, with Audra on her other side, kneel in prayer. They bowed their heads and listened as Pastor Don led Katy through the salvation plan and prayer. When they finished, she looked to find Eddie watching her. A glow radiated from her face, and Eddie realized this was the most beautiful she had ever appeared to him. Emotion choked him as he embraced her, his mom, and sister all together. Soon his dad and Little Joe were there rejoicing with everyone else.

"This is the best Christmas present one could ever get!" Sue exclaimed.

"This makes this Christmas even more special," Pastor Don agreed, asking everyone to bow as he thanked God for another soul brought into the fold.

But why this feeling? Eddie was thinking as they left the church.

Katy's folks asked Katy questions about her salvation experience when she shared with them later that night. Kurt had been to church with Eddie and Katy a few times but had never made a decision to follow the Lord. He had, however, talked to his folks about Eddie's family's beliefs. They had never been churchgoing people, but their association with the Edwards family had left a favorable impression on them. They were glad for their daughter and agreed later they would like to know more about what had brought Katy to her decision. They decided to talk to Hal and Sue about it soon.

CHAPTER 20

The school year ended with all the frenzy associated with that: final exams, Eddie's ROTC final exercises, preparation to go on active duty the following September, and finally graduation! Eddie's and Katy's families drove to Moscow for his Saturday-afternoon exercises. Sue and Hal couldn't believe their oldest son had reached this time in his life so soon. Eddie was excited for the next phase of his life yet sad when he thought about leaving the environment at home that had always been so special to him. He received his engineering degree and his diploma, then said good-bye to classmates.

They all made a hasty trip back to Boise for Katy's graduation Sunday afternoon, where she also received a degree in music and graduated summa cum laude. The two families gathered at the Parker ranch later that night for a celebration. Bob and Joan Johnston were invited as well, along with Jimmy since he had also graduated with Katy from BSU. Eddie had gone to Billy Jones and congratulated him along with Jimmy after their graduation services had ended and was surprised when Billy shook his hand and returned the compliments. Hal and Sue had watched the exchange and had commented that their son was maturing; it pleased them to see this evidence of that.

The next two weeks were very busy with final preparations for the wedding, which was to take place on June 25. Eddie had asked his friend Hopi to be the lead groomsman. Hopi's family had been invited as well, and they all arrived in time for the wedding rehearsal. Kurt and Little Joe were the other two groomsmen. Audra was Katy's maid of honor, with three girlfriends from high school and college serving as bridesmaids. The rehearsal was a time of nervous fun with much laughing as mistakes were corrected and each one learned what was expected of them. The rehearsal dinner that followed was a time of shared memories from each family that cemented together these two families about to become a part of each other!

Saturday dawned bright and sunny with the promise of a beautiful afternoon for the wedding. Katy and Eddie had asked Pastor Don to officiate, but the ceremony was being held at the Parker ranch, on their large and picturesque front lawn, north of Mt. Home. Bill and Katherine Parker had spared no expense for the wedding of their only daughter. Eddie felt as though he was part of a cast on a movie set. He looked at his mother sitting on the front row of chairs as he stood with the pastor at the front. She gave him a tearful smile, and his dad gave him that old thumbs-up.

The music started playing, and the supporting cast filed in. As they took their places, the wedding march began, and everyone rose. Eddie turned expectantly with his heart in his throat. Bill Parker turned between the rows of seats with the most beautiful creature in Eddie's world on his arm. Eddie was completely mesmerized as he gazed at her in her wedding gown. She was gorgeous! He thought, *Lord, are you really giving her to me for my very own?* Her eyes were focused on him, and there was only the two of them in that moment.

Please let her be mine for the rest of my life! he prayed.

The rest of the ceremony was a blur, and by the time the reception was finished, it was late afternoon. Hal had fixed up his old truck for the couple to use for their getaway. Only Hal and Sue and the Parkers knew the newlyweds were going to spend their wedding night in the family cabin at Trinity Lake. Hal and Bill had gone up there earlier in the week and prepared it for the kids' wedding night. Unknown to them, however, Sue and Katherine had made a fast trip up there on Thursday afternoon to make sure everything was prepared with the proper atmosphere for their son and daughter to consummate their wedding vows. The following afternoon, they would leave from Boise airport to spend two weeks in Hawaii for their honeymoon.

Following the reception, the two of them left the group with the explanation of going to change into more comfortable clothes. They weren't really fooling anyone. While they did that, the families kept the guests occupied. They then went out back quietly and drove away from the ranch and left for the cabin. They were filled with nervous excitement and couldn't wait to reach their destination. They had waited for four years for this day. Though they had received spiritual counseling concerning the marital union and both had heard all the worldly talk concerning man and woman, the joy of discovery they shared as they became one, the way God had created them to, left them filled with joy. This was theirs to share together for the rest of their lives.

The two weeks in Hawaii was to be the most precious and carefree time of their marriage. Swimming in the ocean, sightseeing on bicycles, and horseback riding in the interior during the day left them exhausted. They discovered restaurants and food they had never heard of but came to love. Watching the Hawaiian-culture shows, strolling the beaches looking for sea shells, and shopping in the quaint shops took much time, but the intimate sharing together as they explored and discovered the wonders of the marriage union was beyond their expectations. This really had been worth waiting so long for.

CHAPTER 21

The newlyweds returned from their honeymoon to set up house-keeping and get Katy settled in an apartment before Eddie had to report to Camp Erwin, California, for intensive tank training in early September. Katy had applied for a teaching position at Glenn's Cove elementary school in the music department. Upon their return, they had learned she had been hired and would start that job in late August. With both sets of parent's help, they rented and furnished a small home near the town for Katy to live in. As soon as Eddie finished his training and was assigned a permanent unit, they planned to have her come live with him. The time was going to be difficult for them, and they weren't looking forward to being apart. The following two months were both fun and stressful as they learned to adjust to each other and how to establish a routine of living the married life. Eddie was glad he didn't have to leave until Kat had gone to work at the school; that would help keep her occupied, although she was a social person and was always involved in some outside activities.

Saying good-bye was the hardest thing either of them had ever had to do. The next three months were going to be long and lonely. That seemed like forever to both of them before they would see each other again! Eddie's mom and sister promised to stay close to her, and her mom wasn't that far away either; but their arms were no longer the same as being in his arms.

HAROLD SOUTHWICK

Eddie reported to his training unit and immediately began indoctrination classes in heavy armored desert warfare. After two weeks of that, they were assigned to their own specific tanks and began field training. His rank was a very rookie second lieutenant, and as such, he was training to become the tank commander. He soon learned that his crew knew a lot more than he did about the operation of a tank, so he determined to learn from them. As they advanced in the training, he began to love the camaraderie that developed as their efficiency increased. By the time the three-month program was completed, they had become a well-honed fighting team. Their armored battalion ranked high in the final evaluation exercises and was being assigned to the Third Armored Division, Frankfurt, Germany.

Upon learning this, Eddie realized his and Katy's plan to have her join him was going to be delayed until after he was settled in Germany. The ten days he was able to go home on leave before shipping out with his unit covered Thanksgiving Day and was to be the last holiday he would spend at home for a long time. His time with Katy was filled with joy and sadness, made that way because it was so brief and would be their last together for several months. Or so they thought.

Their two families held a special family celebration together for Thanksgiving. The following day Katy took Eddie to the airport, and he kissed her good-bye, all the while feeling a sorrow inside that he couldn't explain. He was reminded of his apprehension the night Katy had accepted Christ and realized he was feeling that way now. Again he could not get a handle on why he felt that way.

The following weeks were spent getting the unit's equipment loaded on ships in San Francisco for shipment to Germany. That completed, they spent the next two weeks at Ft. Ord, California, processing out for overseas deployment. They were then loaded on military transports and flown to Ft. Dix, New Jersey, and then on to Frankfurt, Germany.

They were billeted at the old Gibbs Casern where Eddie's dad had once been stationed. Their shipload of equipment arrived at the docks in northern Germany, where it was loaded on railway flat cars and sent to Frankfurt, being met there by Eddie's unit. They accompanied it on to a base in southern Germany for advanced training exercises. This was a departure from where they had previously been ordered to go. Something was in the air, and a heightened sense of anticipation became evident in briefings all officers were required to attend.

The training exercises they began to undergo were taking on a new intensity; rumors started flying. They were being readied for battlefield deployment; the question on everyone's mind was where. The situation in Iraq was becoming critical. It blew wide open when Iraq invaded Kuwait and seized the sea ports and oil fields.

In the meantime, Eddie had called home to talk to Katy concerning all that was being rumored there in southern Germany. She questioned him about why he was in southern Germany instead of Frankfurt, where they thought at first he was told they would be stationed. She listened quietly to him, asking if she was going to be able to join him there. She expressed her loneliness for him. He told of his own loneliness for her before telling her that no dependants were being allowed to come to Germany at the present time.

"Sweetheart, I wanted to be able to tell you this in person, but since that isn't going to happen, I'll tell you now. You're going to be a daddy!" she said proudly.

"Are you sure, babe?" Eddie cried.

"Of course I'm sure! I missed my last period and started having stomach cramps, so Mom took me to see Dr. Bell. Sure enough, the tests she gave me came back positive! Oh babe, I wish we were together for this time in our lives!" Katy lamented.

HAROLD SOUTHWICK

"This sounds just like what happened with my dad and mom when Dad had to go to Vietnam," Eddie replied.

"I hope you don't have to go to war, but things don't sound good on the news here in the States. Keep me informed, will you, love?"

"I'll call as soon as I know anything and can get a chance to call you again. Go see my mom and dad and tell them about our baby! They'll be thrilled to death! Give them all my love. I'm afraid I'm going to be very busy soon, so I may not have time to communicate with all of you at home as much as I would like to. I'll try to write to you at least once a week, but if you don't hear from me in a while, you'll know we've been sent somewhere else. I can't tell you any more than that. I love you and our new one! Take very good care of yourself for me and our baby, will you, sweetheart? I've got to go." As he hung up, he could hear Katy softly crying.

CHAPTER 22

Eddie loved the beauty of southern Germany and wished Katy could be here with him. There were so many places to go and things to see and do. Her being pregnant right now was an inconvenience, but there wasn't much they could do about it. He was excited that he was going to be a father. He also loved the army, and as his proficiency grew, his confidence as a part of the Twenty-third Armored Calvary Regiment grew. Rumors had continued to circulate that their skills might soon be tested.

———————

Katy's infrequent letters kept him informed of her progressing pregnancy. She told him everything seemed to be going well with the baby. She just wished he was home or that she was with him. Eddie's return letters contained very little information about what he was involved in, but that he was very busy and he missed them too.

His communications with his mom and dad were of a similar nature. He again asked his mom to keep a close eye on his wife, if she would. She always assured him that she and Audra were doing just that. Little Joe was taking care of the yard for her and making sure her car got serviced when needed. He more or less became her handyman when repairs around the house were needed. Hal and Sue always told him to stay in prayer with the Lord and to know their entire family was praying for him and his buddies. They also passed along the news that Jimmy had joined the air force, Hopi had joined the army, and Billy Jones had also joined the army. Eddie wondered if he would ever meet up with any of them over in Germany.

During all this time Eddie had been gone from his wife's side, he had continued to have a vague gnawing in his heart for her and the baby. He tried to pray about it, but his prayers never seemed to go anywhere. He knew he wasn't as close to God anymore as he should be, but he still felt resentment about losing his Grandpa and Angela. Somehow he felt God could have prevented that if he wanted to. He remembered his dad trying to talk to him about all of that, but there was just a lot about God he didn't understand right then. Besides, he was too busy to be able to talk to a chaplain or spend much time in prayer about it. He knew Katy and his entire family was praying for him, and he appreciated it; but his spiritual struggle seemed to get worse, not better.

Meanwhile, his commanding officer called him into the control center one late July morning, "Congratulations, Lieutenant. You have shown great strides in your leadership capabilities, and your tank crew seems to hold you in high regards. So it gives me much pleasure to inform you that you are now promoted to first lieutenant. With the promotion comes the command of your own tank and crew. If you prefer, you will take over command of the crew and vehicle you have been training with since our deployment here. Let me know in the next twenty-four hours, okay?"

Eddie was elated but tried to maintain his composure, "Sir, thank you very much! I can inform you right now that I want to stay with the crew and tank I'm with. We know how to work together and how to depend on each other. Do they know about this, sir?"

"They do, Ed, and they hoped you would want to be their man! So if you'll relax a little and come around here, I'll pin these silver bars on your shoulder. It'll be up to you to get your other uniforms re-pinned."

As Major Ben Croft finished putting Eddie's new insignia on, Eddie snapped to attention, saluted smartly, did an about-face and left the tent. He had been anticipating this promotion; but just like that he held a new responsibility, and the challenge thrilled him! He couldn't wait to let Katy and his dad know. He wondered how Katy was doing. It was about time for the baby to be born.

CHAPTER 23

By mid-August, Katy was experiencing increased lower back pain. In the last two weeks she had been bleeding intermittently, and her mom and Sue were worried about that. The pregnancy had gone well, but they knew this could be trouble. Dr. Bell scheduled her to come in for an exam on a Monday morning, so Sue was going to pick her up and drive to Mt. Home and meet Katherine at the Dr.'s office for the visit. Katherine and Bill came to Glenn's Cove for a Sunday-afternoon barbecue with Eddie's family and Katy. As they were sitting around visiting after eating, Sue noticed Katy becoming pale and agitated.

She suddenly said, "I need Eddie here! Please, can someone tell him to come home? I need him here with me for this!"

She stood up and went to the bathroom, her face contorted with pain. Her mom quickly followed her, motioning Sue to come with them. Hal and Bill worriedly waited for some indication of what was going on.

Sue hurried out to them and said, "Hal, I'm calling the hospital. We need to get Katy up there as fast as possible. She's starting to bleed heavily. Get the station wagon backed up to the door so we can lay her down in the back and elevate her legs. Hurry, we need to get out of here! Bill, Katherine wants you to come help her."

Hal replied firmly, "We better call the ambulance. They can start an IV and give her some oxygen and try to stop the bleeding." He called 911 only to learn that the ambulance was out on another emergency and the backup ambulance was in the shop. Sue and Katherine applied compresses and bed sheets to contain the blood flow, but it didn't seem to help much.

Soon they were on the way, Hal driving as Sue and Katherine made Katy as comfortable as possible. Bill followed in their car. They were just entering Mt. Home when Katy passed out from loss of blood. By the time she was wheeled into the hospital, she was in a critical situation.

Dr. Bell took one look at her and said, "We need to do an emergency C-section. Get IVs going and get her prepped. We've got to get the baby out so we can find where she's bleeding from and get it fixed! Hurry. We don't have much time."

After waiting and praying in the waiting room for what seemed like hours, the Edwards and Parkers noticed the grim expression on Dr. Bell's face as she entered the room. They stood clutching each other as Katherine asked fearfully, "She's going to be all right, isn't she?"

Dr. Bell's reply stunned them. "We were able to deliver the baby successfully. It's a beautiful little black-haired girl. But Katy had gone into a deep coma by the time we had the baby. The blood loss was just too great from the ruptured blood vessel in her womb. I hate to have to tell you this, but we lost her. I'm so sorry. The baby seems to be doing fine. I'll have a nurse bring her out to you for a minute when we have her ready."

Bill caught his wife in his arms as she collapsed against him, sobbing and crying, "Oh God, why, why, she's so young. Oh no, please, no." Bill's mind couldn't grasp the fact that his little girl was dead. How could something like this happen so suddenly? They collapsed in each others arms on the couch, unable to comprehend.

Hal and Sue were holding each other as they cried and prayed together. Sue gasped brokenly, "This is going to completely break Eddie's heart! I hope it doesn't drive him further away from the Lord! I need to call Audra and Mom to let them know. Then we have to figure out how to let Eddie know!"

Hearing that, Bill responded, "I can get a line through the

base out here, to his unit in Germany. Let's see the baby first, and then we'll be able to tell him about her as well. I need to let Kurt know too Oh, God! I don't know if I can do this."

Eddie was just entering the mess hall for breakfast when an orderly from the communications center quickly approached and gave him a salute, "Sir, there is an emergency message for you at the comm. center. Major Croft asks that you come quickly."

A hundred questions raced through his mind as Eddie followed the young specialist. As he entered the room, Major Croft came to his side and led him into an isolated corner where individuals could make calls home.

His concerned expression chilled Eddie's heart as he said, "Son, I want you to brace yourself. Your dad has called from Idaho saying you need to call home. You have an urgent family emergency. We have a line set up for you, ready to place your call. I'll be right out here, waiting to help any way I can."

Eddie was thinking, *Katy's about due to have the baby! Oh God, I hope she's okay!*

As he waited for the call to go through, he remembered the apprehension he had felt that night at the church when Katy was accepting Christ. Did this have anything to do with that?

He finally heard his dad's voice come on the line, "Hello."

"Dad, this is Eddie. What's the emergency? This number isn't our home phone number. Where are you?"

Eddie sensed the struggle his dad was having as he replied, "Son, you need to come home immediately. I don't know how to tell this, but Katy has suffered a very serious problem with the baby."

As he paused, Eddie cried, "She's going to be okay, isn't she? What happened?"

"I'm afraid she isn't going to be okay, Son." As he went on to explain the chain of events, Eddie slowly sank to his knees, his world crumbling around him. "Son, I'm so sorry, but Katy has passed away. Mom and I wish we could be there with you right now. We know you need us!"

When Eddie could finally talk again, he asked through his tears, "Is the baby still alive, Dad? What was it?"

"The baby is doing pretty good, Son. It's a little black-haired girl. Looks just like Katy." Eddie heard his dad's voice break with emotion. His mom came on the phone then, expressing her sorrow and offering her prayers. She asked him to let them know as soon as he would be able to leave for home. Bill and Katherine Parker talked to him next, brokenly expressing their sorrow and regrets.

As he put the phone down, Major Croft placed a hand on his shoulder, saying, "Ed, you have my deepest sympathy. Your dad had told me what has happened. It's hell to be this far away from your wife during a normal birth, but I can only imagine what you're feeling right now. I've got personnel arranging a flight home for you. As soon as they let me know, I'll come get you. Right now I want you to go get what you need to take with you and get ready to leave. I'll have the chaplain come talk with you while you're doing that, okay?"

Eddie thanked him and stumbled out through the center, concerned looks from fellow soldiers following him. When he finally reached his bunk, he slumped on the bed, unable to function. Denial, loss of purpose, grief he had never thought possible, and anger and a sense of being deprived all took their turns flooding through him. *God, why did you let this happen!* He tried to pray as he knelt with the chaplain before leaving to catch a flight to Frankfurt on a military plane. He tried to connect with God but felt only empty and totally alone. The love of his life was gone. What was he going to do without her? In his despair, he had absolutely no awareness that he was now a father; such was his agony. By the time he was on a connecting flight from Frankfurt to Denver, a grimness of soul had settled on him. When he finally arrived at the Boise airport the following afternoon, he was so exhausted his folks hardly recognized him. He felt God had completely abandoned him, and he didn't know why. A cold, heavy hand seemed to be clamped around his heart.

As Hal looked at his son, he thought, *His intense nature and complete dedication are exacting a terrible toll on my boy, Lord.* He hugged his son and shook with his own grief. Sue then pulled Eddie to her, and they both cried together. People passed by with sympathetic glances as Eddie finally pulled away.

The trip to Mt. Home was spent filling Eddie in on all the details leading up to and through Katy's crisis. Sue asked him if he wanted to see the baby first. He replied he wasn't ready for that yet, his manner of speech causing both Hal and Sue to look at him with concern. He asked them to take him to the mortuary; he wanted to spend some time alone with Katy, if they would let him.

While they waited for Eddie, Hal asked Sue, "Are you getting the feeling Eddie is blaming the baby or maybe himself for what has happened? Or do you think he is blaming God?"

"I'm just afraid it's some of each of those things. First it was Grandpa, then Angela was taken, and now this. Katy helped him weather those other two losses, but who's going to help him survive this. She was his pillar. I'm afraid he's feeling God is taking everyone he gets too close to away from him. I have to tell you I'm having a battle about this myself right now." Sue said, squeezing Hal's hand like always when she was extremely disturbed.

Eddie stood looking at Katy's pale, lifeless face as she lay in that cold gray casket, that face that had always been so full of exuberant life and laughter. His anguish was so powerful he wanted to join her there forever. What was there to live for now, anyway?

Katy, he thought, *I've loved you with every ounce of my being and everything I've had to love you with. How am I going to be able to go on without you? We both wanted babies, but you would still be alive if I hadn't got you pregnant.* Deep inside himself some obscure emotion tried to push that thought from his mind, but he was too distraught to respond to it.

When he finally joined his folks again, he found them in prayer. They stood when they heard him and asked if he was ready to go to the hospital to see his daughter. His look of bewilderment and confusion broke him mom's heart.

She clutched his arm and said, "Son, you have to go see your little girl! She needs you to give her a name. You need to see her. She needs her daddy!"

"Mom, I'm afraid to get close to her! I just can't talk about it right now!"

"Eddie, at least come to the hospital and see the Parkers and your brother and sister. They were supposed to meet us there. Maybe you'll feel different after talking to Audi," Hal coached as he led Eddie to the car.

The reunion with the others at the hospital was a time of tears and expressed sorrow and regrets. Audi was finally able to persuade Eddie to go with her to see the baby. She asked the others to give her a few minutes before they joined them.

She watched Eddie as he looked at the little dark-haired beauty. She saw the tears in his eyes and asked, "Do you want to hold her? She's like a feather."

Eddie stepped back with a look of alarm, "No! No, not yet!"

The others joined them then, and Katherine Parker put her arm around Eddie's waist and said, "What did you and Katy decide about a name for her if it was going to be a girl, or did you ever get to that?"

Eddie was lost in thought, seemingly a thousand miles away. He didn't respond until Sue pressed next to his other side, "I think she wanted to name a girl Katrina," he said listlessly.

"Well, what name do you want?" both moms asked at once.

As tears filled his eyes, he turned away, saying, "I want Katy back."

The funeral was a sad, heartrending time. For such a young, vibrant, beautiful woman at the bloom of her life to be taken away when she was needed the most by her husband and her new baby, as well as the rest of her other loved ones, was hard to understand and accept. In spite of that, there was rejoicing by all who knew Christ as Savior that she had come to know him also and was now with him in heaven. Sue and Hal doubted that Eddie was doing any rejoicing at the moment, however.

It wasn't until two weeks later that the baby was brought home to the Edwards' house. Eddie finally took her in his arms and gazed into her dark eyes with an intensity that left his mom speechless. She looked at Katrina and saw the baby staring back at her daddy with wide-eyed wonder!

Sue thought, *Oh, Lord, if I could only tell what is passing between these two right now.* Eddie suddenly turned and left the house with the baby in his arms, strolling down by the horse corrals. A short time later he returned and handed the baby to Sue without a word. She watched as he went to the horse barn, where he saddled his horse and rode off down the trail toward the river, his faithful old dog tagging along.

The anger raging inside his brain was equaled only by the pain in his heart. He was oblivious to his surroundings as his horse carried him closer to the river bank. In his torment, it failed to register that he and his grandfather had spent many peaceful afternoons in this very location fishing and talking. He became aware that he was at the water's edge when his horse stopped and neighed deep in his chest. Eddie raised his eyes toward heaven and a blood curdling scream tore from within him. His horse was so startled he jumped sideways, unseating his rider. Eddie fell near water's edge and lay beating his hands on the sand, spraying water in his face and all around. "God, why are you doing this to me? Why do you hate me?" he screamed at the top of his lungs.

Convulsions shook his body and he began to cry uncontrollably. "Why God, why?" he moaned over and over. God remained silent. Eddie became so exhausted from his horrible journey into the hell of his torment he descended into a stupor. How long he lay there like that he had no idea, stirring only when his horse snorted and began nudging him with his nose. He finally began to return to awareness when he felt Old Shep licking his face. Blaze kept pounding the ground with his front hoof and nudging Eddie with his nose. Eddie slowly rolled over and struggled to sit up. He tried to stand but the trauma of his torment suddenly caused dry heaves to grip his body. That continued until he was left gulping for air. He lay back and sank into a sleep of total exhaustion. When he finally awoke it was turning dark in the east. He took his handkerchief from his back pocket and mopped his face. Curses he had heard others use but seldom ever even thought of using raged within his mind to be uttered. Slowly, rather than scream them as a release, he resolved to never depend on God again for anything. He would make it through this rotten life on his on, come hell or whatever. His last thought before getting up and leading his horse towards the ranch was, *I'm in hell already, so what does it matter.* As he staggered along, Old Shep whined and licked his hand. His horse continued to snort his concern for his master as he followed him. Later, he was unable to remember unsaddling his horse and turning him out to pasture. Old Shep never left his side, watching him with mournful eyes.

Unknown to him, his younger brother Joe had followed him part way to the river and witnessed the terrible drama as it unfolded. He wanted to rush to his hero and comfort him, but some inner restraint held him where he fell in the sage brush and cried in sorrow and frustration. He too, wanted to ask God why. When Eddie entered the house in his disheveled condition, he went straight to his room, ignoring his mom as she reached to comfort him. She watched sadly as he closed his door, her heart aching for him. He was to return to his unit in Germany the following day, and the family knew he had gone to be alone to resolve himself to a life without the one he had adored. They could only imagine the depth of his anger and despair. They were reluctant to ask him about his feelings for his baby. They weren't sure if he even knew just yet. Only his brother was aware of the depth of his despair, and he would never share that secret with any of them. He spent many a lonely night crying for Eddie.

The two families had worked out a plan they hoped would let both sides of the family be involved in baby Katrina's care while Eddie was still overseas. She would be kept at Hal and Sue's place since Audi and Grandma Dot would be available to help care for her. Katherine would come help care for her as much as possible; when she was a little older, she could go spend some time at the Parker ranch. Katrina was a military dependant now, so there would be an allotment sent to help with expenses as soon as Eddie could get the paperwork taken care of. He left home knowing the baby was in a lot better hands than what his would be for a long time. Something was tugging at his heart strings, but he could not have told anyone what it was yet. When his mom asked if she could pray with him before he left, he quietly shook his head no. He gave the baby one last long look, shook hands with Little Joe and his dad, hugged his mom, and went to the car, where Audra was waiting to take him to the airport in Boise for his return to his regiment in Germany.

Eddie spent the long hours on the plane trying to adjust to life without Katy. He couldn't decide if he wanted a relationship with his infant daughter or if he would even come back from what everyone knew was coming in Iraq. Right now he didn't care much one way or the other. His life didn't seem to have the purpose that it had before losing Katy. By the time he reached Frankfurt, he had made up his mind to be the best tank commander possible and let whatever happened determine where his life would go from there.

He welcomed the return to the stepped-up activities as the Third Armored Division continued on its mission to be the best possible. His men soon realized their commander was a different person than the one before. He had them train harder, maintaining their gear and machine continuously, studying and developing battle techniques relentlessly. He told them he wanted them to be the best team to cross the burm and confront the enemy, if they should be sent to the Middle East. They saw the pain deep in his eyes, though he never said anything about home or his loss; he was all business, and they responded to his leadership out of their respect for him.

CHAPTER 24

When word came down in early November that VII Corps Commander Fritz Franklin had been called to Seventh Army Headquarters in Heidelberg, the troops were sure they were on their way to Saudi Arabia. The first unit from the Twenty-second Armored Calvary Regiment began loading trains for German ports on November 19, 1990. The first troops from the Second Squadron, Twenty-second ACR and support elements arrived in the Gulf on December 5 and 6. This was a small wave foretelling the vast flood that was soon to follow. Over the next two and one half months VII Corps would be stretched and pulled in a hundred different directions. For the corps, the main objective was to be in Saudi Arabia and, if need be, attack and destroy the Iraqi Republican Guards. The following weeks were filled with assembling the corps in tactical assembly areas, preparing for war, and conducting desert combat training exercises. As a matter of VII Corps priority, General Franklin stressed attention to fundamentals: agility, teamwork, and discipline. Since these troops had never trained in such desert conditions as these, the days to follow were filled with all that entailed.

Eddie's life had settled into long hours of briefings, field exercises, making sure his tank was properly maintained, and short hours of rest. He had written home before being deployed to the desert, informing his family his unit was being shipped out of Germany. Although they weren't allowed to give details of where they were going, his family knew from news reports that he was in the Middle East.

———————————

Hal was well aware of war conditions and the stress associated with it. Because of that, he became increasingly concerned for his son.

One day as he and Sue were praying for Eddie, he said, "I feel like I'm supposed to call Leslie Davis and talk to her about Eddie. We haven't talked to her since before he finished college. Maybe she can give us some good council."

During the ensuing conversation with her, Leslie asked Hal, "Do you remember telling me about a feeling you experienced several times while you were in Vietnam? I remember you saying it was like a "hand" pointing you toward home during several critical times. You told me it was like God was leading you back home for some special reason. Maybe you should start praying that God would start drawing Eddie back to him and his baby and family in that same manner. I'll pray along those lines with you!"

It was like a light suddenly came on for Hal, and he thanked Leslie. When he shared this inspiration with Sue, she gave him a tearful hug.

"We must be getting old," she sighed. "We should have thought of that ourselves."

———————————

Baby Katrina was approaching her first Christmas with no mother and a father who was half a world away. If what Hal and Sue were afraid of came true, she could be without both of her parents before the dust settled in that godforsaken part of the world.

Hal had nicknamed her "The Kat," and she was growing into a beautiful, dark-haired little girl with a quick smile. She had her mommy's sunny disposition and big brown eyes. The entire

HAROLD SOUTHWICK

family loved her dearly and agreed if Eddie got to spend any time at all with her he would lose his heart to her just as he had to her mommy. They feared he might never get that opportunity, but they covenanted together to pray God would help that to happen. After Hal shared his own story of how God had kept pointing him homeward with that "spiritual hand" with Katy's family, they all made that their prayer focus. Those prayers were to become their anchor and source of hope as the events in the Middle East unfolded in the coming months.

CHAPTER 25

The air war began on January 17, carried out by the USAF, US Navy, the RAF and some French Air Force units. These tactics took the war right to the enemy's centers of leadership, control, telecommunications, transportation, and production centers for weapons. They were all completely neutralized. On February 1 artillery units began to soften up and destroy Iraqi units close to the border where the breach of the twelve-foot-high burm of sand was to take place, allowing the infantry, tanks, and support units to enter into Iraqi territory. The first of some 1,800 prisoners to be taken in the following three weeks were captured. Exchanges of artillery fire across the border as well as Scud missiles fired from in Iraq were taking place over the next three weeks. Eddie's Twenty-second ACR unit along with two armored divisions was kept hidden to the west until February 23. The mission of Twenty-second ACR was to be out front and to provide offensive cover for the movement of the two armored divisions. Therefore, Eddie's group was some of the very first through the breaches cut in the sand berm by combat engineer units; they were to advance to engage the Iraqi war machine. The assault of the First Infantry Division followed up by the swiftly advancing Twenty-second ACR overwhelmed the Iraqi defenders, with many killed or captured. At first, Eddie's steely resolve was rocked by the sheer destructive power of this war machine he and his men were a part of. As they advanced farther into the Iraqi interior, the overall success and the lack of a coordinated defense by the enemy filled them with confidence. As they toughened to the chaotic combat conditions, they resolved to hammer the Iraqi warriors hard and relentlessly and finish this quickly. The precise and destructive power of this tank of theirs amazed his team, and they began to feel invincible. That feeling was shattered somewhat when they began to see some of their own vehicles destroyed and burning, bodies of their comrades laying sprawled in the desert sand. All that remained of some were bits of clothing. It was more than sobering. The advance eventually carried them into contact with Republican Guard units setting up defenses at the Tawalkana security zone. Eddie's team was out front and began to receive heavy enemy resistance. They were maneuvering to engage an enemy tank, and Eddie had just opened his mouth to give the order to fire when their tank took a direct hit. The driver and the spotter were both killed as the shell traveled through the interior and exploded in their ammo hold. Eddie was blown through the open hatch by the force of the explosions and was unconscious before hitting the desert sand. His body received multiple fractures, and by the time he was recovered he had lost a great deal of blood.

He was evacuated, along with other wounded warriors on a military medevac chopper to a field hospital, where he received emergency blood loss control and stabilization treatment. This forward field hospital served as a military emergency room serving to administer critical care to keep the war casualties alive until they reached facilities with more advanced capabilities.

Unknown to him, he was the only survivor from his team. The following morning he was loaded on a military hospital transport plane with some fifteen other injured soldiers and flown to Landstuhl, Germany, the Second General Hospital, US Army, for extensive reconstructive surgery and stabilization before being shipped to Walter Reed Army Medical Center in the States. Eddie had not regained consciousness yet, and it was feared he had sustained some brain injury beyond a concussion.

Some of the best advanced medical doctors and nurses in the world worked at this hospital, and the level of care these tragic cases received saved many who would have otherwise died; such was the case with Eddie. It was determined that he had suffered a severe concussion from the explosion when he was thrown from the tank. He had also suffered a broken left arm, thigh, several ribs on the left side, and a pelvic fracture all caused by contact with parts of the tank as his body was blown through the hatch on the exploding vehicle. . Everything considered, his caregivers thought him fortunate to be alive.

One particular young army nurse took a special interest in Eddie's case

Teresa had become interested in nursing when she had volunteered at an army hospital near her home. She felt there was a ministry opportunity to becoming an army nurse, thus the reason for her being in this particular place at this particular time. Though she considered herself only a nominal Christian, she believed she was fulfilling a need and Eddie presented a particular challenge for her for some reason. She wondered why.

CHAPTER 26

The Edwards family received a call from the department of defense shortly after Eddie's arrival at Landstuhl informing them of his being wounded in action. Sue took the call early in the morning while Hal and Little Joe were out doing chores. As soon as the person on the phone identified herself and where she was calling from, Sue had the sinking feeling all was not well with her son. They hadn't heard from him in several weeks, but that was how he had been since Katy had died. They knew, however, that his unit was one of the first poised to invade Iraq, and the news had confirmed that had happened. After receiving the information concerning Eddie's being wounded and where he had been taken, she hurried to the barn to tell Hal. He saw her running toward him with tears running down her cheeks, and he knew she had bad news about their son.

The next several hours were spent notifying the Parkers, the church family asking for prayers, and trying to find out whom they could call connected to the army to get some updated news of his condition. They needed to let Audra know; she was in Texas attending Bible school. Grandma Dot and Sue's mom were preparing some lunch while Hal, Sue, and Little Joe were on their knees in the living room when the phone rang. As Dot answered, everyone looked at her with worried expressions, fearing the worst.

She motioned for Hal to come to the phone, "It's your friend in Thailand. She wants to talk to you."

When Hal answered, Leslie replied, "Hal, have you heard from Eddie lately?"

"We got the call early this morning that he had been wounded. We don't have any firsthand information about his condition, though. Why do you ask?" Hal asked anxiously. "I've had an over-powering burden to pray for him for several days. God hasn't given me any peace about it and I wanted to call to ask if you know anything about his situation."

They prayed together and talked briefly, then Hal promised to keep her informed and hung up.

"Mom, we better let Audi know what we've heard," Little Joe said. "I'm going to call her!"

After Joe updated Audra, he turned to his dad and said, "Dad, Sis wants to tell you something."

Hal took the phone, "What is it, babe?"

"Dad, Hopi is in Germany now. I just got a card from him. He asked me if I had heard where Eddie is now. Maybe he could go see Eddie if they'll let him. He's a military policeman in Heidelberg, Germany at Seventh Army Headquarters. That's not too far from where Eddie is."

"If he's close enough, he'll go; we know that. Let him know, will you, and have him give us a collect call." Hal told her.

Audi was becoming agitated and said, "Dad, I've got to go to Landstuhl! Katy would want me to do that. I've got to go for little Katrina's sake! Can you help me get a ticket, please?"

"Let me work on it, honey. We'll work out something. Call and let us know if you get in touch with Hopi; maybe I'll know something by then. I think we need to find out more about Eddie's condition and if they think he'll make it first."

"Dad, if he's still alive, I've got to go see him now!" Audra insisted.

"Okay, sweetheart, we'll make it happen." Hal said good-bye with a heavy heart. He called the Parkers next. Bill insisted on helping get a ticket for Audra. He said they would come to Glenn's Cove so they could help the family deal with yet another tragic event.

HAROLD SOUTHWICK

Before he hung up, Bill asked, "Hal, where is God in all of this? The wife and I have been doing some serious thinking about your family's faith and the fact that Katy embraced it the way she did. With everything that has happened to your family and now ours too, we are kind of confused about God's love and how that fits with all these happenings."

Hal was slow to reply. "Well, Bill, we're struggling with this whole thing ourselves, but God's Word tells us that his ways are not our ways and that there are times when we just have to trust him. It's at times like this that it's the hardest thing to do. I don't know what else we can do, though, except to pray, and we all do that. I would like to talk to you more about our faith sometime though."

CHAPTER 27

The young soldier's first sign of movement in more than two weeks was observed with excited gasps by two young women, one sitting by the bed and the other standing over him checking his IVs and his vitals. Audra had arrived in Landstuhl three days earlier and had spent every waking hour at Eddie's bedside. She had met Teresa when the young nurse had come on duty shortly after she came to the hospital. Audra had visited with her and learned that she had grown up in Texas. When she told Teresa she was attending bible school in Ft. Worth, they had a bond. Their conversations had convinced Audi that she was a Christian.

Eddie's eyelids fluttered and then closed again. It was nearly an hour later before he began to stir again, his right hand opening and then shutting again. Audra rang the bell for the nurse, and by the time Teresa entered the room, Eddie was slowly waking up. Audra watched, her heart in her mouth, as he lay unmoving, his half-open eyes looking at the ceiling. After what seemed an eternity to his sister and the nurse, he seemed to become aware of the tubes attached to him and the splints and bandages his body was encased in.

Audra rose slowly and stood over him. "Eddie, do you know who I am?"

His eyes moved slowly to her face, no sign of recognition in them.

HAROLD SOUTHWICK

The military doctor entered the room. Leaning over the stricken soldier, he asked, "Eddie, can you talk to me?"

Eddie's eyes moved ever so slowly between Audra and the doctor, and then he opened his mouth and tried to respond. He couldn't move his head because of the neck brace, and the bandages on the left side of his face limited his view. The oxygen mask covering his face made it difficult to really hear him.

"Nurse, keep a close eye on him; he's coming around, but it's going to be a while yet before he's completely conscious. Audra, it's good that you're here for him to see when he can focus!" Dr. Wilson said as he left the room.

———————————

Audra went through the process of an overseas phone call, going over the things she needed to tell her folks to reassure them as she waited. Finally, she heard her dad's voice as he picked up.

"Hello. Audi, is that you?"

"Yes, Daddy, it's me. I know it's late there, but I just had to call and bring you and Mom up to date on Eddie!" Audra answered, her voice full of emotion.

"Babe, is he going to be okay? What's happening? We've been going crazy not being able to be there and not knowing how he's doing. Mom's about out of her mind with worry, Sis," Hal voiced with a deep sigh.

"Dad, he partially regained consciousness for just a moment about two hours ago but then went right back to sleep. I sat and watched him and prayed and cried for about an hour; then I realized I needed to call you and let you know he stirred. As I stood up to do that, he opened his eyes and tried to focus on me. The nurse came in and we tried to get him to talk to us, but he couldn't. I finally asked him to blink his eyes if he recognized me. Daddy, you know what, it took him a while, but he finally was able to blink his eyes! We were so excited!"

She went on to tell him about Dr. Wilson and his conversation with her. "Dad, we've all been praying that God would put someone who knows Christ in Eddie's life to point him back home, you know. Well, I hate it that Eddie had to wind up here in the terrible condition he's in, but God has put two people who know Christ in his life right here in this hospital to care for him, Teresa, the nurse, and me. I think Dr. Wilson knows about the Lord too. After what Dr. Wilson told me, saying that he sensed that there was a lot more to Eddie's need than just his physical injuries, I think our prayers have been answered!"

"Sweetheart, I'm so glad you're there with him," Hal told his daughter. "Tell him his family loves him and we need him back home with us. His precious baby girl needs him too! I'm going to let you talk to Mom now, but first, do they have any idea when he will be shipped to the states?"

"Dr. Wilson hasn't said, but I'll ask him later today when I see him. Hopi called from Heidelberg yesterday and said he would be here later today again. You remember I told you he's a Military policeman there. He came to see Eddie a couple of days before I got here, but, of course, Eddie was still unconscious. He met Teresa then, and she seems quite impressed with him. I can't wait to see him again! Dad, keep praying for me! I need to get back to school, but I just can't leave Eddie yet. He needs someone from home with him now! I see other soldiers here with no one from home to be there for them, and it just breaks my heart. I think I'm going to stay until they ship him to Walter Reed in Washington D.C. Teresa said that's where the wounded go from here for further care and rehabilitation. I love you, Daddy! Let me talk to Mom now and tell Joe and everyone hi for me. You'll let the Parkers know how Eddie is doing, won't you?"

Hal assured her he would then put his anxiously waiting wife on the phone. He bowed in prayer and thanked God for the news of Eddie's improving condition; because of his own experience with battlefield wounds and all the complications that could arise, he knew his son had a long way to go before he'd be himself again, if that actually ever happened. He made a vow that somehow he and Sue would go to Walter Reed if or when Eddie was sent there. The Parkers would be glad to take care of Katrina, and he could get Stu to look after the ranch for him for a week or so.

After Sue got off the phone, he asked her what she thought of his idea.

"Dad, we really need to go see him." Sue decided then and there she would put the plan in motion. She still remembered how it had helped Hal and Bob Green to have Leslie Davis minister to them in their need in that hospital in Bangkok way back when.

CHAPTER 28

Audra met Hopi in the lounge later that evening. He cut a fine figure in his dress uniform, and Audi was impressed. He listened closely as she told him that Eddie was starting to come around. She had returned to Eddie's room after talking to her folks to find him asleep. When Teresa came in to check on Eddie, Audra told her Hopi would be coming to visit; she noticed the flicker of excitement in Teresa's eyes and smiled. As she and Hopi walked to Eddie's room, he looked at her shyly and asked, "Is that pretty young nurse still looking after our boy?"

"As a matter of fact, she is!" Audi smiled at him. "I told her you were coming this evening to see Eddie, and she seemed pleased. Would you like to take me and her out for something to eat after she gets off work?"

"Do you think she'd go with us?" Hopi asked with a sparkle in his dark eyes.

"I'd bet on it, my dear friend. Hopi, I'm so glad you're here. They won't keep Eddie here much longer, but maybe you can help him. I don't think he'll ever get over Katy, but we've all got to help him move on. His baby girl needs him, and he needs her. She'll never take Katy's place in Eddie's heart, but she can be God's consolation for him." Audi was crying as Hopi put his arms around her.

"I'll do for him what he has always done for me. I'll be the best friend I know how to be. He's always accepted me as an equal, and I'm a better man because of that. Besides, because of

HAROLD SOUTHWICK

him, we're brothers in Christ. Sis, we'll get him through this with God's help. Count on it. Now, let's go see him, and then I want to see if that pretty little nurse will go to dinner with a wild Zuni warrior and you!" Hopi's enthusiasm lifted her spirits, and she felt better than she had in weeks.

Teresa was checking Eddie's vital signs when Audra and Hopi entered the room. She was so intent on her task she didn't become aware of their presence until Audi spoke.

"Is he awake, Tessa?"

As she finished, she turned with a smile and started to speak. Seeing Hopi with Audra, she blushed and said, "Oh, I didn't realize you had arrived!" Turning to Audi with an amazed look, she said, "No one has called me Tessa since I was a little girl. That's what my daddy used to call me!"

Audi beamed. "It just seemed right to call you that! Do you mind?"

"I love it!" the young nurse replied wistfully as she glanced at Hopi.

"You asked if Eddie was awake. He drifts in and out, but that's normal for this type of trauma. His awareness seemed a little better shortly after you left a while ago."

As they stood watching him, Eddie's eyelids fluttered briefly, and a groan escaped his lips. Hopi's face registered a strong emotion as he placed a hand on Eddie's right shoulder.

"Hey, cowboy," he said softly, "Wake up! We've got a steer or two to rope yet!" his unique Indian dialect eliciting fond memories in Audra's mind.

Eddie's eyes opened, and he slowly focused on the face before him. A glimmer of recognition seemed to register, his glance moving to Audra as she moved to Hopi's side once again. He struggled to communicate, his voice garbled. Teresa lifted his oxygen mask, holding it away from his mouth as they strained to understand him. His eyes tried desperately to convey what his voice was unable to utter.

"Take it easy, partner. We're here for you, and these good people are going to help you get better," Hopi said, taking Eddie's hand with a gentleness that brought tears to Audra's and Teresa's eyes.

"I love you, big brother!" Audi's tears fell on his chest as she leaned over him. "Mom and Dad send their love and said for you to get better and come home soon!"

Somewhere down deep inside him, a "presence" briefly invaded Eddie's being. A "hand" seemed to beckon him. As the three with him watched, his countenance appeared to clear with a sense of wonder.

Goose bumps formed on Audra's arms as she became aware that the Holy Spirit was moving in Eddie's troubled heart and wounded mind.

Suddenly Teresa whispered in her ear, "Let's pray. God's at work."

As the two of them knelt at the bedside in prayer, Hopi continued to talk quietly to the best friend he had ever known. As Eddie drifted off to sleep, he joined the two young ladies in prayer.

Dr. Wilson appeared at bedside, taking in the scene before him with keen interest. As a doctor, he knew his medical skills were a gift from the God he loved and tried to serve. He believed prayer played a very important part in the healing process. What he was witnessing here convinced him of what he already suspected. God cared very deeply about this young soldier's recovery. He bowed his own head and joined in the prayer effort underway. Audra felt her burden lessen and tearfully began to praise God, beginning to believe for the first time her brother would eventually be all right.

Those gathered in prayer in that hospital room had no way of knowing that at that very same hour, many miles away, another group had gathered on the front porch of the Edwards ranch house in tiny Glenn's Cove, Idaho, to pray for this very same

HAROLD SOUTHWICK

young soldier. The church prayer team had responded to Sue's call and had gathered at day's beginning to intercede for Eddie until God lifted the burden. *Every wounded soldier should be so blessed.*

CHAPTER 29

A week later, as Audra sat in the passenger section of the military medical aircraft carrying Eddie and other wounded soldiers to Walter Reed Army Medical Center in the US, she reflected on the rest of that eventful evening. She, Hopi, and Teresa had, indeed, gone to a local German restaurant after Teresa had gotten off duty. Eddie had received appropriate medications and would be out for the night, so they felt free to leave his bedside for a while. Audra smiled as she thought about the budding relationship between Hopi and Teresa, longing as she did so, to see her own sweetheart, Jimmy.

After the meal had ended, she excused herself to call home to let the family know about Eddie's improving condition. That, however, was only half the reason she left Hopi and Teresa alone, the other being so they could have some time alone to get to know each other better. When she had talked to her mother, she asked about Jimmy and learned he was currently on TDY in the Washington D.C. area and would be there when and if she got to accompany Eddie back to the US.

Eddie's condition had improved enough to allow his transfer; it was critical that he receive extensive reconstructive surgery and rehabilitation to the left side of his body. In addition to that, he would receive more intensive treatment and rehabilitation for his brain injury and speech problems. He would be confined to the hospital for many months before his treatment would end.

By the end of that week, Audra knew Hopi and Teresa would

be seeing a great deal more of each other. In fact, she wouldn't be surprised if there was a wedding before she got to experience that same event. She was extremely happy for them and thankful for how they had rallied around Eddie and her through those stressful days.

After a long flight, the plane touched down at Andrews Air Base and was met on the tarmac by military ambulances. As the wounded patients were being transferred from the plane to the waiting ambulances, a young air force lieutenant escorted Audra and two others to the terminal. To her surprise, as she came into the waiting area, she spied Jimmy coming toward her, a big smile on his face.

"Oh, Jim, how did you know I'd be here?" she asked as he took her in his arms.

"Your mom let me know, and Bill Parker still has clout. He made a call, and my crew leader let me off to meet the two of you! I was able to secure a room for you at the visitors' quarters on base if you want it for a few days. Hopefully, you will," he said. "Tomorrow morning they'll have Eddie set up here, and you'll be able to visit him for a while, I'm sure. Since the day after tomorrow is Saturday, maybe I can get a pass, and I can show you D.C. after we visit Eddie. What do you think?"

"I'd love that; right now I need a shower and a good night's sleep. But first of all let's get out of here. I need a kiss and a long, warm hug. I'm suddenly totally exhausted." Audi sighed as she took his arm. As she related the details of how Eddie was wounded and what had taken place since then, Jimmy's reaction reminded her of Hopi's. She thought, *The three musketeers: when one hurts, they all hurt.* Their loyalty to each other blessed her heart.

The next evening when Audi led Jimmy into Eddie's room at Walter Reed, he was unprepared for what he saw. His last remembrances of his friend was of a healthy, good-looking young man; the one lying in the bed before him was splinted, bandaged, and attached to lines and tubes like nothing he had ever seen. His shock was clearly visible to Audra.

She hugged his arm, saying, "He looks much better now than he did two weeks ago."

At the sound of her voice, Eddie stirred and opened his eyes. The discoloring around his left eye was less than when she first saw him, but it still looked horrible, and Jimmy was struggling with his emotions.

He moved to the bedside and said, "Hey, pal, do you know me?"

Eddie tried to smile and reached for Jimmy's hand with his right hand. His attempt to talk shocked Jimmy as it had Hopi and Audra. They spent a short time with him before being hustled out by attendants. Although he had received some reconstructive surgery in Germany, much more would be needed on his left arm, leg, and his pelvis. The attending doctor took Audra aside as they left Eddie's room and told her they were going to start further testing on his brain the next day. His speech problems and other indicators suggested damaged areas they needed to explore further.

Audra had a message at the information desk the next morning when she arrived at the hospital. Eddie's attending physician needed to speak with her. It was urgent. As she hurried to Eddie's room, she became increasingly apprehensive. What was going wrong now? She stopped at the nurses' station, where Dr. Mills, the physician who had talked to her the night before, was waiting for her.

"Doctor, your message has alarmed me. What's wrong?" she inquired.

The doctor's expression, though professional, alarmed Audra even more.

"During the night your brother became very agitated and feverish; then, not responding to medications, he lapsed into a coma again. Tests indicate he has developed inflammation in the brain and it is swelling. We need to do what is called a craniotomy, which is to remove a small section of the skull on the affected side so there will be room for his brain to swell without doing more damage. We believe this will also facilitate treating his speech problems and aid in the therapy he will need to undergo for that. I need your approval to proceed since you're the nearest relative present. I can do the operation without approval if necessary, but I think it wise to ask you for it. We have him being prepped right now, so I'm kind of in a hurry."

Audra's voice quivered as she replied, "Doctor, you do what you have to do. His family all wants him well, and if it takes this, then they will all agree with my decision. Please go and do whatever he needs done. I'll be praying for him and for you as well."

Dr. Mills thanked her and added somewhat grimly, "Ms. Edwards, I have no choice but to tell you that your brother is in very serious condition right now and there is no guarantee this operation will succeed. There is a distinct possibility he may not live. I'll do the best I can." With that, he turned and hurried away.

CHAPTER 30

Audra stood with her head in her hands, tears once again dimming her eyes. Suddenly she thought, *No, I won't accept that verdict. Lord, please, you've brought him this far; please bring him back home.* As she hurried to the telephone, she thought, *I've got to convince Mom and Dad to come back here right away even if they can't afford it.*

As soon as she heard Audra's voice, Sue knew Eddie's condition had grown worse.

"What's happened now, sweetheart?"

She motioned for Hal to pick up an extension as she waited for Audi to continue.

"Mom, you and Dad better get on a plane and get back here. Dr. Mills just informed me as I came into the hospital a few minutes ago that Eddie became feverish and agitated and lapsed into a coma during the night. He said tests show inflammation and increased swelling in his brain so they need to relieve the pressure and let his brain swell up. They're starting what he called a craniotomy, which is removing a small section of the skull over the affected area so his brain can have room to swell, hopefully without more damage."

Audra took a deep breath and added with a sob, "Dad, are you on there with Mom?"

When he replied, she continued, "The doctor just told me there's a very real chance Eddie might not make it. Daddy, we can't let that happen! Have Grandma activate the prayer chain

HAROLD SOUTHWICK

and let the Parkers know too. Please hurry back here. I need you with me. Jimmy is going to come in later today, but I need you. I'm about to the end of my rope!"

Hal and Sue took a taxi to Walter Reed directly from the airport the following morning. Audi was waiting for them at the information and visitor's center. As they were getting their bags from the taxi, Sue commented, "I had no idea there were so many buildings here. Which one of them is the hospital where Eddie is?"

"Here's Audi, so I guess we'll find out soon," Hal said, looking around.

As they embraced their daughter, her drawn face spoke volumes. "Has there been any change since we talked last night, Sis?" Hal asked.

"Like I told you last night, he came through the craniotomy okay, and Dr. Mills said his inflammation is responding to medications; but they're going to keep him in a drug-induced coma for a while as they work to get the swelling down. He's waiting to talk to you both when we get to the hospital. We could have this taxi take us over there." Audi explained.

Later, standing at Eddie's beside in intensive care, Audra stood back and watched her mom and dad as they stood looking at their oldest child. Their agonized faces said it all. They would gladly trade places with him if it were possible. The helplessness of not being able to do anything was tearing them up inside.

She moved between them and put her arms around them. "Mom and Dad, we have to keep believing and keep on praying!"

"I know, sweetheart. It's just so hard to see him like this now when he's always been so healthy and on the go. What's scaring me even more now is that Little Joe is talking about enlisting in the army as soon as he graduates this spring. I couldn't take it any more if something happened to him on top of all this." Sue wiped tears from her eyes as she squeezed Audi's hand. "I just hope Eddie will even want to get well, losing his wife and their dreams; they were all-important to him."

"That worries me, too," Hal said. "But he has to get to know his beautiful little daughter! That could do wonders for him. She could be God's bridge between Katy and the future for Eddie if we can figure out how to get him through this."

CHAPTER 31

The Edwards had made arrangements to spend two weeks in D.C. with Eddie. Audra had missed a lot of school and needed to return to Texas to catch up so she could graduate at the end of the current semester. Hence, she left at the end of Hal and Sue's first week at Walter Reed. She promised to forget the rest of her school year and return to D.C. if Eddie got worse again. She made her mom promise to keep her informed.

By the end of their second week, Eddie's swelling had abated, and Dr. Mills decided to take him off the meds keeping him in a coma. He wanted to see if Eddie would wake up on his own. The doctor wanted to observe his reaction to seeing his parents, if there was any at all. Hal and Sue were allowed to stay with him in his room through the night following him being taken off the meds. Hal was standing at a window, looking but not seeing the landscape outside. His mind was back in Vietnam, remembering those moments when he was in the process of waking out of a coma. He was suddenly gripped anew by the confusion, pain, and fear that had assailed him as he became aware of his surroundings.

Hearing a stirring on the bed behind him now, he turned to see Sue leaning over her son. He watched with wonder as she stroked Eddie's brow and spoke softly to him. Hal recalled with deep emotion the powerful attachment Sue and Eddie had always shared. Could that powerful cord of love pull Eddie out of the coma into her presence now? Hal began praying for that to happen.

After a time, he heard his wife cry softly, "Oh, Dad, look. He's trying to open his eyes!" They sat watching for a long time before his eyes finally came open and he tried to focus.

Leaning next to him on the bed, Sue said, "Sweetheart, your dad and mom are here. Do you recognize us?"

Instead of recognition, what they saw in his eyes was pain and confusion.

Trying to hide his disappointment, Hal murmured, "Well, at least he's waking up. That's better than anything we've seen since we got here."

Dr. Mills entered the room. Going to bedside, he said, "Oh, good. He's coming around. That's what I wanted to see this morning."

"But, Doctor, he doesn't seem very alert!" Sue's response caused him to turn to her with a nod of his head and an understanding smile.

"I completely understand your concern and agitation. This is your dear son, and your feelings are completely normal. However, Eddie's level of consciousness right now is about what we expect after the operation and the induced coma. We will run tests on him very shortly, but I think he's on the mend, with a long way to go yet, of course. I'll be having the nurses take him down for testing within the hour, which will take a good deal of time. If you have anything you want to do or see here in D.C., I think we can find you some form of transportation. We should have Eddie back in his room by mid-afternoon." Dr. Mills shook Hal's hand as he turned to leave. "Rest assured; we will do our very best to get your son back to as near normal as possible." The doctor had believed for a long time that most people had no idea the ordeal being wounded in combat created for the wounded as well as their families.

Hal and Sue were reluctant to leave the hospital, but rather than sit and worry, they decided to go see some of the city. A young soldier entered the room and told them he was their escort for the next few hours. As a result, they were able to drive by the White House, the Capital building, and other places of interest that they had heard about for so long. Upon returning to the hospital, they found Eddie back in his room. He looked pale and worn. Sue could only hold his free hand and fight back tears. Hal sat on the side of the bed and talked to him, watching for Eddie's response. His left eye was still somewhat bloodshot, and the surrounding bandages kept them from being able to read any expressions he might have, but it seemed there was a flicker of recognition in his right eye. He tried to utter something as Sue bent to hear better, but only garbled sounds came forth. Hal watched as Eddie's eye filled with tears and an expression of frustration emanated from him.

Dr. Mills laid out for them the plan the military medical staff had set in place to meet Eddie's needs and the timeframe they were looking at for his recovery. As they shared a parting goodbye with their son before leaving for the trip home, they thanked God that he seemed to be more alert, but they were heavyhearted for his mental and spiritual condition. Dr. Mills complimented them on their daughter Audra, what an impression she had made on the staff taking care of Eddie. He also thanked them for the sacrifice their son had made and was making for his country. He promised to keep them informed with Eddie's progress, and then he prayed with them before they left.

Sue left feeling hopeful yet worried she would never again see her son the way he had once been. Hal left wondering if the objective for which his son and so many others had paid such a high price to obtain was really worth the cost. The cost was being extracted not only now, but it would be ongoing well into the future of many such as Eddie. He knew for sure that his family's life would never be the same. He only hoped that the God he had come to love and trust over the years would somehow prove trustworthy where his son and his little granddaughter were concerned. He remembered his dad saying at times, "It's a dang long road that doesn't have a turn in it!" Well, it seemed that it was about time for a turn in the road his son had been asked to travel.

Hal missed his dad as much today as he did the day he had passed away. He knew the rest of the family, especially Eddie, did as well. But that was an expected part of life. The loss of Angela had shaken the family to its core, but they all knew she was in a much better place now and was perfectly normal in her new abode. The tragic chain of events that took precious, beautiful Katy from them was still a raw, open wound for them, as it was for the Parkers. To be leaving their son now, not knowing if he would ever recover completely, left Hal and Sue both with a weariness of soul and spirit that almost overwhelmed them. Hal thought, *Lord, we could use a little turn in our own road right now as well.*

CHAPTER 32

In the weeks following Hal and Sue's return home from Walter Reed, the reports they received concerning Eddie's progress were encouraging as far as his physical improvements were concerned. He was soon able to undergo much-needed bone reconstruction surgery. His left arm, leg, and pelvis all had been repaired and his ribs were beginning to heal nicely. His head injuries were continuing to improve, and his response to mental stimuli each progressive day also improved. Dr. Mills became more pleased each day and relayed that information to the Edwards family when they called for an update. As soon as Eddie was able to get up from the bed and sit in a wheelchair, his physical therapy began, soon followed by speech therapy and efforts to reactivate his memory processes. Each form of therapy employed a different therapist, Eddie becoming their sole focus for the portion of each day he was assigned them.

To anyone observing these individuals carrying out their assigned duties, it was immediately obvious they were doing more than just a job. This was their mission in the overall war effort. As a result, they were soon personally caught up in the progress and success of Eddie's rehabilitation. As soon as was appropriate, flash cards were used to promote enunciation as well as to help stimulate the memory process. While Eddie worked hard at the physical therapy and showed continuing improvement, his speech therapist began to notice despondency as he struggled with his memory and with his ability to pronounce basic words.

She was a very positive person and a good encourager; hence, she worked hard to keep him moving forward. Slowly his pronunciation began to improve, which should have perked him up some, but she continued to sense his despondency. After consulting with Dr. Mills and the therapy staff, they decided to question Eddie's folks concerning anything that may have happened to him before being wounded in action.

In the meantime, Eddie had a visitor at the hospital in the second month of his rehabilitation. When the tall young soldier walked into his room on this particular afternoon, Eddie was sitting, looking out the window, oblivious to anything or anyone around him. He was still in casts on both his arm and his leg and pelvis, and he had wraps around his rib cage; so it was with an effort that he turned to respond when he heard a voice from his past.

"I hope you don't mind my coming to see how you are doing, Soldier."

Recognition registered in his eyes as Eddie tried to respond verbally, mixed with a degree of astonishment! "Bi … Bil … Bill, whaaa … doi … n erre?"

As he struggled to rise, Bill Jones came to his side saying, "Hey, man, don't get up. I just wanted to come by and say hi. I'm TDY here at Walter Reed, learning some advanced medical techniques for skeletal reconstruction and rehabilitation. Jimmy Johnston had told me you were here being put back together. It looks like you've gone through a heck of an ordeal. I'm going to be here awhile, so if you don't mind, I would like to come see you again one of these days." He extended his hand to shake with Eddie and continued, "I really need to talk to you about something very important to me if you feel up to it one day soon."

Eddie struggled with some emotion and finally took his old adversary's hand. As they shook, Billy was shocked with the lack of strength in Eddie's grip. *This guy used to be one tough son of a gun*, he thought. *War is hell.*

In the days following Billy's visit, Eddie's memory improved, and his ability to pronounce words improved dramatically. In direst proportion, however, his listlessness and inner turmoil increased. He would lie in his bed, unable to sleep, or sit in a chair in his room, staring out the window. Flashbacks of his tank exploding and the screams of his driver in the split second before oblivion engulfed him, haunting his dreams. He hadn't been told, but he instinctively knew the rest of his crew had not survived. He lay in his bed slowly remembering his torment before combat had begun. A vision of Katy began to move across his mind. As his memories became more vivid, he began to wonder if his preoccupation with his wife's death had hindered his ability to lead his tank crew effectively. As he considered life without Katy, he began to wish he had been killed along with his men. At least he would be in heaven with her now if heaven was really his destiny.

During one of his darkest nights of lonely struggle, longing for a miracle to bring Katy to him, a vision of a miniature Katy began to move through his mind. Somewhere deep inside him he sensed a quiet knocking on a door he had slammed shut. A troubling question came to him: *What lies behind that door?* A vague curiosity began to form, followed by an alarming sense of dread and fear. As he lay there in the dark room, a "hand" seemed to suddenly beckon him, "come home." As he drifted off to sleep at last, his parting thought was, *what's at home for me now?*

CHAPTER 33

Back home in little Glenn's Cove, Idaho, the reports from Walter Reed were causing a sense of "what can we do now"? Audra had finished Bible school in Fort Worth and had returned home. She was urging her folks to let her take Little Joe and go see Eddie again. In the midst of trying to raise enough money for the two of them to go, the family received a call from Dr. Mills. His questions about Eddie's mental attitude prior to being wounded, along with a suspicion that Eddie had suffered some tragic event, confirmed what Sue and Hal had feared would happen; he lacked motivation to become whole again. The fighting spirit he had always possessed in sports and other things just wasn't there to help him overcome and win the toughest battle of his life.

The Parkers came to the ranch the evening following Dr. Mills' call for supper and to see baby Katrina. As they were discussing Eddie's situation, Katherine quietly suggested that Eddie needed to see his little girl; maybe she could arouse his will to live again. Hal instantly agreed with her. He wondered aloud if Eddie even remembered Katrina, or if he had mentally blocked her memory from his mind. They had all suspected that her birth being connected to Katy's death was a key element in Eddie's emotional and mental condition. After much prayer and discussion, Bill Parker suggested he would pay for the tickets for Katherine, Sue, and Audra to take Katrina to see Eddie. Sue and Hal agreed with Audi that it would be good for Little Joe to see his brother and see firsthand the realities and the consequences of war.

HAROLD SOUTHWICK

Bill Parker had sat listening to the talk going on around him, not saying much. When a lull in the conversation presented him an opportunity he said, "You know Hal, Katy had told Katherine and me about you being wounded when you were in Vietnam. Now your son has been wounded in another war. Is there some kind of a parallel in this or is it coincidental?"

Hal sat in deep thought for a long time before answering. When he finally did, he sounded confused. "When I went to Vietnam, I didn't know much about what it meant to be a Christian. Looking back, I can see that everything I experienced over there moved me closer to God. I don't know if that had anything to do with me being wounded, but I doubt it. I think God just used it to help me grow up. It also helped me meet Leslie Davis. I think Eddie's situation is completely different. He was raised in our home and taught about being a Christian from the very beginning."

Everyone else had become quiet as they focused on what Hal was saying.

Bill asked, "How does that make what happened to him different?"

"Eddie has always worked hard at doing what's right. I'm beginning to think he has developed a misguided belief in some kind of a works-rewards system where God is concerned. I hope I'm wrong but I'm starting to think he may feel that God is punishing him by what's happened to so many he's loved. He started growing away from God when Grandpa died and it has just gotten worse when Angela and then Katy died. Eddie was running away from God and I was trying to grow closer to God, so I don't think that's a true parallel. His getting hurt may or may not bring him back; I don't know. I sure hope so."

"Amen to that," Bill acknowledged. The others nodded their agreement.

The Edwards had been hard-hit with expenses helping Audra go to Germany on top of her school expenses. Their own trip to D.C. had further added to the outgo. Added to that, ranching wasn't all that profitable at the present time. It had never been a means to riches. Hal dug deep into their cash reserve and bought a ticket for his youngest son.

As he thought about all that had transpired in the life of his family, he realized his younger son had always seemed to be in the background. That realization caused him a wave of guilt. He shared those feelings with Sue, and they agreed it was past time to change that. Joe had been a big factor in Angela living as well as she had for those brief years they had had her with them. He had always been willing to help on the ranch and never seemed to ask for much. Besides, he loved and admired his big brother greatly and had suffered just as much as the rest of the family from Eddie's trials. This would be good for him and hopefully for Eddie too.

Katrina was just over a year old now and had become the center of attention for the entire family, not just because of the circumstances surrounding her, but because of who she was. Her daddy hadn't seen her since Katy's funeral and had no personal connection with her and no idea what she was like. Sue hoped "Little Kat," as she was called, would be what Eddie needed. Little Joe was as taken with Little Kat as Eddie had been with Angela when she was a baby. He was delighted he was getting to go along on this trip. He was going to be a big help in caring for the baby and keeping her occupied.

It was another three weeks before all the details could be worked out, and the five of them were on their way. Many prayers had been said and best wishes offered by the church family as they left with burdened but hopeful hearts. Hal wished he could have gone along, but the ranch needed him. His mom and Sue's mom were both in failing health and needed someone close as well. It just wasn't possible to be in two places at once. Somehow, this was the way it was supposed to be, and he accepted that.

His good-bye to Sue was typically Hal. "Wake him up and get him headed home."

"I'll do my best." Sue sighed. "I wish you were going with us!"

As Audra hugged him, she murmured, "Dad, you know how much I *love* you. We both know how close Mom and Eddie have always been. Well that's how I feel about you. I want you to take good care of yourself. You always work too hard, and you need to know how much this family needs you, you hear me?"

Hal gave her a long hug and a wry grin, with a lump in his throat.

"Dad, we're going to get big bro back home! I still believe it, okay?"

As Hal watched them all walk down the corridor in the airport, he was startled to see that Little Joe wasn't little anymore. He was several inches taller than his mom and Audra, who was the same height as Sue. Audra's long dark hair fell to her waist, and he realized anew she was a beautiful young lady. She looked just like her mom except for the color of her hair. In spite of all that had happened in their family over the past long months, down deep in his inner man he knew he was a blessed man, and he thanked God for that. He also knew that what they were undertaking with little Katrina was the right thing to do.

Suddenly, he sensed the presence of the "hand" on his shoulder, and he turned and walked away with a feeling of peace he hadn't felt in a long time!

CHAPTER 34

Eddie's pelvic fracture had mended enough for him to start therapy to strengthen the skeletal muscles. The multiple fractures of his left leg had delayed his ability to stand, and his left arm injuries hadn't allowed him to aid his legs by using a walker. But now, after several surgeries and manipulation therapy to keep his muscles from atrophying, he was slowly beginning to stand and take some tentative steps. His rib fractures were mending well but were still tender to touch. Over all, the therapists and Dr. Mills were satisfied with the progress.

After the doctor had talked to Eddie's folks concerning his mental attitude, he decided to take the bull by the horns, so to speak, and challenge him. He already knew his family was bringing Eddie's baby girl to see him, and he wanted to lay some mental groundwork to get Eddie's thoughts off himself and his situation.

One morning after therapy sessions as Dr. Mills came into check his progress, he straightened up and said, "Well, young man, you are on the mend quite well considering the shape you were in when you arrived here. We have a long way to go yet, but with hard work and the desire to make it, you can get back to a productive life. What concerns me is your mental condition. I have talked extensively with your parents and your sister. You are more fortunate than many soldiers who come in here all tore up from war."

As Eddie started to bristle, the doctor raised his hand and

continued. "I know about the losses in your life, and I understand how that has affected you. I can't give you any answers about why God allows things like that to happen. What I do know is that God still loves you and so does your family. You still have a great deal to live for if you're man enough to accept the challenge. I'm not a theologian, but from what I know about God, you can at least try giving your heartache to him and ask him to heal you, inside as well as out. My pastor tells me that part of the process of maturing as a Christian is to accept the burden God gives us to carry and go on with what he has for us to do. Do you think you're man enough to try doing that?"

As he stood waiting for a response from Eddie, he worried that he had laid it on a little too heavy. He observed the battle going on behind Eddie's eyes and saw the trembling of his jaw. Then, almost imperceptibly, his jaw began to set and his look firm up, and he said slowly, "I … try … harder."

"I knew you would. I understand you have a beautiful baby girl at home that you don't even know. I want you to think about getting well so you can get to know her. She really does need you, and you need her a lot more than you have any idea about right now." Dr. Mills laid a hand on Eddie's shoulder and left the room.

———————————

Eddie sat there for a long time, giving consideration to what he had just been told. He experienced the whole range of emotions those words evoked, not the least of which was anger; but finally, a feeling of giving up all that burdened him started to clamor for attention. As tears began to dim his eyes, he bowed his head and began trying to pray for God's help. Words didn't come easily, and while he was trying to let his thoughts convey to God his turmoil and needs, the most beautiful sound assaulted his ears. He turned to the window to see a cardinal bird, its red breast glistening, singing as he had never heard a bird sing before. The hair on the back of his neck stood out, and goose bumps covered his entire body. God was speaking to him through this beautiful creature, beckoning him to come, come back home.

He remained facing the window long after the bird flew away, not seeing with his eyes, but looking inward. Stillness of mind, soul, and body engulfed him, and for the first time since his grandpa died, he felt secure in letting go of his grief, fears, and insecurities! He began to realize the walls he had tried to protect himself behind had failed. They had only isolated a part of him.

He returned to his bed and lay down, sinking into a deep, untroubled sleep that had eluded him for so long. His exhaustion had destroyed all his defenses and the miraculous processes God had designed were moving forward. The rest he now was able to enter into began a renewal of his entire being.

So deep was his sleep he was unaware of those coming to check on him. One nurse called her supervisor, only to be told to let him sleep. Dr. Mills had left emphatic instructions. Eddie was undergoing a healing far beyond any that they had the ability to administer or to assist.

———————————

Hours later, he awoke with a start. To his surprise, dawn was breaking in the east, and the first rays of light were filtering through the window on that side of his room. He lay there for a while and suddenly realized he was looking forward to what this day held for him. He wanted to get on with his speech therapy and to really start working to rebuild his strength.

He drifted back to sleep easily and didn't awake until a nurse brought breakfast to him. Although hospital food was notoriously unappealing, he ate everything before him, which the nurse took note of. She gave a big thumbs-up as she took the tray back past the nurses' station and smiled.

Dr. Mills stopped in on his morning rounds later and discussed Eddie's progress again. He made notes on his clipboard chart and expressed encouraging words before adding, "Oh, by the way, you have visitors waiting to see you. I'll send them in on my way out." He smiled as Eddie gave him a questioning look. "You'll be pleased!"

CHAPTER 35

Eddie sat expectantly in his wheelchair, glad to have visitors for a change and wondering who they might be. He hadn't thought about him much for a long time, but he suddenly hoped Little Joe would come see him. He was totally surprised when Joe walked through the door, stopping with his typical half grin on his slender face. The look of concern and love in his eyes spoke more to Eddie than any words would have, and his face lit up with a smile. He wheeled his chair toward his brother as Audra entered behind Joe, smiling as she took in the scene of her two brothers. In spite of the bruising still evident on the left side of his face, he showed surprise and delight as Joe leaned down and embraced him.

Neither had uttered a word, but now Eddie tried to speak, "Bro … I been wa … ann.ng … see … you! A fleeting look of frustration crossed his face and just as quickly disappeared. Audra took note with an uplift of her spirit. Big Bro was definitely doing better than when she had last seen him.

"I've wanted to see you too, big Brother." Joe spoke haltingly as he struggled with his emotions. "From what everyone has said, you've been through hell, but it looks like you're starting to do better, huh?"

"Yup!" Eddie replied, looking Joe up and down, adding, "You ta … er." Seeing Audi standing next to Joe only emphasized how much his little brother had grown since he had last seen him.

Audra gave him a big hug and said, "Look who's here to see

you!" Eddie received another surprise as Katherine Parker came into the room, wiping tears from her cheeks.

"Oh Eddie, I'm so glad to see you! You look so much better than I expected. I'm so sorry for all that's happened to you. Bill and I love you and hurt for you." She leaned down and hugged him for several moments. As she stood up, she turned saying, "Someone else has come to see you also."

Joe and Audra stepped aside, watching Eddie's face as their mom came into the room carrying Baby Katrina. Sue's look was one of hopeful anticipation as she turned the baby so her son could see his little daughter face-to-face for the first time since Katy's funeral.

"Son, here's your little girl! Isn't she beautiful?" Sue said with pride. Stepping forward, she knelt in front of Eddie's chair and whispered, "I love you so much, Son, and I hope you'll be happy to see your baby again." With that, she held the little wide-eyed girl out to her daddy.

Everyone watched with held breath as Eddie sat silently looking at the beautiful little miniature of the girl he had loved so strongly. Finally, looking at his mom for a long moment, then back at Katrina, he reached out with his right hand for his baby, tears filling his eyes. Sue carefully sat the baby on his lap, watching his rapt look of wonder. With a sob, she wrapped her arms around them both and kissed Eddie's cheek. Wrapping his left arm, cast and all, around his mom as best he could, they both broke down and wept. Katherine cuddled Audra and Joe to her, and they all cried along with them.

When Sue finally sat up, Katrina looked first at her grandma and then at her daddy for a long moment. Suddenly, her face broke into a bright-eyed smile. Eddie's breath caught in his throat as he returned her smile. That was the same smile Katy had given him the first time he had seen her. In a flash of memory, he was back at the fair grounds in Glenn's Cove, talking to Kurt Parker when that beautiful little gal with the long black hair walked up, turning with that radiant smile on her face. His heart had been captured then, only to be left broken and frozen by her loss. In his grief, he had vowed to never let it be captivated again. Now, as he sat taking in the wonder of this little girl on his lap, all his resolve began to melt, and something powerful and appealing began tugging at his heart strings. Out of nowhere, he sensed a "hand" beckoning him, "come home."

When everyone was seated, Katrina reached for Joe and went to him. Sue watched as Eddie's eyes followed Katrina. She would've loved to know what he was thinking. "Little Kat" settled in Joe's arms, then turned to look back at her daddy, her expression seeming to say, *Look who's got me now.* As all in the room watched the silent exchange between baby and father, her little face lit up in another brilliant smile. Sue's heart filled with gratitude to God for what was happening here in this quiet hospital room. Different emotions were evident on Eddie's face as he watched Katrina for several long moments. He opened his mouth once to say something but couldn't seem to speak the words he wanted to. They all sat observing his struggle, unaware they were trying to help him form those words. Eddie noticed this and gave a little shrug and dropped his eyes.

Audra went to him. Kneeling in front of him, she said, "It's going to be okay."

Although the medical staff had talked to the family, it was hard for them to grasp the fact that Eddie's memory and his ability to put his thoughts into words were still affected by the trauma to his brain. His ability to reason normally was getting better, but it would be many long months before he would be able to function as before, if ever. Katherine Parker picked up on these aspects of Eddie's situation intuitively. The fact that she was not blood related aided her objectivity; she thought perhaps she could share some insight that would help his family deal with what still faced them as well as motivate them to become creative in how they helped him. They were already experienced along those lines from working with Angela. She could tell that bringing Katrina to see Eddie had been a very good start in that direction.

In the course of the conversation going on, Eddie looked at his mom with a question, "Where ... Dad?" The sudden concern in his voice caused all eyes to turn to him.

Sue instantly understood what motivated the question, "Dad's just fine, Son. He had to stay home because of the workload at the ranch. He wanted Joe to get to come see you, but he sent his love and prayers."

Watching Eddie's mind working to process this information and to stay focused on what was being said made all of them realize what a high cost these young soldiers were asked to pay for the safety of our country. It was obvious he was becoming weary. One of his nurses came in to check on him and told them he needed to rest. After prayers and tears, they promised to return later.

―――――――――

That was how the following several days were spent before the family had to return home. To the normal mind, it seemed odd that Eddie seemed to spend so much time studying his little daughter. It was as if he was trying to figure out exactly who she was and how he should relate to her. Katherine gave them some insight when she mentioned that Eddie didn't have a history of relationship to Katrina for his damaged memory to draw on as he did with the rest of them. It was obvious by the time they left that he was becoming attached to her as she was to him. That was what they had hoped for, and it gave them strength to face the long days and trials they all knew still lay ahead. The good-byes were especially difficult because the growing bond would be interrupted.

HAROLD SOUTHWICK

CHAPTER 36

Several days later as Eddie was being returned to his room from a therapy session, Billy Jones met them in the hallway. After asking if he could accompany them back to Edie's room, he asked how Eddie was doing. His reaction to the answers he received seemed genuine and sincere; it was obvious that something had changed in his life.

When they were alone in Eddie's room, Billy asked, "Ed, do you remember when I visited with you a couple of weeks ago?"

Eddie's response was slow in coming. It took time to process the question and try to remember. Finally, he nodded and said, "Think ... so."

"Well, because of your injuries, I know you're having trouble remembering and communicating. I just wanted to come tell you what has happened to me. You know that I never liked you when we were going to high school together. What you probably never knew was why. Well, I always envied you for what you seemed to have. I always thought you were a goody two-shoes who thought he never did anything wrong, and I felt just about everything I did was wrong. I wanted what you had, but I was too proud to ask you what that was." Billy paused and took a deep breath. "While we were at Boise State together, Jimmy Johnston and I talked about you. He asked me what my problem with you was, and I told him what I'm telling you now. He told me about Christ and your relationship with him. That got me started thinking about what I needed in my own life. I met a Christian in basic training who finally persuaded me to accept Jesus as my Savior. A lot of things have gone on in my life, but I am happier now than I have ever been. I would like to have you as a friend and a brother in Christ now and seeing all that has happened to you in the last couple of years I think you could use a new friend. I'm sorry about your little sister and also about what happened to your wife. I can't say I know how that feels or how to deal with it, but I just want you to know I'm praying for you. If the God I've come to know is who I believe he is, I can't help but believe that he has something good for you in life yet. I pray you will let him show you what that is."

Eddie sat looking at Billy for a long time, slowly processing what he had been telling him. After a period of time, Billy saw moisture in his eyes, and he reached for Eddie's hand. As they shook hands, the wall between them crumbled, and a look of appreciation and acceptance came to Eddie's face and eyes. "Thanks … I … I … !" Eddie struggled to say.

"You don't have to say anything, Ed. Thank you for listening to me. I just hope we can become good friends someday. I have to go now, but I wanted to come see you before I left. I'm leaving for my home base back in Texas tomorrow, but I'll try to stay in touch." With that, Billy asked if he could say a short prayer.

Eddie sat thinking about the visit, about how God used people even when they weren't aware of it, and about what the future had in store for him. His mental abilities needed a lot of time to return to normal, but down deep in the places that made Eddie who he was, his soul continued to stir.

Each of the hospital rooms was equipped with a sound system connected to broadcasts of various kinds. Eddie had never used the one in his room, but he had a need to hear some soul soothing music for a change. Music had long been one of his crutches and after meeting Katy and becoming acquainted with her passion for it, he had come to appreciate it even more. He wheeled his chair over to the system control and searched for what he wanted. He came across a station playing Gospel music and left it on that station. Moving back to the window, he sat starring out; the calming of the music softly washing over him. A longing to enter into the flow of life had been knocking at his heart's door since the day he had heard the bird singing outside his room. He slowly became aware of the song playing as the refrain penetrated his reverie, *whispering hope; oh how welcome thy promise, making my heart in its sorrow rejoice!* He sat lost in the promise of those God appointed words. Their import slowly registered on his battered and needy mind and heart and his remaining fears, doubts and anger began to melt away. His memories returned to that afternoon on the river bank back home after Katy's funeral. He recalled with horror the anger and resentment he had screamed out at God. In some of his more lucid moments since regaining consciousness in this hospital, he had cringed at the memory of that time. His unresolved anger and hurt would quickly blot those moments of guilt out, however. The mental, emotional and spiritual toll had finally become unbearable and his resistance to God crumbled. He finally released it all as he collapsed in great shuddering sobs, his head on his arms lain across the window sill. The purging was so intense it was like a searing, purifying fire as it surged through him. When he finally became aware of his surroundings, he was completely exhausted. He returned to his bed and lay down. Almost instantly he sank into a deep, soul, mind and body renewing, and rebuilding sleep; a precious gift from God for his creation.

CHAPTER 37

Almost a full year later, Eddie was declared rehabilitated enough to be released from military hospital care. He had been transferred from Walter Reed four months previously. His physical wounds had healed sufficiently, and his mental and speech abilities had greatly improved. Dr. Mills had complimented him on his dedication to working hard and getting better. He attributed that to his family bringing his little daughter to see him and to his positive reaction to Dr. Mills' council. As a result of that, he was able to be transferred to a military hospital in Denver, Colorado, for the remaining recovery procedures to be administered. Members of his family had been able to come to visit him there once, and now he was anxious to go home.

Only Audra knew for sure what day Eddie was to arrive home. She and Jimmy had visited him in Denver, Jimmy being stationed in Colorado Springs now. Audra made a dual-purposed trip to see both Jimmy and Eddie. While there, Eddie and she planned the surprise return home for him. He would fly from Denver to Twin Falls, catching a bus there for the rest of the way to Glenn's Cove. The Greyhound buses went right by the ranch driveway, so he would have the driver stop and let him off there. Audra would be watching for the bus at a pull-off down the road and would hurry home from there to be a part of the homecoming.

Eddie had talked to the bus driver while they were stopped in a little town thirty miles up the road, so the driver knew where to stop. As they approached the lane leading down to the ranch

HAROLD SOUTHWICK

house, Eddie was both anxious and eager about his homecoming. When the bus stopped and the driver got out to retrieve his bag, several people who had heard him relate some of his story, gave him a hand of appreciation. He thanked them and shook hands with the driver, then stepped back as the bus pulled away.

Taking a deep breath, he picked up his bag and crossed the highway. The duffle bag was heavy, and he had to stop to rest several times. His strength was still not back to normal. As he wiped his face with his handkerchief and thought about the last time he had been home, the memories of his loss rose up to hammer him once again.

As he stood staring at the house situated in front of the outbuildings and corrals, memories flooded his mind, and a lump lodged in his throat. His gaze stopped on the suspended swing on the front porch where he and his family had spent so much time together when he and his siblings were growing up. A vivid memory of the first time he had sat in the swing with the most beautiful girl he would ever know overwhelmed him momentarily. He hung his head and prayed that the God who had pursued him so relentlessly would not desert him now.

His determination to finish this last leg of his journey home returned, and he picked up his bag and continued slowly down the driveway toward the ranch house. As he reached the front gate, he noticed that the fence could use some new paint. *Dad must be slowing down,* he thought. The squeaking of the front gate brought someone to the front door. He saw the curtain part and his mom look out to see who was there.

With a cry to the others in the house, she threw open the door and rushed onto the porch.

"Oh Eddie, you're home! Oh thank God, you're finally back home!" As the rest of the family came out and crowded around them, she cried, "Oh Dad, our boy has finally come back home!"

As the rest of the family hugged him, Audra drove into the yard, exiting the car with a big smile.

Hal looked at her and then back to Eddie. "I wondered where

you were going in such a hurry. You knew he was coming home today, didn't you?"

"Yup! He wanted to make this last leg of his journey home on his own, and so we planned it this way so he could do that!" Audra beamed.

Then she went into the house and returned, holding little Katrina in her arms. Stopping before Eddie, she held the beautiful little girl out to her daddy, "Tell your daddy hi, sweetheart!"

As Eddie took her into his arms, she smiled that bright Katy smile and exclaimed, "Hi, Daddy!"

Eddie buried his face in her hair and uttered a silent prayer. *Thank you, dear Lord. I'm finally home!*

HAROLD SOUTHWICK